Lone Star Odyssey
First Steps

David Wilson

This book would never have happened without the support of my beautiful wife and our amazing children.

Thank you for everything.

Prologue

Lone Star Odyssey - First Steps

14 March 2005, Mashhad, Iran

"Are all of our people in place for Operation Qiyamah?" ask the Supreme Leader Ruhollah. "Yes, all of our faithful are in place and will remain at their assigned locations until all of them have mastered the local language and basic English. We are on track and within the time line you have set forth," replied the grey haired Islamic Revolutionary Guard Corps General, "They all were handpicked from volunteers among the faithful and will be watched over by the most devoted from our Islamic Revolutionary Guard Corps."

4 Aug 2009, Mashhad, Iran

"Supreme Leader Khamenei, the time has come for the next phase of Operation Qiyamah," stated the young major in the uniform of the Islamic Revolutionary Guard Corps. Raising an eyebrow and glancing around the council chamber, the Supreme Leader gestured for his Chief of Staff. The Chief of State rose and approached the Supreme Leader, bending over so he could hear the Supreme Leader's commands, "Remove everyone from the council chamber, make sure everyone present knows that to utter anything they may know or think they know about Operation Qiyamah to anyone outside this chamber is death." After everyone was escorted out of the council chamber, the Supreme Leader commanded the IRGC Major to continue.

"Supreme Leader all of our IRGC-QF (Quds Forces) paramilitary trainers and personnel working under business and religious covers are in place. As ordered our IRGC-QF members will be focused on developing relationships with the local youth of Arab origin, who will be recruited as potential intelligence and militant recruits. The family groups recruited to accompany God's warriors have been carefully selected from within loyal families and will be relocated to Canada and Mexico with the sole purpose of assimilating into the local culture and establishing small businesses; such as automobile repair shops and muffler shops." The reason automobile repair shops were chosen were they had all of the necessary tools for the men to hone their skills in constructing bombs, which included the powerful and deadly armor-piercing explosively formed penetrators or EFP's that Iran had become infamous for in Iraq. The assigned families were going to provide cover for action and cover for status for the men assigned from the elite Iranian Quds Force and to provide them trusted couriers for sending and receiving clandestine messages from their controllers within the Iranian Government. The rest of the briefing took almost two hours, "Major blessing be upon you for the update. Please have the target list updated and proceed with the next phase of Operation Qiyamah. May we both remain on this earth to see the fruits of our labors."

Northern Mexico, Fall 2013

If any of the various US alphabet agencies had been watching closely, they may have realized that over three dozen small family owned automobile repair and small appliance repair shops in towns and cities in northern Mexico closed in early August. The families all contacted the local Mexican cartels and paid the exuberant fees without arguing over the high prices of getting them across the United States border and for transportation to large US cities scattered across the West Coast and Southern United States. The cartels coyotes realized very quickly the people were not Mexican, but their money was good as anyone's, so who cares if a bunch of Arabs attempting to look and act like Mexican's crossed the border into the United States.

Canada/Northern Border US, Fall 2013

The routes had been chosen carefully and vetted by unwitting refugees several times over the last two years. The guides moved slowly, driving the current refugees slowly across the rugged terrain. No one talked, but the children were wide eyed and slightly scared as the guides had told them if they wandered away from the group that they would just leave them for the grizzly bears for a snack. The group had been moving since before daylight and they all were cold and uncomfortable with the children forced to sit on the laps of the adults in the six passenger ATVs. The guides had passed the word they had crossed the border about 15 minutes ago and only had another hour or so before meeting their contacts.

US Congressional EMP Hearings, Washington D.C. 2017

Quotes from the EMP Commission: "We all know that a single nuclear weapon detonated to an altitude of 500 kilometers could produce an EMP that would blanket the entire continental United States, potentially damaging or destroying military forces and civilian communications, power, transportation, water, food and other infrastructures on which modern society depends. In fact, I think it is the ultimate terrorist threat." Dr. Wood had referred to a robust EMP lay down over our country as a giant continental time machine which would move us back a century in technology. Dr. Wood was ask, "Dr. Wood, our population today in this distribution could not be supported by the technology of a century ago," and his unemotional answer was, "Yes, I know. The population will shrink until it can be supported by the technology." The electric power network is probably the most fundamental of all the nation's critical infrastructures, all of which depend on the energy delivered by the electric power grids. Assessment of the commission on the electric power grid is that that grid is in danger of functional collapse during an EMP event over a very wide area.

Operation Qiyamah (Chicago Teams) Fall of 2018

During the fall of 2018, over the course of several months, small groups of four to five young to middle age women arrived in the Chicago area. Each group was under the control and driven by a middle age man. Housing arrangements had already been set up and each of the groups was assigned a general area within Chicago and a target within that general area. Overall there were a total of five groups assigned to the Chicago area, consisting of a total of 24 females. None of the females were allowed to leave their residences alone and English was the only language they were permitted to speak. False identification and work history paperwork were provided for them to study and memorize. Daily classes were given at each of the residences.

Team 2 was made up of four females ranging from 26 years old to 36 years of age and had been assigned the South Lake Shore Drive area of Chicago. Within this area, the team had been assigned four targets, all of which were Nursing Homes or Assisted Care Facilities. After completing their training and memorizing all of the fake background information, each of the young ladies applied for work at their assigned target. All of the girls had applied for janitorial services and were willing to work the night shift; all were hired within a month. After working at each of the facilities for just about two months, they all submitted applications at new nursing homes and assisted living facilities. All claimed they were moving was the reason for the requests, when in fact their mission was done at these facilities and they had other targets to service. As all of the women had been excellent workers, their managers gave each of the women excellent references.

As the women of Team 2 switched to jobs at new facilities, they set about establishing a normal work pattern much as they had done at the first job. After a week on the new jobs, the women had collected as much information as they needed to begin the new operation. The women began the process of bringing in one device per female, each evening and concealing the small devices as instructed by the elder male group leader. The devices were identical, a small dark colored plastic package about six inches square and weighing in at around five pounds. Each package had small fan vents on all four sides and self-annealing tape on the top and bottom of the device. A safety pull ring was located on the front of the package and was pulled out only after the package had been placed in its hiding position. Each of the small box were marked "Property of the City of Chicago" and were labeled as a Radon Detector.

None of the women involved knew what were in the packages. The only thing they had been told is that though their efforts, many of the infidels would die. By the end of the six months period, all of the teams combined had placed over 20 of the packages inside each of the fifty facilities where they had worked. Each of the packages contained approximately three ounces of SARIN gas in a liquid form. Once activated by pulling the pen, a countdown timer would take over. The plastic boxes were sealed and contained an old fashion mercury anti-tamping device made out of a thermostat. If anyone found any of the devices and tampered with them, it would be the last thing they ever messed with. The timer on all of the devices were set to go off at exactly at 1:00 PM the first day of May 2019.

Operation Qiyamah (Chicago Teams) minus 60 days

The women working in the nursing homes would use their spare time in making victim activated improvised explosive devices. Most of these were children toys, such as stuffed animals. The items used the same construct as the devices they used in the nursing homes and medical facilities, but without the timing device. When a victim, more than likely a child pulled the ring, the device would activate. There were only two types of devices, one with SARIN and one made with a military hand grenade. The hand grenade being used was the V40, originally made in the Netherlands, but used by both the Canadian and US armed forces until recently. It was small about the diameter of a golf ball and only weighed 4.8 ounces, yet powerful, with a lethal blast radius of five meters. The women paid close attention to detail as they made the devices, carefully straightening the pins in each of the devices so very little effort would have to be made to pull out the pin. Once the pin was pulled on a SARIN device, the device activated and a small glass breaker driven by a powerful spring would be released to drive into the small vial of deadly nerve gas. Even though it was a small vial, it would continue to kill for several hours after the vial was broken. After they were finished with their mission at the nursing homes, the terrorist teams would scatter across the US, seeding areas with these devices. They all knew there were many other teams in other areas of the United States doing the same thing and that something big was going to happen soon. With the addition of their random terror attacks along with the United States government and law enforcement attempting to deal with other terror attacks the chances of them being caught was small, Inshallah.

Operation Qiyamah minus 30 days, Washington D.C.

Hamid sighed as he rushed into his corner office at Impact Venues, LLC. There were a million and one things to do to get ready for the Washington Mall venue scheduled a month from now. As he rushed into his office he failed to realize that he had a visitor sitting calmly in one of the high backed chairs in front of his desk. Startling slightly upon realizing he had a visitor, he relaxed when he recognized his visitor. Rounding his desk, he sat down, smiled, and leaned back in his chair, "Yes Uncle, what brings you to Washington?"

May 1st, 1:00 PM, Washington DC, Capitol Hill

The protest rally had been scheduled for over a year and preparations had begun several months ago and was being billed as the largest civil rights gathering in Washington DC since the late 60's. Black Lives Matter officials, along with Al Sharpton, Jesse Jackson, Farrakhan and numerous other so-called leaders of the black community were present. A crowd of over 25 thousand had gathered on the Mall to hear the speeches about everything they claimed was wrong with the United States. All of the major TV stations were broadcasting live with their talking heads attempting to put their own spin on the event. DC and Capitol police had been reinforced with police officers from jurisdictions all over Maryland and Northern Virginia and riot police forces were standing by to make sure the protest didn't turn into a full blown riot.

The guest speakers had just arrived and had been seated on the grandstand. The master of ceremonies walked to the podium and was going over the order of events when the grandstand disappeared in a brilliant flash of light and noise. No one would ever know for sure how large or what type of explosive was used, nor how the bomb or bombs got past security, as the investigation was never completed. But whatever type of bomb it was, it detonated under the grandstand with enough force to kill or wound anyone within an 80-yard radius. Afterwards, the police estimated over 400 people were killed and over 230 were wounded from the grandstand bomb. In some ways it was lucky that the crowd was so tightly packed around the grandstand. The tightly packed bodies of the first five or six rows of protesters soaked up much of the blast force. After the initial shock, panic took over the large crowd with everyone running away from the blast area. Many of the injured resulted from the crowds trampling those that fell. The panic quickly turned into anger and the crowds began smashing anyone or anything in their path. The media platforms were initially not effected by the blast as they had been set up approximately one hundred meters south of the main stage. Each of the networks had contracted the same company to erect their camera platforms so their reporters could see over the people occupying the mall grounds. The majority of the network cameras were set up on the eastern and western edges of the mall. As the reporters were recovering from the bomb blast under the grand stand, a series of explosions began going off under the networks platforms. When the explosions finally stopped, not one of the networks platforms had been spared and no one near or on the platforms survived the attack. Complete chaos erupted and the surviving network camera crews and reported located on the edges of the mall captured every bit of the horror and confusion. First responders attempting to get to the victims were set upon by the angry crowd resulting in the withdrawal of almost all of the medical personnel until the police could get the crowds under control. Many of the scared attendees attempted to take refugee in the Smithsonian Museums that line the Mall. This path was one the rioters used also as the police began pushing them off the Mall. Before the small guard forces inside each of the museums could react and lock the museum doors, the rioters basically overran the few guards stationed at the museum entrances and entered the museums.

No one knows who began the destruction within the museums, but the National Museum of Natural History was hit the hardest with the entire second story wing of gemstones destroyed. Really don't know what someone is going to do with the Hope Diamond but I doubt it is going to be worth much right now. As always much of the looting and destruction didn't make much sense, priceless painting and historical artifacts were destroyed or ruined and fires were started in many of the museums.

Later that afternoon an anonymous phone call to the Washington Post claimed a pervious unknown white supremacy group was responsible for the attack on the Mall. In their statement they claimed this was the beginning of the war to cleanse the United States and make it safe for the white people. Whether the claim was true or not did not matter, the individual calling had certain facts about the attack that no one up to that point had, such as the scaffolding for the network platforms had been packed with explosives made from distilled hydrogen peroxide and ammonium nitrate.

As the news networks began reporting the claim of who was responsible for the Mall attack, other claims came in from many of the major cities across the United States. Waves of terrorist bombing and gas attacks were being reported and as the news of these hit the airwaves, a number of assassinations timed to coincide with the news took place across the United States. Many of the attacks were tipped off to the press just prior to the attack, making sure the media covered the attack. Several of the networks talking heads made comments suggesting the coverage of the attacks only made everything worse, but bombs and bodies were news and they continued to report the attacks. As most of the network news reports of the attacks took place at residences of famous Black leaders in politics and the entertainment business, the networks were slow to pick up on the retaliation attacks taking place in many of the cities across the nation. Racial tensions already high before the attacks exploded into savage, brutal open warfare.

Mass race riots broke out across the United States. Within hours many of the major cities were being looted wholesale and many were on fire and out of control. Governors declared martial law and activated the National Guard. Results varied on whether the Guard personnel showed up for duty or just showed up long enough to grab as many weapons and ammo as they could before disappearing back into the night. By midnight the President declared Martial Law within the lower 48 states with a 8:00 PM to 6:00 AM curfew and ordered the New York Stock Exchange to remain closed until further notice, and suspended all federal funded schools and universities until further notice.

As the riots took firm hold on most of the larger cities within the United States, several major terrorist attacks took place across the country at major fuel holding points and refineries. One such attack resulted in over 1200 deaths and countless missing was the Ravensworth Station Attack, in Fairfax County, Virginia. No one knows exactly what happened other than someone at the facility called the police and reported that several masked men had taken over the pumping facility at the Ravensworth Station Reservoir. The call left many of the younger policemen puzzled, as they had no idea what the Ravensworth Station Reservoir was, let alone why someone would want to take control of the facility. Local law enforcement was on the scene within minutes and the Fairfax SWAT was called in. The chief engineer of the plant was called to the site to explain to the SWAT Commander exactly what the team was facing. He explained that the Ravensworth Station Reservoir was an underground storage facility that stored over 13 million gallons of liquefied petroleum gas (LPG). The storage cavern was constructed or drilled back in the early 1960's and was over 400 feet deep. Normally, the gas is kept in a liquefied state by a water cap to maintain geostatic pressure. If the water pumps were shut down and the pumping equipment left on the entire area would soon be covered in, well basically, propane. One spark or open flame would cause the entire area to go up. Just about the time he finished explaining this, massive clouds of what appeared to be smoke began bellowing out of the open windows of the pumping station. The SWAT Commander ordered everyone to evacuate the area but it was too late. The resulting explosion could be heard as far away as Philadelphia to the north and Richmond to the south, and registered between 3.5 and 4.0 on the Richter scale. The damage to the Braddock/495 overpass closed the outer loop to traffic and started forest fires that destroyed several neighborhoods in the immediate area.

Later that same night several small groups of men in white panel vans started their vehicles precisely at 0100 AM. Earlier that day the men had driven to predetermined staging locations near several of the water pumping stations servicing the Washington DC Aqueduct project. Two of the vans headed towards the Dalecarlia reservoir near Great Falls, Virginia. This was their main target, with the other vans targeting the smaller pumping stations scattered across the district. They would all regroup for follow-on targets after the night's work was finished. For years security studies had warned how vulnerable the United States water infrastructure were to attacks, but security upgrades were expensive and no one had ever seriously attacked any major city water supply before. The terrorist leader had been surprised that all of the information he had needed to plan the attack had be easily found on the Internet. The entire water system to include maps of the system were downloaded and provided to each of the teams. He was pleased that none of the teams would have to use any explosives to completely disable any of the systems. A few smashed computers after shutting down the pumps and a few minutes with sledge hammers would do enough damage that within minutes there would not be enough pressure in any of the systems to provide water to most of DC residents and cut off any chance of the fire departments to stop any fires using the hydrants in the city. The Dalecarlia Reservoir was the main treatment plant for the district's drinking water. After treatment the water is then pumped to reservoirs all over the district. The two vans pulled up to the main building at the Dalecarlia Reservoir, five men exited from each van, three from each van were carrying an AK-47 slung across their backs, and with suppressor equipped .22 pistols in their hands, the remaining men carried sledge hammers and tools to assist in the planned destruction. The terrorist leader had ordered his men to kill all the workers at the plant, with the rational being that the workers were some of the only people that could repair any damage they did. The ten-man team moved quickly and efficiently, eliminating any of the workers they came across before arriving at the control center. After killing everyone on duty within the control room, the leader moved over to the master control panel and began shutting down all of the pumping equipment. After everything had been shut down, the team destroyed all of the computers, control panels, and backup systems. Making sure the team recovered all of the hard drives from the computers the team turned their attention to the pumping equipment. This scene was repeated at all of the pumping stations the group had targeted within the district. By 0400 AM, calls were coming in from all over the district reporting low water pressure. By daylight all of the terrorist were finished and headed west to a remote assembly site outside the 495 Beltway picked well in advance. They would remain there until signaled to carry out their next attacks.

At almost the exact same moment the terrorists started their vans for the attacks on the DC water supplies, twelve semi trucks started their engines at a truck stop in Baytown, Texas. The semi trucks had been leased almost six months prior and had carried several legitimate shipments of contracted supplies. But tonight was the reason the trucks had been leased. Earlier that day, right after the attack on the Mall in DC, the semi trucks with 50-armed terrorists had pulled into the ammonium nitrate plant just north of Waco, Texas. As the plant was normally closed on the weekend, the terrorists made short work of the two-man guard force at the main gate of the complex. The terrorists had rehearsed the plan many times over the last two weeks. The loading warehouse was large and easily allowed all twelve of the semi trucks to back up to its own loading bay. As the trucks came to a stop the rear doors flew open and five ATV's sped off the trailers to their assigned positions. All of the terrorists had been trained in their jobs and some headed to get fork trucks and others headed out to provide security and to plant demolitions around the compound. The terrorists had detailed plans of the plant and it only took them a little less than four hours to load all of the semi trucks with the material they had come for. Det cord was rigged and layered into the sacks as each of the pallets were loaded onto the trucks. Once the trucks were loaded, each leaving enough room for the ATVs to reload into the trailers, the trucks all pulled out and headed south. While the trucks were being loaded, some of the terrorists had spent the time to carefully plant explosives at predetermined spots in the chemical plant. Thirty minutes after the last truck pulled out of the chemical plant gates the entire compound exploded into a small mushroom cloud. Windows were blown out of houses as far away as five miles and the sound of the explosion was heard as far north as Dallas.

The semi trucks pulled out of the truck stop in Baytown and headed towards the ExxonMobil Baytown petrochemical terminal just two miles south of the truck stop. The Baytown Refinery is the largest refinery in the United States and is one of the world's largest industrial complexes. The lead semi truck slowly pulled ahead of the other trucks as they approached the terminal. The main gates of the terminal was a hard left hand turn off the highway but the turn was wide and allowed the lead truck to maintain a steady thirty miles an hour and it turned hard into the main gate. No one at the plant was really expecting trouble and the main gate crumbed like tin foil upon the impact of the semi truck. While the damage to the truck was enough to kill the truck's engine, the speed of the impact carried the gate and truck out of the path of the other trucks coming in behind it. None of the trucks stopped to check on the first truck, they all had predetermined positions and they headed for their targets. The terrorists in the first truck finally got the doors open on their trailer and started to unload their ATV when the guards opened fire on them. Under normal conditions the reaction of the guards would have been more than adequate as all five of the terrorist were hit and down within seconds. But these were not normal times and one of the five was able to detonate his suicide vest that in turn detonated the truck load of ammonium nitrate, killing all of the guards at the main gate before any of them had had a chance to report the attack. It took the eleven remaining trucks less than ten minutes to find their targets, park their trucks, jump on the backs of the ATVs and speed off to their planned egress routes. None of the terrorists returned to the main gate, they all had planned routes out of the terminal though the security fences. All of the teams were miles away and headed to safe houses when the terminal explosion tore Baytown apart. The Baytown terminal was one of the largest of its kind in the world. Dozens of massive tanks, some as large as 88 meters in diameter and a height of almost 20 meters each holding over a million gallons of gasoline products, paint thinner, finger nail polish remover, and other petroleum products exploded in a chain reaction. The explosion was estimated to be the largest non-nuclear ever in the United States; the death toll was in the tens of thousands, with many more seriously injured. Hospitals in the area were overwhelmed with the injured. The Texas Governor called out the State Guard and requested support from the Federal Government.

Over the course of the next six hours additional attacks targeting electric grids, water supplies, gas and oil holdings and pipelines, train tracks, major tunnels and bridges, black and Hispanic leaders and major left-wing Hollywood stars took place in at least 12 major US cities. Low income apartment complex's were fire bombed and many intercity neighborhoods, schools and malls that had never experienced drive by shooting were hit with multiple acts of murder. The women and teenagers that had lived in northern Mexico and Canada for the last few years had remembered their training and committed many acts of atrocities before the night was done. The teams of women with their male driver had split up and dropped off their homemade IED's. With so many terrorist attacks being reported the police systems were over loaded. Hundreds of police officers and first responders died because no one was warned about the poison gas and IED's. Many of women committed attacks with suicide vests strapped in place and attacked any public gathering they could locate. All of the attacks seemed random, but created rage wherever they touched as some type of evidence was clearly left at every scene showing whom was responsible. All evidence pointed towards right wing radicals or militant black groups. This fed the hate and anger from all sides. The more one group would deny the attack; they in turn would be accusing other groups of committing acts of terrorism against their own interests. Attacks against targets of opportunities, many including children were perpetrated on the second day, school buses across America were either blown up or were found with bombs attached, creating mass panic among parents. As America had been gradually moving towards a two income society, with all the schools closed across the nation, at least one of the parents had to stay home from work, adding to the hysteria.

By the end of the day after the attack on the DC Mall, every cop, fireman, or first responder in the nation dared not go into an intercity neighborhood without body armor and back up. Many of the firemen refused to respond to certain neighborhoods due to their trucks and personnel came under fire each time they tried. By the next morning after the DC attack America's cities burned out of control. Most of the law enforcement, fire fighters, and first responders had not shown up for work the following morning, they had families that had to be protected from the madness gripping the nation. Billions of dollars of damage to the nation's infrastructure was done and with no end in sight.

Chapter One

After spending the last four and a half years working in Afghanistan I some how found myself driving back to the last place I wanted to be, Washington D.C. Such is life; in my line of business you have to go to where the work is. There is almost never any shortage of work in my expertise and normally the pay is very good, the down side of this is most of the jobs requiring my skills are in the worst areas of the world. And I have been to most of them, Haiti, Somalia, Iraq, Afghanistan, Sudan, if you name it and it's a shit hole than I've probably been there. But as I want to be able to occasional go home to Texas I took a job near DC.

After retiring from the Big Green Machine (Marines) I figured I would work for some government agency for a few years than retire retire. I was at that point where all I wanted to do was kick back on my ranch in Texas, watch the kids grow and enjoy life. Yes, I worked for a couple of different three letter government agencies for a few years after retiring at 38, even attempted to go back in the Marines after 9/11. They said no thank you at the time. So after 9/11 the money for contracting jobs was getting crazy and became very attractive, so I jumped to the contracting world. Been there ever since, jumping from job to job, some lasting several years, some only a year. Wherever the money was best and the job wasn't boring and it was worthwhile at least in my opinion. I have always had a problem with boring jobs. I most often get myself into some type of trouble if I get bored and I now always try to move on once I begin getting that bored feeling. It normally goes like this, go overseas for an exciting and well paying job for a year or two, return to the States and work for a year or so, then off to the next adventure. That worked great until I got married again. This time I found a keeper. She is smart, beautiful, funny, and understands my world of work as she was "in the business" for about ten years before she decided it was time for us to have a family. Now I'm a few years older than her, well actually several, but I agreed to one. Ha, God is still laughing, we ended up with triplets. Don't know how she did it but she pulled it off, but she carried them for almost the full term. Wouldn't trade them for the world, now, but that first few months were hell (but great), as they were little eating and shitting machines. But they are growing fast and are all smart as hell, healthy, and good looking (thank God they took after their Mother).

Anyway, that is why I ended up staying so long in Afghanistan this last time and why I'm heading back to DC. I have always sworn to never work up here again, but here I am. The last time I worked up here the job actually turned out to be a great job and I stayed until the program ended. The small company I had been working for had been brought out by one of the large defense contractor firms and they immediately ran the program into the ground. That is why I took the job in Afghanistan and ended up staying for over four years, as the money was good and with the arrival of the triplets I figured I'd best make as much money as I could, while I could. But as good as the job was, the government decided to do a drawdown and stop all combat operations so my billet was replaced by a government position. So I headed back to Texas to spend some catch up time with the family.

After kicking around Houston for several months looking for a decent paying job, nothing turned up and I ended up heading back to the DC area, it was that or a job in Tampa or Bragg. Neither of which paid anywhere near what a guy in my line of work can make in DC. It wasn't perfect, but then nothing ever is. I hated to be away from the kids so much, and it did put a hell of a lot of stress on my wife. But it is what it is. The new job wasn't difficult and it did appear to be interesting, plus it wasn't downtown DC or Kabul. At least, I hoped anyway, it looked like I would be able to get to my new building, it was located near BWI, and the area was far enough away from Baltimore that the area should not have the widespread riots the downtown areas were experiencing. Pulling my vehicle into a parking stall in front of the Hampton Inn, I resigned myself that this would be home until I could find somewhere to rent or lease or arranged to stay with one of the many guys I know from the Corps. It seemed like almost all of the guys that stayed in the business after the Corps ended up in the DC area after retirement. The good thing about this new job (besides the decent pay) was that it was not downtown DC, have I said that before, don't want you to get the impression that I don't like DC, no really I HATE DC. So anyway the riots should not really affect me. At least that is what I thought as I checked into my hotel less than 1/4 mile from my new office and headed up to my room to lay down to get some much needed sleep before my first day at a new job.

SHTF Day One - 1230 AM

My first thought when I heard the electronic lock on my hotel room door click was someone was attempting to break into my room. As I felt around searching for my pistol, I glanced at the clock on the nightstand and saw the power was out. Not surprising with all the rioting that has been going on for the last 24 hours. So far the area I was in had not been affected, but it was only a matter of time if the government couldn't get things under control. Finding my Glock 17, I eased out of bed as quietly as I could and quickly moved to the wall across the room nearer the hotel room door. After standing and listening for about 30 seconds I could hear nothing outside my door and no other attempts were made to open the door. Not that anyone could as it was double locked, with the deadbolt locked and the small joke of a panic bar engaged, plus the rubber doorstop I always traveled with under the door. Still I knew I had heard the electronic lock disengage. I stood there for another minute and then turned to retrieve my headlamp and flashlight from my go bag that was sitting on the unoccupied second bed. I pulled on my sweat pants and running shoes and stood to go check the door. As I moved to the door I heard voices from the room next door. It was the guy talking to his wife or girl friend attempting to calm her down, I had met them in the hallway as we were both checking in at the same time, he was telling her to go back to sleep that the electronic lock on the door was not working but the dead bolt still worked.

Walking over to the door, I kicked the rubber doorstop out of the way and disengaged my deadbolt and panic bar, sure enough the electronic lock was not working and the door opened as I turned the handle. Is that normal I thought, not knowing at the time that I would have that same thought many times over the next couple of days until I realized it was the new normal. After checking the hallway, I went back into my room and eased the door back shut, I made sure the deadbolt was engaged, the small worthless panic bar was closed and my door stop was back in place, I returned to bed in an attempt to get back to sleep. As I was laying there tossing and turning in my attempt to get back to sleep I realized what was wrong, there was no background noise of any type, upon realizing how quiet it was I really got a bad feeling. No noise of any kind, normally there would be the low rumble of traffic on I-395 and of course the noise of jets landing and taking off from BWI every few minutes.

The hotel I was currently staying in was sandwiched between I-395 and BWI airport. It was the closest I could get at a reasonable rate to my new work building. After lying in bed for a few minutes the quietness began to weird me out a little so I threw back the covers and climbed out of bed. As I was getting up to look out the window I felt more than heard a jolt run though the hotel rooms floor followed closely by a muffled explosion. Before I could cross the ten feet or so across the room to the window, two more distant explosions closely followed the first explosion. I moved to the window but realized my room faced away from the direction the explosions had come from. The window faced south towards Washington DC and BWI was to the east about one mile in a straight line from the hotel. I was more than a little surprised to see a glow on the southern horizon, it didn't look like the glow you normally see from a distance city, but more like the glow you would associate with a large forest fire. Realizing the power must be out, not only in the local area, but it looked like power was out for the District also. Standing there for a couple of minutes revealed no clues to the cause and I returned to bed. Contemplating the situation I dismissed my gut feeling and wrote it off to the power being out because of the riots.

Looking back at this moment I'm going to blame all my years in Iraq and Afghanistan for my slow comprehension of what was going on. Assassinations, protests, power black outs, explosions, glows on the horizon from fires were part of a normal day in Kabul or Kandahar or Baghdad. I just turned away from the window and went back to bed. Hey, I never claimed that I was a rocket scientist, I said I worked for a couple of three letter agencies, not four, and I had to be up early and into work for a staff meeting first thing. I needed my beauty rest and yesterday had been a long day.

SHTF plus 6 hours

I glanced at my Afghan special Rolex (which by the way has been going strong for over 9 years now) and wondered why my alarm on my iPhone had not gone off. I knew I had set it and had added a second alarm 15 minutes after the first to make sure I got up on time. My first alarm should have gone off at 0445 followed by the second at 0500. It was now 0505 and neither alarm had gone off. Slightly aggregated I reached over and punched the button on my phone to show me the time. Nothing, nada, the blank face of the phone just stared back at me. Now I was getting into one those moods, thinking Apple had pushed an update causing my phone to shut down after updating it. What if I hadn't woken up in time to the staff meeting? That would have been great, the new guy late to his first staff meeting. Just great, I would have to go by the IT department later today and kick one of the nerds. Hey, don't judge, it's not like I would really do something like that, I do like to think I'm one of the good guys, but that doesn't mean I'm always one of the nice guys. I have always tried to live by the rule; if you cannot do something smart, do something right. Anyway, I hold down the button on my phone to restart it, hmmm, nothing. Maybe I didn't hold it down long enough, second try same thing, nothing, third and fourth try, nothing. Next I pulled out my iPad. Same thing, wow, sometimes I'm a little thick, next up I pulled out my laptop, no luck, by this time I'm cussing Steve Jobs and everything Apple. So by now I'm wide-awake and the gears are beginning to turn. Reaching over to the lamp next to the bed I attempt to turn it on with the same results as my electronics. Cussing to myself I stood and made my way to the curtains in the room and drew them open. Complete darkness met my eyes, but the darkness did confirm that all of the power was out in the area. Going back to my go bag I rummage around and pulled out my LazerBrite glow tube and switched on the white light section of the tube, while at the same time congratulating myself on packing it in my go bag.

After switching on my LazerBrite, I sat and pondered on the events over the last five or six hours. First the power went out around 1230 AM, I quietly cussed and wished I had checked my phone at that time. Second I realized that the power going out should not have affected the electronic lock on my door. It was battery powered. Following this line of thought was leading me down a path that I really didn't want to think about. I got up again and went back to the windows and studied the skyline. It was still dark, really dark. There was not a single point of light anywhere. This sucked.

I decide first things first and headed into the bathroom to see if there is any water pressure.

SHTF plus 7 hours

After completing my rather lukewarm morning ritual of shit, shower and shave and getting dressed I headed back over to the window to take a look outside. I had dressed in my green CRYE pants after pulling the knee pads out of them, no use drawing anymore attention without need, my LOWA boots and a polo shirt, with the power out I wasn't going to get dressed in a suit when my work building would be closed as long as the power was out. I also didn't want to go full combat mode until I verified for myself that this was in fact an event worthy of being called a SHTF moment. The sun wasn't over the horizon yet but it was light enough to see shapes. The first thing I saw were the columns of smoke pretty much across the whole southern horizon and than noticed a few people wandering around the hotel parking lot talking and gesturing to their cars with their hoods up. While no one has ever confused me with Einstein I can do basic math and can tie my own shoes without help most of the time. Power out, none of the electronics are working, cars won't start, this is beginning to add up to one huge nightmare. The timing could not have been worse for me, 1,400 hundred miles from my family and home. Pushing that thought away as hard as I could, I knew time was very important and I needed to get more information quickly.

None of the smoke columns appear to be close enough to be a danger to the hotel so I slipped my Glock in its Tier One holster and struck two spare magazines into my left back pocket, I left my shirt tail out to cover the holster and grabbed my flashlight and headed downstairs. (Before all you 1911 guys toss this because of the Glock, I will explain. I am a 1911 guy, however since my near eyesight has gone, I had to switch to a Trijicon RMR on all my pistols. Also have you ever shot a 3-Gun Match, it is hard as hell to keep up with 20 round mags versus 8-10 round mags. Anyway, now I use a custom Glock 17 and 19 for most of my day-to-day carry.) After entering the hallway and shutting my door the darkness was complete. Pressing the button on the end of my Surefire flashlight I lit up the hallway and I again mentally cussed knowing I had not packed any extra batteries for it. But on the good side I guess that answers the question on whether LED bulbs would stand up to an EMP. Making note of how many doors were between the stairs and me in case I had to find my room in the dark, with that finished and wanting to save power I spotted the stairway door and turned off the flashlight. Shoving the flashlight into my pocket I felt along the wall to the end of the hallway and entered the stairwell to head downstairs. I wanted to stock up on any high calorie pogie bait that I could before it was all gone. Walking down the stairwell, I came out near the front desk and immediately headed over to the alcove where they had a fairly well stocked snack section. Grabbing all the bags of nuts they had and several of the Milky Way bars and bags of M&M's, along with a Diet Coke that was still fairly cool I carried it all to the front desk. The clerk began to protest that he could not sell anything, as the cash register was not working. I waved a couple of twenties under his nose and told him to keep the change. Next I headed into the breakfast area and went over to the juice machine and checked to see if the machine was working. Jackpot, filling a cup I quickly drank the whole cup and refilled the cup a second time. There were bagels on the counter and I loaded one up with cream cheese. Carrying all of my supplies I headed back up stairs to my room. I had only been away from the room for a couple minutes but entering the room I set down the bagel and supplies on the bed and checked the room, as it had been unlocked the whole time I had been downstairs. Moving one of the chairs over so I could see out the window I sat and ate my bagel and cracked open my diet coke. I took my time knowing it might be a while before I had either again. As I sat and ate I watched the guys in the parking lot attempting to start their vehicles. They were wasting their time switching out batteries, trying batteries connected in series, nothing worked and I thought to myself, those things are nothing but big paper weights. Finishing my bagel I began to think though what my own plans were. It was a long way to get home to my wife and kids down in Houston and to make things worse I was unfamiliar with the area I was in right now. My first priority was to get some better equipment and hopefully a long gun. That meant finding a sporting goods store before the hordes of people realize what was going on and the real rioting starts. Well that's easy I thought, I know of only one sporting good store in the area that had everything I needed and that was the Bass Pro Store at the mall. Finishing off the diet coke I stood and headed over to begin organizing what little gear I had.

I first dumped all the gear in my bug out bag out on the bed. Than I began to seriously pack all of my gear, not that I have all that much useful stuff with me, back into the bug out bag. Being that my new job was in Maryland, I had planned on being very, very low key with what gear I carried in my bug out bag. Just what I had with me now would be considered a felony, as in go straight to jail and throw away the key, in normal times in Maryland. With martial law being declared in all the major cities I would need to be careful to avoid any roadblocks. What I really needed was to find someone that knows what the hell is going on. I know at least a dozen people in Northern Virginia that would know what was going on, but they are all down in the Fairfax area or DC area and might as well be on the moon. It was clear that the attacks at the mall and around the nation were just the first stage of a planned attack with the second stage being an EMP type device or maybe we were just extremely unlucky and was hit with the mother of all solar flares and it was just a coincidence it followed the terrorist attacks yesterday. I can pretty much discount the solar flare theory as we would more than likely have seen some type of advance warning either from the government or from one of our allies. I cannot imagine that an enemy would only strike a part of the country, whomever had done this would have probably hit us with multiple strikes high up in the atmosphere or with just one massive EMP weapon at least 350 miles up over the center of the US. I could also not see just hitting the US and none of our allies, at least striking our major allies like the Brits and Aussies. I'm wondering now if our allies had been hit the same way with attacks against their minority populaces. Whoever came up with this plan knew what they were doing. Start civil unrest, then cut off all the power, an instant recipe for wide spread chaos.

Glancing out the window the columns of smoke had combined into one mass black cloud covering the Southern horizon. I have not been outside yet but I would imagine the same is to the north. Just my luck to be struck between two of Americas most violent prone cities. I needed to get moving before the hordes of people begin moving out of the cities and into the countryside. Which I mused would not be long based on the smoke coming from the major built up areas. Once that happens it will be extremely difficult to move freely and any stranger would become a threat and target for the locals of the area.

It only took me a few minutes to divide the useful stuff from my meager supply of clothing and equipment. I could kick myself for not bringing more gear, but my original plan was to only be here for a few weeks than fly back home to Houston for a few days and return with more of my "stuff". But to waste time right now playing the "what if" game was a complete waste of time and time is now one of the most important items that I could somewhat control. I mentally went over what I have on hand, my three day pack with an empty 100 oz water bladder, a 27 oz. stainless steel Klean Kanteen, a Sawyer Mini Water filter, my custom Glock 17, with one 16 oz Nagel bottle of HP 9mm ammo (about 120 rounds) and six loaded Glock magazines, my war belt with triple mag pouch's for the pistol mags, one pair of LOWA Desert boots (a life saver at this point), a lensatic compass, my Petzl headlamp, a small flashlight with two spare batteries, my Warbonnet Blackbird XLC hammock with my Warbonnet Super fly tarp, a Solo camp stove packed in a one quart pot, 100 feet of 550 cord, a small roll of gorilla duct tape, a signal mirror, one firefly IR marker, a zip lock with some medical supplies, (a tourniquet, one large sterile bandage, one chest seal, several Band-Aids, some Neosporin, a half dozen tampons and some sanitary napkins), two small pocket knifes (neither suited for this situation) but better than nothing, my never leave home without them, my all around use everywhere TOPS Brothers of Bushcraft 6 inch knife and my Mercworx Shiva for those times you just really have to stick something or someone, and a non waterproof light jacket. Last but not least, strapped to my three day pack is my (what my wife calls) zombie ax but is called a Tramahawk by Zombie Tools out in Montana. She got it for me as a joke after I had shown her the website, but it has turned out to be almost indestructible and useful in so many ways it is hard to count. It's a small hand ax, bigger than a normal tomahawk but not by much. Just an excellent all around tool to have when you need to bust something up. I next tested the headlamp after putting batteries in it. It worked fine as did the flashlight, there had always been a lively debate on whether LED flashlights would survive an EMP event, but so far both of mine had.

I keep pushing away thoughts of my wife and the triplets. Did this attack effect down into Texas also? If it only affected the East coast than they are fine, if not there is nothing I can do other than get there as fast as I can and just hope that her brother and Father each had headed that way to get her and the kids. I know because of the timing of the event that she and the kids would have been home and the neighbors will help out for as long as they can. Thank God my next-door neighbor was a good old boy and knew which way a round goes into a gun. There is food and water in the house to last for several weeks, but not enough for the winter. I also knew that her Father would move heaven and hell to get to my wife and kids. I reassured myself that her Father would get them to his ranch and that he was pretty well supplied for an event such as it was. I pushed it away, no time for this right now, I needed to move.

I checked the time and saw it is already almost 7 AM. I need to get moving to secure some of my immediate needs before I begin my trek back to Texas. I wish now that I had stopped by Bass Pro at the mall last night. Of course that is a moot point now, but I had planned on stopping and didn't because of the traffic and now I'm in the worst possible position I could be in. My first concern is to get my hands on water and a map of the local area. While the hotel still has some water pressure I would really prefer to get some bottled water for the bladder. I'm sure I had seen some bottled water down in the breakfast area that I would grab on my way out. After that I need to hike over to the Bass Pro Shop about 3 miles from here. It is the only place I know of around here that

12

will have most of the things I need. As I am not familiar with the area and on top of that this is Maryland home of some of the worst anti gun laws in the land (well that might be a slight exaggeration but not much of one). The how of getting the gear that I need from a closed store I will have to deal with once I get there and assess the situation. This could be a real problem if the looting had already started but I don't think it will start for another day or two. I hesitate for a few seconds before reaching over and grabbing the knee pads I had taken out earlier, stuffing them back into their proper places, I next pulled out my inner belt to my war belt threading it into my pants loops, than throwing on my combat suspenders and drew those on over my arms and shoulders. After securing the suspenders to my inner belt, I slung my war belt on and settled it into place. I slide the other spare mags into their mag pouches, before putting on an oversized lightweight long sleeve shirt. Hopefully I won't be stopped and searched as this would lead to a straight ticket to the local jail. Maryland is death on concealed carry and what I am carrying would be considered an "arsenal" in this state, but if this event is what I think it is I don't have time to stand around waiting to be sure.

I carried my two suitcases down to my now worthless car and threw them into the trunk of the car on the slight chance I was wrong about what had taken place. After making sure my rental car was in fact dead, I locked it up and shouldered my pack. My first stop was the lobby to check and see if they have any maps of the local area. Entering the lobby area there was a small group of people gathered at the front desk giving the clerk a hard time. One man in the group stood out, as he was the loudest and also the fattest, directing a string of foul language at the dis-leveled clerk behind the counter. As I walked in the conversation dies down for a second, than the fat man begins yelling again at the clerk, "Listen bitch I want a shuttle van here NOW! I have a flight to catch in one hour and

I have to be on it!" I'm immediately impressed on how well the young lady is handling the irate man, she simply replies in a calm tone, "Sir, all of our vans will not start and until the phones begin working again there is nothing I can do to assist you getting to the airport." This reply at least temporarily shuts up the obnoxious fool as he moved away muttering to himself.

As I approached the counter the young lady immediately began to tell me, "Sir, we do not know when the power or phones will come back on line." I just smiled at her and said, "I know, would you happen to have any maps of the local area?" She relaxed slightly when she realized I wasn't going to yell at her or ask for impossible things, "Sir we have these," pulling out a pad of large scale area maps. "Is it ok if I take a couple of these," I ask. "Of course," she said and pulled two copies off of the pad and handed them to me. I once again smile and said, "Thank you, also do you have any bottled water available?" At this she also smiled and just pointed towards the breakfast area. I walked over to the breakfast area and checked out what they had put out since I was down earlier. It looked like the hotel had pulled out all the stops in an attempt to appease the disgruntled customers. There were large containers of several different types of dry cereal lined up on the counter and several pitchers of milk and orange juice. I walked over to an empty table and dropped my daypack. Reaching into the bottom pouch I pulled out a couple of quart zip lock Baggies. Moving over to the cereal I filled both bags with Frosted Mini Wheat's (my favorite), again don't know when these might come in handy or when I would get a chance to have them again if ever. While they might not be the highest in nutrition, it would provide calories and fill my stomach in the coming days. Stuffing them back into the bottom pouch I returned and filled up a bowl and added milk and grabbed a large hand full of sugar packs. Retrieving

14

another zip lock I dropped in the sugar, returning to the condiments area and grabbing a couple of hand-fulls of honey packs, this while receiving a few dirty looks from the surrounding tables. Oh well, you can't please everyone all the time and right now I needed to get what I could to survive the coming hard times. Sometimes you just have to do what you have to do to survive.

December 1990, USN/USMC SERE Course, outside of Brunswick, Maine

It was cold. Like really cold, there was a 30-inch base of snow and more coming in by the minute and we were getting ready to depart the compound. The instructors attempted to keep a close eye on us as we were given a coke can to fill with the items we were going to be able to take with us on the survival phase of the course. I had been training for this my whole life and I knew I could leave out of here without anything (ok don't get crazy, anyone needs the right clothing in weather like this) and survive just fine for the four days, but they, our instructors, don't play fair. They handicap those of us that know what they are doing by teaming us up with another person. Where one person can survive, it doesn't just make it twice as hard to keep two people going it makes it three or four times as hard. I have been in the woods hunting and trapping since I was big enough to carry traps for my Grandfather. And trust me, these instructors might be hardcore, but they were nothing compared to my Grandfather. So I stuffed everything I could into the can, my socks, and down my t-shirt. Nothing big enough to stand out but hey if you're not cheating your not trying. Plus I knew I was going to need all the advantage I could get with the shave tail Navy Lt they had teamed me up with. I still didn't know how he was going to climb up and down these mountains with being so full of shit, that whole I'm a Naval Fighter Pilot shit. Ok, don't get me wrong I love the guys when they are up in the air bombing the rag heads, but when they are on the ground they are a pain in the ass. Anyway, those 300 or 400 extra calories I was able to hide away might make a hell of a difference over the next few days. It was then I knew how true the old saying was, eat when there is food, drink when there is water, don't stand when you can sit, don't sit when you can lie down. Anyway, with the one rabbit I was able to twist out of its burrow with a stick and the extra calories I was able to hide, the fly boy and I were able to make it just fine during the survival phase, even if those bastard instructor did screw us on the rabbit turn in (it was against the rules to eat any rabbits if you caught one, you turned it in and were reportedly traded a small vat can of stew for it. Our vat can was half empty. Bastards).

Finishing the cereal in my bowl, I got up and tossed the bowl in the trash and grabbed a paper cup and walked over to the orange juice. Standing there I drank two cups of it down. I was really feeling the need to get on the road before something delayed me further. Moving over to the tub of bottles of water I picked up five of the bottles and headed back to my table pulled open the top of my day pack and untwisted the cap on my camel Bak. Quickly dumping in the five bottles I capped off the bag and zipped up my daypack. I sensed someone move up close to me and I looked up to see the girl from the front desk standing there. She eyed me for a few seconds than walked over to a cabinet under the drink counter and pulled out another case of water. She grabbed another six bottles and walked back and set the bottles on the table. Unzipping my pack again I stuffed the bottles inside and closed the bag. I looked up and said, "Thank you". She hesitated than quietly ask, "Do you know what is going on?" I looked at her and motioned for her to follow me. I walked out of the lobby carrying my pack out into the alcove by the front doors. I answered her in a low voice, "Ma'am, if what I think happened did in fact happen, thing are going to get really bad around here and they are not going to get better in a long, long, time if ever. This isn't from any riots from the attacks yesterday. This appears to be a follow on attack and this time we were hit with an EMP device of some type. I don't know by whom or why." She started to interrupt me but I held up my hand to stop her, "Ma'am you need to get somewhere safe really soon, gather up as many supplies like food and water that you can because by tonight or no later than tomorrow all hell is going to break loose. If the thugs and gangs have not already figured it out they soon will and there is not going to be any help coming from the government." She turned a little pale and shook her head in denial; "We have power outages all the time. Maybe the government shut down the power after they declared martial law last night." I stopped her again, "This is not just a power outage. Think about it, have you ever seen a power outage that also stops all the watches and phones, kills all the cell phones, causes the cars to stop working and knocks jet airlines out of the sky. Not only that, I'm sure anyone with a pace maker or implanted medical device that was battery powered is dead by now. Anything ran by computer or microchips and was hooked to the grid is fried. Open your eyes; this is not a normal power outage. The only thing that could do all of this an EMP." This just elicited a blank stare, which in turn triggered frustration in me, "Ma'am I don't have time to stand here and fully educate you on what an Electro Magnetic Pulse or EMP for short is. There are only two things that can cause an event like this. One is a high altitude nuclear detonation and the other is a massive coronal solar ejection from the sun. Right now it doesn't matter which caused the EMP. What does matter is that within a few hours it is going to be complete chaos when people begin running out of water and food. Most people have less than three days of food in their homes and almost no water. Most won't know how or where to get potable water once the water pressure goes away. They don't know that bleach has a very short shelf life, or that they can use pool shock to purify water. And the water pressure will go away very quickly without the pumps working. At that point the normal people will panic and the lawless element will prey off the weak and unprepared. The thugs and gangs will be completely out of control. Even the normal people will begin doing things they would never dream of doing when their kids are hungry or crying because they are thirsty. Every store in the area will be looted by tonight and people will be killing each other for a candy bar a week from now." "But what about the police and the government? Isn't that what FEMA does, they will come in and help the people and the Army or National Guard with keep the gangs under control," she countered. It was this kind of reasoning that really always rubbed me the wrong way, "What about them?" I fired back, "Not only are they at home with no way to get to work and even if they could do you think they would leave their own families unprotected? They know what is going on and I guarantee they are gathering all the supplies they can to try and ride this out. You need to gather as much of this food and water as you can and get to your family as soon as possible. Quit worrying about these people here at the hotel. Most of them will be dead or dying within the week. I know that sounds harsh but you need to open your eyes and realize you can't do anything for them." Gesturing at the horizon, "Where do you think all of that smoke is coming from, every transformer in the city shorted out and most of them started fires, the cities and built up areas are burning. Didn't you hear the planes crash last night? What do you think knocked all of them out of the air? The reason they crashed is that everything electronic just shut down. Get home and protect your family." She just shook her head and said, "No the police and

18

government will get this under control." I just smiled and said, "Good luck." I picked up my pack, slung it on and headed across the parking lot not willing to waste any more time and effort on attempting to convince her just how very wrong she was. Looking back now, I was wrong, it was much, much worse than I ever imagined.

Chapter Two

SHTF Plus 9 hours

I know the mall is about three miles as the crow flies but about four miles if I follow the roads. I plan to head to the mall in as straight of a line that I can. I'm already thinking about what items I really need to make it back to Texas. Right now at the top of the list is a good pair of wire cutters as I stare at the seven-foot high chain link fence separating me from the direction I'm wanting to go. I follow the fence for a short distance and find a place I can crawl under it. I can already see another fence just like the one I crawled under several hundred yards south of me and running parallel with Highway 195. Maybe two or three good pairs of wire cutters and a small set of bolt cutters, these fences are going to get old really fast. If I had to I can always climb over but I'm not as young as I used to be. Turning 55 this year didn't mean much to me as I don't feel any different from when I turned 35 or 45. I not much of a runner anymore but I still attempt to stay in pretty decent shape, just ask my wife, she will confirm that round is a shape, she can really be a smart ass, just one of the many qualities I love about her.

Once I get up on the highway I think what I really needed right now was a good mountain bike, I would have to keep my eye out for one I can burrow. There has always been a lively debate among the prepping/survival community about what is theft/looting and what is scavenging when the shit hits the fan or SHTF. Not much debate with me right now, I would not/will not take something by force from its rightful owner but I will scavenge whatever/whenever I can. My only purpose in life right now is getting back to my family as quick as I can by whatever means I can. Right now I have to get outfitted for the long haul and get the hell out of this area and get west to the Blue Ridge area before heading south.

I do have a few additional skills picked up growing up in the county, my twenty years in the Marine Corps and added to by the next fifteen years of contract work in the Middle East. As I walked south toward the mall I recalled the conversation with my wife about taking this job in the Socialist State of Maryland. I attempted to come up with every excuse not to go to Maryland, I'd have rather gone back to the rock pile (that's Afghanistan for you non-military types), oh I'm sure most of the people who reside in Maryland think it is a great place, I just happen to disagree, so sue me, last time I checked this is or was a free country, that is unless you are in Maryland and want to conceal carry a firearm to protect yourself and your family. But that was yesterday and from what it looks like the clock just got reset to sometime around the mid to late 1800's. Anyway I was driving my wife crazy and had to get back to work. I had been home since the end of May, pretty much closing out my honey do list, and she was ready to smother me in my sleep.

I know that four and a half years sounds like a long time to be deployed but the pay was good and the mission was worthwhile. The unit was made up of some of the best each of the services had to offer and it was never boring. Plus with the triplets growing fast I needed to bank as much money as I could between riding lessons, gymnastics, karate, dance, swim lessons, and the beginning of private school. Yes, I need to get home as fast as I can. My wife is one of the smartest people I know and does have some good skills, but outdoor survival is not one of her strong points. While she can and has done all of the survival schools and is a decent shot with both a handgun and a M4, her idea of camping is at a four star or above resort, complete with spa and room service. Again based on the time of the event, she would have been home with the kids and more than likely our neighbors were home too. If anything, my neighbor is as prepared as I am to defend his family and I know he will keep an eye on my family also. Between the supplies he has and the ones I have stored at the house they should all be fine for a good period of time. At least they are off any of the main highways that will become a nightmare with all of the people pushing up out of downtown Houston. At least not anytime soon, but I really do need to get there before it becomes necessary to bug out of there. Her parents are about 50 miles away, but knowing them they will do whatever it takes to get to them.

I get to the next fence running along side of 195 and find a hole large enough for me to crawl under. Even though the event took place around 1230 AM last night, there are several dozen cars and trucks stalled in view on the highway. I take a couple of minutes looking into the interiors of a few cars closest to me to see if there is anything of use to me but as luck would have it, I didn't see anything. That is until I spotted a work truck about 50 yards away. You know the kind that has tool compartments in place of a normal truck bed. I cautiously move up to the truck and check the area to make sure no one is in the area. Finding some tools would be a huge find and would potentially save me a lot of time down the road and was worth the time now. Kneeling down next to a car, I drew my Glock from the holster and did a quick press check to make sure that I had one in the pipe and was ready to go. After re-holstering the Glock I stood and slowly approached the truck. I just knew all of the toolboxes would be locked and hopelessly wished I had my pick kit with me. After all the time and money the Department of Defense spent on my training and practice I finally have a situation where I really needed my pick kit and didn't have it with me. TV shows and movies always make it look so simple and easy to pick a lock. Anyone that actually knows how to pick a lock knows it takes hours and hours of practice to develop the "touch" or "feel" to be able to pick a real lock. Of course there are tricks to a lot of locks, especially the cheap ones, but really most locks are only made to keep honest people honest, not to keep out trained professionals. The old saying, opportunity makes a thief, is not really true, honest people don't steal other people's stuff, whether it is locked up or not. I think of last week when I got to my new job. As soon as I arrived they assigned me to a cube and of course all of the desks and cabinets were locked and no one knew where the keys were. It took me an hour or so of messing around with my penknife and a heavy-duty paper clip but I was able to unlock all of the drawers and cabinets. Defiantly not a time record for opening up such simple locks but I'm out of practice.

As it turned out all of the thoughts of picking locks was a waste of time as well as brain cells. Upon trying the first bin it flipped open at a pull of the handle. Inside hanging in plain view was a key on a bright yellow fob marked "Truck 4 tool bins". I immediately looked around scanning the area, hardly believing my luck and thinking ok this is too easy, I'm about to get hit with a lighting bolt or something, because I just do not have this type of luck. But then again, I will take it the easy way for once. I glanced up and said, "Thanks," never know when I might need to beg a favor.

Yes, I will admit it, I have been called or you might say earned the title of "gear whore". I just can't resist a new gadget or tool. Most new gadgets turn out to be junk or worthless, but once in a while someone develops something that is worth having and keeping. The only reason I mention this is because the vehicle I had just found was obviously a plumber's truck and had just about any tool you could dream of. Now my problem was what to take and what to leave. There were so many scenarios running though my mind, but I needed to "choose wisely". Right now I was kind of feeling like that guy with Indiana Jones trying to pick the right cup, I would need the right tools for the right job, but didn't know exactly what the job was. The next 24 hours were critical to my chances of success in getting home. After that, much of the gear and supplies would be harder if not impossible to find. Right now any kid with a .22 rifle was far more deadly than I was. Not that I'm too shabby with a handgun but really anything over 25 yards I would have to kindly ask the target to stand still for a couple of seconds so I could shoot him. I don't think I'm going to get many of the thugs and gang bangers to cooperate with me. I really need as AR-15 or better yet an AR-10. I mentally kick myself for not traveling with my own AR, but had talked myself out of it as I needed to take all of my suits and crap for work. I had to already pack two bags with all of my work related clothes (worthless now) and my heavy winter dress coat (even more worthless now). More so I didn't want my wife to think I would be spending all of my free time on the range, at least not until the money began flowing in again.

So after doing another scan of the area, again seeing nothing moving in the area, I turned my attention back to the truck and the tools. I began by making a pile of any tool I thought might be useful. A set of screwdrivers, a hand full of zip ties, a small crescent wrench, a large crescent wrench, a crow bar about three feet in length, a medium size set of bolt cutters, tin snips (could come in handy for cutting into duct work), a box cutter with a small box of new blades, a small set of glass cutters (can you say "Jackpot"!!) complete with a four inch suction cup, a three pound ball peen hammer, a hacksaw with a pack of four new blades, a set of Allen wrenches, a small vise grip plier, a large vise grip plier, two cold chisels, a tool belt, a coil of .5 inch rope complete with safety harness, a tape measure, four road flares (never know when you might need those), a can of WD40, a couple of rolls of duct tape, and last but not least a small portable cutting torch setup. The gauges showed full on both the oxygen and the acetylene bottles. Of course portable is a relative term as the set weighed about 30 pounds.

December 1978, Camp Lejeune, North Carolina

I remember right after I got to my first unit at Camp Lejeune, North Carolina that I learned what man portable is. I was straight out of Infantry Training Company and was assigned to H&S Company, Heavy Weapons Platoon, 2nd Battalion, 6th Marines, when an old Gunny told a bunch of us boots (means new guy in the USMC) that a 106 mm recoilless rifle was man portable and just to prove his point he had us do gun drill all morning. Set it up on one end of the parking lot, simulate firing, break down and carry it to the other end of the parking lot, setup, repeat, repeat and keep repeating until the Gunny got tried of standing around and giving us advice and telling us how we were all shitbirds and worthless to his beloved Corps. Maybe his jaw just got tried, he was a complete ass but he really knew that 106 mm and the M2 (Ma Deuce for you old timers) .50 caliber machine gun. Never to this day have I seen anyone set the headspace and timing on an M2 as fast as Gunny could do it. But to answer the question was the 106 man portable, just about like a fighter jet, with enough Marines just about anything is man portable, still doesn't mean I want to carry the damn thing by myself.

I was a little surprised to see the size of the pile of tools I had selected. A quick calculation put my collection at about 30 pounds not counting the cutting torch and tanks. But hey, I was only going to have to hump the stuff a couple miles and I'm a fairly good size guy, 6 feet 2 inches and roughly 230 pounds, I can handle this. Ok, right, I have to get rid of some of this, even if I wasn't going to walk right up and kick in the door in board daylight I would need some of this stuff but not all of it. My rough plan was to arrive in the area and watch the place until it got dark, then attempt to enter the store somewhat surreptitiously. Yes, I do know what that means, if you don't look it up.

Making my choices, I decided against the tool belt and some of the larger tools. I double checked the cutting torch tank levels, cracked the acetylene valve and squeezed the striker a couple times in front of the nozzle. The acetylene lit with a pop sounding unnaturally loud in the quiet morning air. I quickly cracked open the oxygen tank and the smoking flame turned into a jet of first red then blue flame about three inches in length. I shut down the oxygen tank than the acetylene and rewrapped the hoses around the tanks. I hefted the kit, not too bad, maybe 25 or 30 pounds; I can handle that for a couple hours. This thing would make quick work of any door lock. Much better than breaking out a window, which in this silence could be heard for a long distance, even after taping it up first. Stuffing the remaining tools into my backpack, I slung on my pack, bent over and picked up the cutting torch and headed south along the shoulder of the road.

The quiet was eerie, no vehicle or people noise of any kind, the only sound were my boots hitting the pavement. After about 20 minutes of walking, I hit the train tracks that run towards BWI, as they were running southwest to northeast, I decided to follow these as the likelihood of running into people along the tracks was much lower than staying on the highway and they would not take me though any residential areas. Right now I did not want to have anymore contact with groups of people than I had too. Plus it made for much easier walking than attempting to cut directly across country. As I walked my mind once again drifted to what had happen. I couldn't help but think that whoever did this they had picked an excellent time to strike as the government was pretty much shut down for the holiday and long weekend. After the attacks targeting black leaders, most of the major cities had been overwhelmed

26

with rioting and looting. But most of America would have been home or wherever they had taken off to for the holiday. Many of them would've done exactly what I had done, just rolled over and gone back to sleep thinking the government would get things settled back down and that the power outage was due to the riots. It was good the EMP event happened late on Sunday night, Monday would've been one of the busiest travel days of the year. But with that said it also stranded many critical government and professional types away from their places of work. This will further complicate any effort of assistance from the federal government. Congress was not in session, so many, probably most, congressmen and senators were away from DC and would be stranded at whatever location they were currently at. I would think that at least some of the military vehicles and aircraft were hardened against EMP but so far this morning I have not seen or heard a single vehicle or aircraft. In fact since leaving the hotel this morning I have not heard a single human made sound. The silence again reminded my that I had to get clear of the major built up areas here in Maryland and get west to the Shenandoah Valley. A couple of rough plans were forming in my mind, one I could hit the Appalachian Trail and take that south or maybe hit one of the major train rail lines and follow that south, or two I could head over and hit one of the rivers that flows into the Mississippi and take that all the way to the gulf. Either way winter was going to catch me and slow me down. I would worry about that later, right now I had to get clear of the DC/Baltimore area.

Breaking out of my daydreaming I realized the tram track had turned almost due south. According to my map I should be about one mile from the mall area. As the train track turned south it gave me a good view of the southern horizon. Thick black smoke was rolling across the horizon to the south and southwest. From my viewpoint most of the fires appeared to be in the direction of the District with only one close by. The close one was maybe a mile south of me and appeared to be dying out. I was torn between checking out the fire and continued on towards the mall, which was to my southwest.

According to my map the railroad spur breaking off to the west would be my best route to take but if I continue south on the tracks they would run directly into the Route 176, which would also take me to the mall area and would take me near the smoke column to my south. The more I thought about it the more I wanted to take a look at the site and talk to any first responders to find out what they know about the event. After about 10 minutes walking along the tracks I moved into a wooded area to the west of the tracks that were moving back south. I wanted to be able to observe what I thought was a crash site before I approached the first responders or investigators from the FAA. I also want to drop off my tools and equipment before approaching the site. No need to answer questions that I didn't have to as all the equipment I was currently carrying might raise a few eyebrows.

Once again I wanted to kick myself for traveling without my normal bug out bag. I had pulled out some of my stuff because I was already going to be taking so much with the two bags of dress and winter clothes I needed and I didn't want to have to worry about everywhere I would have to drive in Maryland, let alone doing it with a bunch of what the Maryland PD would call prepper junk. My original plan was to fly home in a couple of weeks, just for the weekend, and bring back a few more things. My normal kit would have had my bino's in my pack but I had pulled those out along with my snares, fire kit, main water filter, and most of my emergency food and first aid. With the thought being that I would get it that weekend when I went home.

Chapter Three

When I was directly across from the crash site, I stashed my tool bag; cutting torch and backpack under a small bush pile and made my way back to the train tracks. I'm no stranger to bad scenes having seen about the worst kinds of horror in the aftermath of terrorist attacks in Iraq and Afghanistan. I have seen more than my fair share of death but what I saw after I came out of the woods shocked me to my core.

While I'm not an FAA investigator by any means, it was clear fairly clear what had happened. Just to the east of the track bed with scattered fragments of the last one-third of the aircraft. I could not determine the size of the aircraft other than it was a large aircraft, the kind that had three row seats on one side and two on the other. It appeared to me that the pilot had the nose up and the first thing to hit the trees was the tail section. There were suitcases, seats (many still with bodies or parts of bodies strapped in) and fragments of fuselage along with the tail section scattered from near the railroad track to as far as I can see into the wooded area directly to my front.

My next shock was where were the rescue crews and the first responders? It'd been nine to ten hours since this plane crashed and as far as I can tell no one had been at the crash site. It seemed like a bad movie set that was way, way over the top with cheap special effects. Small fires still burned here and there, rows of seats filled with bodies slumped over were scattered every which way, some completely intact while others were hard to tell if it was a man or woman. Most had been spared from the fires but several were badly burned. As soon as that registered with me, the smell hit me and I had to swallow hard. The smell of burnt human flesh is unlike anything else on earth and almost nothing is worse.

I moved into the debris slowly attempting to not disturb anything. From the look of things no one had survived the initial impact, at least not anyone in the tail section. Luggage was scattered everywhere as I move forward. I noticed a couple of the new model Army rucksacks and I made a mental note to check them on my way back. Don't judge, from the look of things no one on this flight was going to be worrying about checked baggage. And all I had was my daypack, a large ruck would be very helpful to me.

That was when I spotted the two long sand colored pelican cases in the debris. I quickly moved to the cases and pulled them from the wreckage. Without looking any further, I walked back to the large rucks and adjusted the straps on one and slung it on my back. Picking up the two pelican cases, I moved rapidly back across the railroad tracks and stopped once I got back into the tree line. Dropping the pelican cases I shrugged off the ruck and turned back to the wreckage. Again I know many would think how dare him stealing from the dead, but I really doubt those soldiers would hold it against me for using what they left so I can get back to my family. As of right now those things in those packs and cases meant nothing to the men who had once owned them. Now that my mind was made up I move quickly back to the area that I had found the pelican cases. A quick search revealed several more cases and I knew that these belong to soldiers returning from Afghanistan or Iraq and had been traveling with their weapons. With the current situation it was best that I secure these weapons to keep them from falling into the hands of thugs or criminals who would use them for evil deeds.

It is amazing how the human mind can rationalize during times of stress. Anyone dealing with situations where they have very little or no control or are going through an experience that involves physical hardship, psychological trauma, and/or deprivation of what is normal can react or lash out in other than normal behavior. As any experienced interrogator can tell you there are a couple of different ways of coping with high levels of stress; emotion-focused (passive avoidance-based coping strategies using denial or disengagement from a problem, or attempts to evade difficult circumstances and the associated emotions) and active problem-focused (approach-based coping strategies using active engagement with stressful problems or circumstances, or attempts to actively problem solve when presented with a difficult situation) but that is a complicated subject for another day. Those whom choose to use passive avoidance-based coping strategies will more than likely become victims during a SHTF situation. Why may you ask is this important? It should be obvious, denial of problems solves nothing, such as the desk clerk back at the hotel, oh the government will have all this under control in just a few hours, no more like ten to twelve years if ever. More than likely she will still be saying that as she dies from hunger or dehydration.

Looking one more time at the carnage, I picked up another pair of pelican cases and the remaining rucksack and moved back across the tracks passing the first pair of cases and ruck and carried them back to where I had stashed my pack. I added the cases and pack to my own and returned to get the rest of the cases and the other pack. I was tempted to go back and grab more, but I remembered what one of my sergeants had once told me, the greediest pigs get eaten first, so after looking at the crash site one more time I turned back to my newly acquired gear.

After returning to my gear I did a quick reconnaissance of the immediate area. As far as I could tell I was all alone with no residences within my view. I wanted to get out of the area as soon as I could so I pulled out the bolt cutters from my tool bag and cut the locks off of all four of the pelican cases. The first case was a surprise and a little disappointing. I would have loved to be able to take it but under my current situation there was just no way I could. It was a SAW, a squad automatic weapon, complete with the cleaning kit and sling. No ammo, which I knew there wouldn't be, as most soldiers have to turn in all their ammo when traveling on commercial aircraft. I have quite a lot of experience with a SAW, as I had quickly turned in my M16A2 in Somalia and checked out a SAW. I have always hated to be outgunned and given the opportunity, more firepower is better. But the thought of humping a SAW for 1400 miles was a no-go. Plus the thing needed belt fed ammo, yes I know it can use regular M4 magazines but I would have to find government issued metal magazines, as the SAW would quickly eat the top off of P-mags or any other plastic magazine. Additionally being fully auto would result in me being out of ammo five minutes into any kind of firefight. No, not a good idea.

The next three cases yielded three M4's with the standard 14.5 inch barrels, one M9 Beretta 9mm, and two Sig Sauer P226's, better yet all of the M4's had ACOG optics on them and each of the M4 cases had six empty P-mags. I quickly inspected the three M4's and chose the best maintained one. The ACOG looked to be in good shape, but I pulled another one off one of the other M4's as a backup. I also pulled the bolt carrier group and charging handle out of one of the other M4's. You never know when you are going to need a spare part. Between the four cases I was able to put together a pretty good cleaning kit. One of the guys had had a bore snake, which I added to my cleaning kit. Again I gave a quick thanks to the soldiers. I gathered the gear I would not be taking with me, that is the SAW, the two M4's, the Beretta and one of the Sig's and secured them back into a couple of the pelican cases. After concealing the cases under the brush pile I turn my attention to the two rucksacks.

The first thing I did was unstrapping the body armor from the first ruck. It appeared to be in good shape and after slipping into it; it fit fairly well and could be adjusted to fit me if I decided to keep it. It had pouches for eight M4 magazines and four pistol magazines. I shrugged out of it not deciding on whether I wanted to keep it or not. Right this second, not. I didn't want to get into any type of fight that the advantage of body armor would outweigh the speed I would sacrifice by wearing it. If I were driving no question I would take both vests, but as it was looking like I'd be walking most of the way, and if it comes down to water, food or vest than the vest loses.

I next opened the outer pouches of the rucks. The first pouch held a pair of shower shoes and a container of foot powder. Tossing the shower shoes, I shook the foot powder container, good mostly full; this went in the keeper pile. Next came a shaving kit I zipped it open and tossed the toothbrush put the toothpaste in the keeper pile, along with the tweezers, floss, small mirror and a couple of new razors, not that I planned on shaving any time soon.

By the time I had gone though everything in the two rucks, I had a considerable pile stuff to keep, stuff that was nice to have and stuff to toss. The big items I came away with was an almost brand-new modular sleeping system, an almost new Gore-Tex rain suit in large (it might be snug for the first week or so but I figure I was going to grow into it as I would undoubtedly lose some weight over the next few weeks), two pouches, a Tasmanian Tiger chest rig, one wooly pully (that's a wool sweater for you civilian types) in my size that would come in handy in a month or so when it started getting cold, six relatively new pairs of boots socks, one pair of almost new size 11 jump boots not that I would trade them for my LOWA's, but a good backup, a watch cap, a heavy pair of winter gloves, two Klean 32 ounce stainless steel water containers, one Life straw bottle that looked and smelled new, one cold steel Tanto knife with an 8 inch blade, one K-bar almost new, a bag of cotton balls with small canister of Vaseline, one of these guys really had his shit together. One e-tool with case, a Gerber multi tool and a total of four MRE's.

I sat and went over each piece of equipment to include the rucksacks. After choosing the one I wanted, mainly I took the one who's water bladder didn't smell sour and I slipped the ruck on empty and made all of the adjustments I needed to. I was getting a little nervous having spent the better part of two hours at or near the crash site. Now that I knew what I wanted and didn't want I stuffed the unwanted stuff into the second ruck and that went under the brush pile besides the pelican cases. I dumped my daypack and begin emptying water bottles into the rucks water bladder. After filling it I dropped in eight water purification tabs just to make sure in case of bladder was contaminated from dirty water. It would not do much for the taste but better that than to begin the trip with a case of the runs. I would give the tabs a couple hours to do their magic before I drank from it. I really am not too worried about it as the bladder smelled like it never was used before. Filling the bladder reminded me that I had not drunk anything all morning since leaving the hotel. I drank both of the 12-ounce bottles left over from filling the bladder. I next moved on to the magazines and tested each one of them. I kept 12 M4 magazines and all six of the Sig Sauer magazines. All of them were clean and appeared to be well maintained. I slid eight of the M4 magazines into the chest rig along with four of the Sig Sauer magazines. Grabbing my bottle of 9mm's I quickly loaded all four of the mags and slapped one into the Sig Sauer. The Sig went into the drop down leg rig and the rest into my new ruck along with the two empty Sig magazines. I glanced at my watch and saw that it was almost one o'clock and a sense of urgency began to drive my movements. I reloaded the ruck with as much speed as I could, combining my original gear with my new gear. From the original tools I kept only a small crescent wrench, a medium flat screwdriver and a Phillips screwdriver, a small pry bar, and the bolt cutters from the tool bag. Once loaded I grabbed the chest rig and slide into it adjusting the waist strap so it would not interfere with my war belt, I dropped my headlamp into the left hand pouch of the chest rig, along with a couple of tampons, a chest seal, one large bandage with blood clot and a tourniquet into the right hand pouch. Jumping up and down a few times to settle the gear in the place, I made a few adjustments and again jumped up and down a couple of more times to settle the gear again and was satisfied with the lack of noise. Grabbing my ruck, I bent over and slid my arms into the straps of the ruck and flipped the ruck over my head. Pulling the shoulder straps snug I then hooked my waist belt and tightened it. Walking around in a small circle and making sure everything was riding okay and not making any real noise. Last by not least I then swung the two-point sling over my head and glanced round one more time. Pausing for just a few seconds I gave a quick thanks for the service of our soldiers and gave them a last nod. Their bad luck but it was a Godsend for me and really upped my chances of getting back to my family in Texas. I had no idea what was next, hopefully finding some ammo for my M4 and Glock. With that thought in my mind I undid the waist belt and slid off the ruck. I returned to the weapons pelican and removed the other Sig and Beretta and secured them in my ruck. Might come in handy for trading and if not I could always cache them along way. With a final adjustment I once again began walking south towards the mall area as it was only place I knew within 60 miles that had everything I needed.

After following the rail tracks for about a mile from the crash site I came to where the tracks intersected with Highway 100. Turning west I continued on towards the mall area feeling more and more exposed. So far I've not seen any other people moving in my direction but had seen several groups of what appear to be teenagers heading in the direction the mall. That was not good. I planned on waiting until dark to enter the mall, however if there were a lot of people at the mall I would have to make my move as soon as I could. Any break-in would be attributed to them and would keep anyone from looking for a single individual. Every couple minutes I would do a complete scan of the area. Other than the small gangs of skateboarders the area appeared to be empty. I used the time in between to go over my mental checklist of items I needed. Top of my priority list was 5.56 ammo for my M4, I would first load some mags and get my M4 fully operational. Second, 9 mm and grab a few more magazines for my Glock. If they had left out the pistols I was hoping to snag another Glock, maybe another 17 as a backup. That is what I normally carry as my tactical pistol. One of the best all around useful handguns ever made as far as I'm concerned. I wished again I had bought my Glock 19 as a backup, it already had a good RMR installed and sighted in and I trusted it as I have about 3000 rounds though it. But either way I needed a couple hundred rounds for both the 9 mm's and at least six hundred rounds of 5.56. I know that sounds like a lot of ammo but I really, really hate being without ammo.

First Gulf War, two days before the breach into Kuwait.
           The message came into the 8th Marine Regimental S-2, 10th Marines had reported they had several suspicious individuals in their custody that they had caught attempting to sneak out of Kuwait into Saudi Arabia. They were requesting for someone to come out and take them off their hands for interrogation. The request was passed on to our team. There were two Counterintelligence (CI) sub-teams assigned to the 8th Marines, which made a total of six CI types and our two

Kuwaiti interpreters. 10th Marines had sent an MP vehicle with a mounted M-2 (.50 caliber machine gun) over to "guide" us into their perimeter. As most of our guys had been busy most of the day it was decided that myself and the other sub-team commander would take our interpreter and take care of the incident. It was already late in the afternoon and total darkness comes quickly to the desert. This makes navigation difficult at best, even during the day there are very few landmarks, at night it is almost impossible. The best you can do is attempt to follow an azimuth. You have to remember that this was before GPS was common. Most of the times back than this was accomplished by having someone sit on the hood of the Hummer with a compass and give the driver hand and arm signals in a mostly vain attempt at navigation (also to keep the driver from driving into some poor unfortunate grunt's foxhole, they were a bitch to see at night). But the MP driver claimed to "know" the way and off we went to accomplish our mission. True to his word the MP was able to get us to the outer perimeter of our destination. The problem being the canon cockers had laid in a hasty mine field that afternoon and it was not clearly marked for safe passage. It was determined that our best course of action was to halt in place and wait until daylight to proceed. Of course by the time we stopped we were already into the edge of the minefield and that meant no getting out of the vehicles for any reason. If you have never had the pleasure of attempting to sleep in a military Hummer, well unless you have done it, it is hard to explain how uncomfortable it is and it is not something you need to add to your bucket list. Anyway as nature would have it, it wasn't too long before a couple of the guys began to complain about needing to relieve themselves. There are only a limited numbers of ways this can be done from inside a crowded Hummer. It was finally decided the best way to do this was for them to climb out the back and stay in the tire tracks. Yes, kids join the Marine Corps and see the world. Anyway shortly after solving this major problem, our Iraqi friends decided they had too much armor in their inventory and launched their one and only attack of the short war. Of course the location of their attack was the gap between the 10th Marines and the 8th Marines and just happened to be exactly where we were sitting in the middle of a minefield. Needless to say it got a little exciting for a few minutes. Oh, did I forget to mention that when we deployed, Uncle Sam only sent us over with side arms, our interpreters had M-16's, so that gave us a total of two 9 mm pistols, two M-16's and two AT-4's. Where you ask is the logic of issuing us AT-4's but not rifles, please I'm sure it made sense to someone, somewhere. Anyway the MP Hummer did have an M2 machine gun and the two MP's were armed with both M-16's and pistols but it was all pretty worthless against an armored battalion of T-55 and T-62 tanks. Our only chance was to hope they would not see our two Hummer's in the dark. We were just getting ready to bug out when the 10th Marines made that a moot point. The Iraqi's breached the berm about one click (1000 meters) to our north but never made it beyond 500 meters from that original breach. Did I fail to mention that the 10th Marines were an artillery unit? As the Iraqi's poured though the breach, the Marines lowered their 155 mm artillery tubes to ground level and opened fire. Long story short, there was nothing but a bunch of scrap metal left. The 10th Marines hammered each and every tank south of the breach into just so much junk. It was the most terrifying yet beautiful sight I have ever witnessed. We were about 400 yards to the west and maybe 100 yards behind the artillery tubes. When a 155 mm hits a T-55 at point blank range, well what can I say there really isn't too much left, maybe a piece of track or a road wheel but that's about all. The artillery was firing in volley and each time the six 155 mm's would fire it was like the world exploded, the

38

concussion even as far away as we were felt like it ripped the air from your lungs. The awe of it was completely mesmerizing. No words can really ever do it justice, it was just as we say in the Corps, it was fucking magic.

Bottom line is I am not a fan of being under-gunned. More is better, bigger is good and more and bigger is really, really good. Like I said earlier, I would love to have an AR-10 vice an M4, but I will stick with the M4 because I can carry more ammo. I might change my mind if I can get my hands on a SCAR in .308, but more than likely even if Bass Pro has one they would only have the 10 round magazines for it, this is Maryland after all.

As I continued to skirt the highway it took me about an hour to get within sight of the mall. Upon getting close I cut south across to the edge of the woods bordering Highway 100. I would need to cross over to get within sight of the store. At least the timing of the event had been during a time with low traffic, there were not a whole lot of cars within sight on the highway. I stood and watched the area for several minutes. Ideally the best spot to watch from was from the wooded area directly to the east of Bass Pro. The drawback to this was I would have to cross several roads and the likely hood of being seen was high. I really needed to get eyes on before dark to see any activity around the area. I decided that I would break down the M4 and conceal it in my pack so not to draw attention if I was spotted crossing any of the roads. After breaking it down I had to repack my ruck to make room but it was do this or stash the M4 and I really do not want to do that. Putting the ruck back on I stood and watched again, seeing nothing I moved across Highway 100 as quickly as I could while at the same time keeping my movements slow enough that it would appear I was not in a hurry. Quick movement draws attention as does moving too cautiously as it appears to be sneaking or as my Dad would say, "Up to no good". After crossing the highway I scouted around and found a couple of downed trees that still had the rootball attached. Both appeared to have blown down recently as they still had their leaves. I dropped my ruck and climbed up onto the closer of the two root balls and pulled out the small set of bino's I had found in one of the rucks from the airplane. I swear if I can I'm going to al least attempt to get word to the SFC's family to let them know what happen to him and thank them for his sacrifice. With his bino's I was able to get a fairly good view of the roads leading into the mall area and the front entrance area of the Bass Pro.

After a quick once over I was amazed to see no one and the glass doors of Bass Pro appeared to still be intact. From my vantage point I could not see the boat sales area but as far as I could tell there was no damage to any of the boats sitting out front. That thought caused me to think for just a second about the possibility to use a boat to get home but just as quick I dismissed it. One, I didn't have the knowledge and skills to sail a boat from Baltimore to Houston and I didn't want to waste the days it would take to get to the harbor to maybe find a suitable boat, maybe I might be able to figure out how to sail one by myself, and maybe I might be able to find the supplies I would need to manage the trip by water. Way too many maybe's for me. While I am extremely confident in my land survival skills, I was not that confident in my limited, read non-existence, sailing skills.

Under normal hiking conditions I know I could average 12 to 15 miles a day given the terrain in this area and some luck. That is as long as I didn't have to scavenge for food or water or twist a knee or develop blisters. I know, I know, you are thinking that's not very far. Backpackers on the AT often average 20 miles or more a day. Well wake up and smell the roses, this isn't some pleasure hike with a box of supplies waiting at the next post office, or a store where you can

40

resupply. But let's say this is Burger King and you want it your way, so 20 miles a day it is, even if everything goes perfectly and I don't have any trouble at all, I'm only going to cover approximately 220 – 240 miles before I'm completely out of food.   It is approximately 1400 miles to Houston, TX. Also above all else, I must find water every day. Easy, there are a lot of streams, rivers, lakes and ponds in eastern Virginia, right? But it really isn't about finding the water that is the easy part; it is how you handle the water. One drop of the wrong water could end your trip, forever. Pick up the wrong bacteria (read cholera), or amoeba (dysentery), or protozoa (giardia), by drinking contaminated water or absorbing through a scratch or cut and you will be down for the count without the proper medical treatment. Four-fifths of all illnesses in developing countries are caused by water-borne diseases, with diarrhea being the leading cause of death among children. With no power, where do you think all the sewage is going to end up once all the pumping stations stop. If there is one item you do not skimp on that is your water equipment. I still needed at least one more stainless steel water bottle, along with at least one more method to filter water, and as last resort, have a back-up bottle of water purification tablets or a small bottle of beach.

I made myself relax and settled in to watch the area. It was at least two hours until the sun went down and I had no intentions of doing anything until well after dark. Actually I thought if there is no activity between now and dark I might make my move about an hour after total darkness. Hopefully the cloud cover would hang around, but even if it doesn't there is not much of a moon anyway. The more I thought about it the more I wanted to get in, get out and get some distance before morning. Each day the situation was only going to get worse and worse and the faster I could get out of the built up area surrounding Baltimore the better.

Movement caught my eye and I brought up the bino's for a better look. A group of teenagers on skateboards came into focus. There were six of them, typically they would have gone unnoticed but these were not typical days and any group of people could be a threat. As I watched I saw the group approach some of the parked cars. They moved slowly by the cars and appeared to be looking into each of them. After stopping by one car, I couldn't tell exactly the make or model but it looked to be an Accra or Infinity, they moved off a short distance and appeared to have a conversation before moving on to the south and out of sight. Looked to me like they were scouting out which vehicles to come back too after dark. That could be a problem, but I would really like to avoid them if I could. That way any break in's might be attributed to them and would keep anyone from looking for a single individual.

Every couple of minutes I would do a complete scan of the area. Other than the small gang of skateboarders the area appeared to be empty. I used the time in between to go over my mental list of items I needed. Ammo first priority, 5.56 first, load some mags and get my M4 fully operational. Then 9 mm ammo, if time, grab a few more magazines for the SIG. I had to keep reminding myself not to get too greedy, take only what I needed and get out. Get the ammo, move to the camping area and get a good water filter and a spare filter. Ideally I could grab a couple Platypus GravityWorks or a Katadyn Vario, along with a couple of Life Straws, but whichever one was there and also had an extra filter was the one I would grab. The best thing about the Platypus was you did not have to expose yourself for long to get water. All you had to do was take the dirty water bag, fill it from the water source and then you could move back to cover and filter it later. Next up would be food, grab and stuff as many Mountain House meals and bags of beef jerky as I could get into my bag. Than over to the back packing stove area, hopefully they would have a some solid fuel cubes, I have my Solo stove, but I really did want some of the cubes as they didn't create as much smoke and as I would be in or close to built up areas for a while I did not want to attract any more attention than I had too. Later I would be traveling in areas that would have plenty of natural fuel.

Next up would be a good quality sleeping pad for my Warbonnet hammock. The Warbonnet is a double-layered hammock with the ability to slide a sleeping pad between the two layers. In my younger days I did a lot of camping, mostly with old army shelter halves. While in Afghanistan I was turned on to using a hammock system. When most people hear the word hammock they conjure up an image of a large backyard hammock. But a good backpacking hammock system is something else entirely. While a decent one-person bivy tent could be found for around one hundred dollars. A Warbonnet or Clark 4-season hammock system with all the whistles and bells run about four hundred, but once you ever try one you will be listing all of your tents on Craig's List. My wife and I were over at one of the SF guy's house for a cookout and he was showing his Warbonnet off and my wife could see it in my eyes when I turned to her to explain why I needed one. She stopped me before I could open my mouth and said absolutely NOT. End of that conversation. As I already had one, I didn't argue with her. She always gave me a hard time about any "prepper stuff", she really didn't care but she just didn't want to hear about it. I did not have an under or over quilt for my system, but I had spent the extra money on a Super Fly and all of the Dutchware for it. For those of you that have never messed with Dutchware, they take accessories and make them better, I don't have time to explain how valuable their devices are for rigging a hammock, tarp or rain fly. Again another one of those things that make living on the go so much easier. I would keep my eyes open for an under quilt as the weather would be turning cooler at night and the only real draw back to a hammock is that it is not the warmest without the right add ons.

I wish I was not in Maryland for the hundredth time. Any other Bass Pro in the world would have traps and snares, but probably not in this one, this is Maryland, can't have any of those nasty traps that harm the local wildlife. I wonder where they all think their small dogs and cats run off to, yes as shocking as it is, those pets didn't run away or get stolen, they become fast food for local coyotes or bobcats that roam freely in the local neighborhoods. "Oh look honey, see that beautiful wild animal, I wonder where Muffy is, he should be back by now, he just went outside to potty." Morons. I would grab a roll of electric fence wire and make some snares. Snares and traps are quiet and don't expend a lot of energy. I'm fairly confident I can at least find some old steel traps once I hit the countryside of Virginia. I also need to grab a set of Troy flip down or offset sights for my M4 as it does not currently have backup iron sites. I'm a firm believer in redundancy. I've never had a Trijicon device go bad on me, but I have been known to be a little rough on gear. Just never hurts to have a backup. I wouldn't pass up an RMR either as the ACOG has a mounting spot for one. Don't know if the EMP would've shorted them out but it is worth a shot if one is lying around. Also will attempt to get a good suit of camouflage if I have time along with a good set of long johns and winter gloves. I would really like a camo Gore-Tex jacket. I almost laugh out loud I can hear my wife, is this a need thing or is this a want thing. What I really need is to get in and out of Bass Pro as fast as I can. Lastly, I need to grab a bunch of AAA batteries for my headlamp and a new flashlight along with maybe a good weapons light for my M4 if they have any. At least my headlamp didn't get burned during the EMP as I had gotten in the habit of never leaving batteries in it after ruining a Petzl by leaving batteries in it for a couple of years.

Glancing up I saw the same group of boys approaching the front of the Bass Pro from the North. They slowed as they weaved between the boats but didn't go near the big bay doors and quickly moved on pass the front of the store moving more or less in a straight line back to the car they checked out earlier. I wondered what their fascination was with this one car when I could see a couple of much nicer vehicles parked out front of Bass Pro not to mention the new four wheeler still parked outside of the front doors of the store. Looking back now this should've been an indicator to me. Trained observer my ass, maybe the government didn't get their moneys worth when they sent me to all that training. It didn't take long before they demonstrated why this particular car was of interest to skateboarders. The car was sitting all by itself and was one of those low-slung aerodynamic models. Perfect for using as a ready-made skateboard ramp. I just about jumped out of my skin when the first kid hit the car. By the time I got my binos up all I could see was a skateboard flying though the air and a body on the ground to the side of the vehicle. My first thought was that someone had shot him but then I saw the kid slowly get his hands under himself to push himself up into sitting position. I could hear the other boys laughing and making fun of him.

I have spent some time on in-line skates but growing up in the country never presented much of an opportunity to learn how to skateboard. I do remember one year my brother or cousin got one for Christmas. This is not one of the new modern skateboards; this one was about 6 inches wide with metal wheels. We were all at my Grandmothers and the only concrete was the sidewalk running from the front porch to driveway. It couldn't have been over 35 or 40 feet of sidewalk ending in the gravel driveway. However there were posts on

45

either side at the end, oh did I fail to mention they were brick columns really about 3 feet tall topped by cement Swan planters. The first trip down the sidewalk by one of my older cousins ended up with him flat on his back with one of Grandmother's Swans neck and head in one hand and his other hand attempting stop the bleeding from the back of his head. Grandpa's wood furnace took all of about two minutes to reduce that skateboard to a pile of ashes. That's about the extent of my experience with skateboards. Obviously the kid and his friends had much more experience as the next kid landed on the hood when up and over the windshield across the car's top and barely glanced off the trunk and somehow landed graceful on the ground as he pumped his hands in the air as he circled back towards group. I really was impressed; it was something like you would see on TV. I'm pretty sure the owner would not have been impressed but given the events of last twenty-four hours I really couldn't fault them. Not that they probably actually knew that the car was worthless at this point but I didn't feel to bad, figure let them have what fun they can before reality sets in. But I did hope they moved on before long. There was only about an hour before it would be completely dark and I wanted to get a move on as soon as possible.

While the boys continue to trash their new jump ramp I climbed down and began to organize my gear for my own little excursion. From the ruck I pulled out my now empty daypack, a roll of duct tape, my new watch cap and my Petzl headlamp. I stuffed my Larue OBR hat into the top of my ruck and cinched the straps down tight. I already had on my military flight gloves and made a mental note to grab a couple more pair if I find any inside the store. I go nowhere without them. There are many brands that claim this and that about how good their gloves are, but for my money I have always liked the military flight gloves for shooting and all around wear. While

46

they don't stand up to hard manual labor that's not what they were made for. They are like a second skin yet allows you the finger dexterity to do most things without having to take them off. I finished up the Power Bar and drank some water for my ruck bladder. While not tasting like spring water, it was drinkable and I didn't have to worry about any problems with it. If time permitted I would refill with water from bottles inside the store prior to leaving. As I finish up I again heard the clatter of an out-of-control skateboard hitting the ground and laughter from the group. Glancing up I saw another victim lying flat on the ground holding his arm. The other boys were gathered around pointing and gesturing at the boy on the ground. A couple of them went to help him up and I heard a yelp a pain. Laughter dropped off as quickly as it had begun and I thought to myself that the young lad just about picked the worst time in recent history to break or fracture his arm. With one of the other boys carrying the kid's skateboard they all began moving towards the South. I glanced down at my watch and set back down to wait out the sun going down. Taking one more glance at the disappearing boys in the distance I thought about what my Grandfather would've said if he had observed the incident.

Summer 1970. My grandfather and I pulled in the small country store just outside of a small town in the Ozark's. We had stopped so he could pick up some Good Money Twist Tobacco, which was his preferred chewing tobacco. I mentally urged him to be quick because I was excited as is my first time ever going with just him to go bass fishing. As I sat in the truck while he was in the store two teenage boys on bikes were approaching the store from town. They were moving along at a pretty good clip and turned in the store parking lot just as I heard the bell attached to store doors jingle as Grandpa exited the store. I glanced back around as I heard a short scream and the clatter of metal on gravel. I stared in amazement at the cloud of dust and the mess of tumbling bikes and boys emerging as a hot summer wind drove away the dust clouds from the scene of accident. By this time my Grandfather had reached the driver door and was opening it to get in. I said, "Wow did you see that?" He glanced at me then over to the two boys gingerly picking themselves up off ground. Both were bleeding for multiple scrapes and one had most of his ass hanging out where his pants were torn. He was the one in the most pain and was holding his right arm tightly to his body. The second boy was picking up their bikes and pushing them over to the side of the store. The storeowner was outside by this time yelling at them about how stupid they were. As we pulled out of the parking lot Grandpa cocked his head and looked at me and said, "Boy, you're going to learn the most people are only good at one thing in life." He paused in thought and of course being 10 years old and being impatient I ask what are most people good at. There was no humor in his voice and he rarely told jokes so I knew he was serious, he gave me the same look he had when he looked at the boys at the store and said, "Most people are only good at one thing and it is turning perfectly good food into shit." My smile quickly faded as I looked at him, he was completely serious. It was one of those moments between us like he was judging to see if I was one of those people.

Chapter Four

With all my kit packed and ready to go I climbed back to my perch on top the root ball and continue to watch the area. Dark clouds had begun to move in and hopefully would bring some rain. I was ok with that as the temperature was mid 80s, the rain would help with the fires and help keep people inside. With the wind picking up from the south the strong odor of burning buildings carried on it. Watching the clouds build up I figured the rain would reach me in about 30 minutes or so. I would wait until the rain began to make my move to the storefront. With the smell of smoke I did add to my mental list to grab a couple boxes of N95 masks if I could find them. I could not recall ever seeing any in Bass Pro, but I'd only been in the Maryland store once so they might have them and I just didn't see them. I also reminded myself that I needed to stock up on Quick Clot and if they didn't have that some tampons and feminine pads from the ladies bathrooms just in case. There are not many medical bandages that work nearly so well for gunshot wounds. Just one of those things you never want to use but if you ever need one, enough said.

I stood up and hopped down as the first raindrops hit. Shouldering my ruck I moved to the edge of the trees as the rain began coming down in hard-hitting sheets. Well I thought, I did want it to rain, as all the noise from the rain would cover any noise I was going to make. One more look around produced nothing of interest or any movement. With the rain pouring down I couldn't have seen a semi truck coming from any further away than 15 or 20 feet so I took off for the front door at a slow shuffle. My desert LOWA's boots quickly became waterlogged, and I decided right than that after the ammo and food, some waterproof boots were in order.

Don't get me wrong; my LOWA's are the most comfortable pair of boots I have ever owned. I had never had a pair of LOWA's till my boss over in Afghanistan, who was an SF type and really had his shit together, told me to order a pair after I was bitching about a new pair of boots I had just gotten from the PX. Now I was wishing I had ordered a pair of the waterproof LOWA's but as it didn't rain much in Afghanistan there wasn't really a need for it than. Lot of good wishing does now. It only took me a couple of minutes to cross the parking lot from the trees. The front doors were pretty much as I remember them with two sets of double doors leading into an air trap followed by another two sets of double doors. As I didn't want to breach two sets of doors I followed the front of the building around to the boat area. There the entire walls were made up of huge multi section roll up doors so the boats could be moved in and out of the show room. Luckily the area was covered and watching the area for a short time revealed no movement. The noise of the rain would cover about anything short of a gunshot, with that thought in mind my eyes fell on the landscaping surrounding the boats. I moved over to the area surrounding the nearest pond and picked up the top-landscaping block. Carrying it back to the roll up door, I dropped it and pulled out a roll of duct tape. I began taping up the second tier window of the rollup door. Tapping on the glass it didn't appear to be made of break resistant laminated glass as far as I could tell. I hesitated and looked around again to check the area, seeing nothing but the rain pounding down, I picked up the landscaping stone and stepping back I shot-putted the stone into the taped window. The window bowed in but was strong enough to hold together. I picked up the stone again and taking a couple steps back I lunged forward throwing the stone as hard as I could. The entire pane caved in and popped out of the frame; so the glass had been made out of safety glass and the stone skidded across the slick concrete

50

floor of the boat showroom making enough noise to wake the dead, which is if they were inside the store. I quickly grabbed my backpack and stuffed it through the window and immediately followed it inside. It was dark as hell in here I thought. Grabbing my backpack I slid my arms into the straps and moved over to squat down by the back of a Boston whaler on display. I pulled out my Petzl headlamp and after making sure the red filter was in place I held it around the end of the boat shining it towards the closest aisle.

The response was immediate and I almost lost my left hand. The crack of a high powered rifle was deafening even in the big store as it whipped by my hand and punched a nice neat hole in the window pane just above the one I had smashed in. My mind registered the muzzle flash somewhere to my right and appeared to be elevated. Examining my hand to make sure I still had five fingers, I attempted to massage away the tingling from the near miss. After making sure my hand was intact and still functioning, I reached back and drew my Glock. At least no one could come up behind me, that is unless someone came up from outside, now that was a comforting thought. Glancing back at the window I broke, I realized that I could not move from behind the boat without silhouetting myself against the backdrop of the windows. Whoever the shooter was they must not have been in place when I busted the window out or he would have nailed me coming in. So what to do now? The area I was in was backed by the dim light coming in from all of the windows and it would be extremely risky to attempt to make it the 70 or 80 feet to the beginning of the clothing section. Well when working from a position of weakness - bluff. I really think the moron who came up with that saying had never been in a no win situation but what the hell I couldn't think of anything else and I damn sure did not want to get shot today. Slowly I loosen the straps of my ruck and eased it to the floor. Making sure my lower body was behind the boat trailer's double axle I called out in normal tone, "I'm hoping that is the normal way friends greet friends around here." From the darkness came a chuckle, "Well I take it you're still breathing. The real question is, are you leaking blood on my clean floors." I chuckled back in reply, "No sir, no blood, but I will recommend not to taste any of the water on the floor because it is not all rain water." This time when the response came, it clearly came from a different location. Maybe a little closer and at least a few feet higher up. "So what do you know a polite thief, I would suggest you get out the way you came in," the voice said out of the darkness. "So I can leave? Does that mean you won't shoot me the second I silhouette myself against the window?" I said. Again the location of the voice came from a slightly different angle, "I didn't say that I merely made a suggestion is all."

I really didn't like the way this was going, as from the changing angle of the guy, it wouldn't be long before he had me outflanked and I said as much, "Sir, I'd really appreciate if you would stop moving to my right. I'm not really in the mood to get shot tonight and all I wanted was a few supplies to help me on my way back to my family down in Texas. My triplets will be pissed as hell if I don't make it back in time for Halloween." The voice called back, "So I had you pegged for a no good southern from the time you began talking. What brings a reb this far north anyway?"

"What else, work," I said, "and trust me, I'm not here because I want to be, plus the weather really sucks up here. Oh and by the way I'm only paying for the one window I broke, the other one is on you!" When no reply came I continued to hope that if I could keep this guy talking he would be less inclined to shoot me. I ask, "So who didn't pay the electric bill, or couldn't you find someone up here that knows how to write?" Still no response, but it did elicit a chuckle that sounded like it came from ground level and a lot closer. I stayed where I was behind the trailer wheels without moving, straining to hear the slightest sound. A slight squeak of a rubber sole shoe sounded about 25 - 30 feet away and from behind one of the larger pontoon boats. It was so dark in that area all I could make out was the upper outline of the boat.

The man finally spoke again, "Are you armed?" I thought about that for a couple seconds than replied, "Would you believe me if I said no." "Not likely," he called back. "Well in that case I'm armed and have a little experience from my 20 plus years in the Marine Corps." This got another chuckle, "Just my luck, struck here without power and a damn jarhead breaks into my store, you do know we don't carry crayons for sale." "Hey I was not breaking in," I replied, "I'm on a rescue mission, I heard there was a crazy old man in here that needed help." The invisible man laughed out loud this time and added, "Not only a jarhead but a smart ass jarhead, it's starting to look like it might be a waste of a perfectly good round of ammo, when all I have to do is give you a sharp object and you would more than likely cut yourself and bleed out." Taking a guess I said, "That's an awful long sentence with some big words for a squid, I'm impressed."

After a few seconds he responded, "I'm going to throw out a light, please step into the light and lay your weapons on the floor. Place your weapons, including any knives, on the floor with the muzzles pointed away from me. Kneel down and cross your ankles and place your hands on top of your head." I snorted and replied, "Oh my god, not only a squid but a master at arms, really, kiss my ass. I don't give up my weapons to no man. I'm just here to get some supplies so I can get home to my family in Texas. If I were you I would grab all I could and get the fuck out of here. This place is going to be ground zero for some of the worst looting this country has ever seen and no one person is going to hold them off. Once people realize that no help is coming and the lights are not coming back on, they will descend on this place like locust and take everything that is not nailed down. And once people get pissed when everything is stolen they will burn this place to the ground. Most out there still don't know that it was an EMP or even what an EMP is and that we as a country are totally screwed. So what's it going to be, do we talk or do we dance. Either way is good with me, but lets get on with it as my feet are wet and I want to get on some dry socks."

"How do you know it was an EMP?" the guy asked. "Think about it," I said, "The only thing that could completely shut down watches, cell phones, pacemakers, the electrical grid, vehicles, planes, everything. Only an EMP could do that, oh I guess it could have been a massive solar storm, but I doubt it was, as someone would have spotted it before it hit the earth. And most planes and military equipment are built these days to withstand most solar events. At this point I don't know who attacked us or the intent behind the attack. I don't know if we retaliated and the whole world is this way or if only the East coast was hit. But if that was the case we would have seen the rest of the military responding to this. So yes, it was an EMP and things are going to be hell hereabouts within about another 48 hours. I want to be long gone by then. Where do you think people are going to head when there is no food or water at their homes? The locals are going to descend on this mall like a swarm of locust. The only real question is will they burn it first or loot it and burn it afterward. I don't know about you my friend but I do not want to be here when the mobs arrive."

"You don't exactly paint a rosy future do you," the man stated, "So what do we do now, I really don't want to shoot you, blood is so damn hard to clean up and any amount bigger than a dime has to be considered hazmat so what do you propose, my friend?" I replied, "How about I leave you my USAA credit card and an IOU for all the gear. If the lights come back on, charge me the full price for all of it. How does that sound?" "Oh, the hell with it," the man said and I saw movement to my front. At first I tensed ready to lunge to my left and begin firing, but instead a headlamp came on and began moving towards me.

The man said, "Give me a hand moving something in front of that broken window. We don't want to give anyone any bad ideas." Dropping the muzzle of my Glock I holstered it and slide my headlamp on and pushed the switch to turn on the red light. I said, "You might want to use a red light when moving around in here, people will not be able to see it outside unless they are right at the windows. That white light can be seen across the parking lot." The man laughed and turned to me sticking out his hand, "I'm Don Johnson, the manager of this fine store." I reached out and took his hand, looking the man up and down. He had a good firm grip and appeared to be in his early 60's. About 5'10", with short cropped dark hair that was losing the battle to gray and not carrying much extra weight. I replied, "I thought you worked down in Miami, I'm Talon Clark and its good to meet you." Don groaned loudly, "Wow I have never heard that one in what, oh, since sometime yesterday." Letting go of my hand, he laid his Sig Sauer AR-15 on the boat trailer fender and walked over to the rear of the Boston Whaler. He turned and ask, "Well are you going to give me a hand or not?" I moved over to his side and he gestured at the large box sitting behind the boat, "Lets get this over to the window and stack another on top in front of that window. I will put another one of the motion activated trail cameras down here to the side of the boxes so we will know if the boxes move," Don said.

"Ahh, is that how you knew I was around?" I ask. "Hell no, you made enough noise that I could hear you from the can when you broke out the window," he laughed, "Your lucky it took me a couple minutes to finish up my business and get over here or you would never have had the chance to make it inside. So you can thank my overactive bladder for your life. Because I sure would have shot you and did in fact attempt to shoot you. As I was shooting at what I thought was your head."

"Well you can thank your bladder for me," I laughed, "I don't hold a thing against you for trying to shoot me when I came in, now if you're thinking about trying it again, now I would have to take that you don't like my bubbly personality and might have to try and foil your plan."

If you have never attempted to carry on a conversation with someone that is wearing a headlamp it is hard to do. Normally we always face one another when we talk to another person. If you're both wearing headlamps then you keep blinding each other even using the red filters.

After some pulling and pushing we finally got the two large heavy boxes stacked in front of the broken out window. I laughed when I saw what the boxes were or should I say had been, gas generators. Although given enough time, knowhow, and large quantities of the right gauge of copper wire you might be able to rewire the generator motor so that it would work. Don glanced at me and said, "You ok?" I smiled and said, "Yes, just found it ironic that we were using these big paperweights to the block the window." Don glanced down at the boxes and immediately saw what I was talking about. "So you figure none of these will work?" Don ask. "I really don't know, but it has been one of the major questions for years, will generators survive an EMP. Guess it just depends on the strength of the EMP. Considering how strong this one appeared to be, no I don't think they will. I would think you would have to do a complete rebuild, including re-wrapping the motor, replacing any capacitor, maybe even have to replace the points and of course replace or bypass any electronics. Yes, pretty much a complete rebuild. Of course we won't know for sure until we try one. Although I would have thought the trail cameras would have been fried also, so maybe they would work," as I looked at Don questionably.

"Na, you're probably right, the trail camera's on the floor would not work, but I dug around in one of the shipping containers out in the warehouse. The containers are sitting on pallets so they were not touching the ground." I nodded, shipping containers made pretty fair Faraday Cages if they were set up right or in this case, lucky and said as much. "So what else was in your Faraday Cage?" Don said, "You said you were a Marine, but you seem to know a lot about what is going on and what in the world is a Faraday Cage?"

I laughed, "I don't know all of the math behind the concept, but I do know the basics. Just about anything made of a conductive material, such as a metal trash can or a shipping container can be made into a Faraday cage. As long as the material inside is not touching the outer skin of the container, and the container is grounded, the electromagnetic field is canceled out somehow. As far as I'm concerned it's fucking magic, but it works. What we don't know is how it will affect modern things like LED bulbs, electronic scopes and anything with microchips. I do know that all the cell phones in this area were affected, along with the cars and computers and of course the whole electrical power grid. If this was an EMP than it really depends on what type of weapon was used and at what altitude the device was detonated at. I have seen different studies say different things but the most common was if a 200-250 megaton weapon was detonated over Kansas at a height of 225 to 250 miles than most of the United States would be affected. Leaving only Alaska and Hawaii with working electrical grids. You put that together with all of the other terrorist attacks that have taken place over the last couple of days, this was differently a man made attack. I don't know by whom, or for what purpose. But as far as I can tell, they were at least fairly successful. I could go into greater detail but right now we don't have a lot of time to waste standing around talking."

Holding my hands out to my sides I just shrugged and said, "Just a dumb old grunt trying to get back to my family in Texas." Don huffed again, "Yea right and I've believe as much or as little of that as I want too, but I do have some land I want to sell you down in Florida too. So what were you doing up here in the Baltimore area?"

I bent over and gathered my day pack up and stuffed it back into the top of my ruck sack, "Don could we move over to the ammo area while we are talking, I really need to get what I need before the little zombies show up. I really admire your work ethic and that you are hanging around protecting the store but you do not have enough guns and ammo here to keep the people out when they show up, that is unless you are willing to kill kids and women to possible keep them out. But of course if you do manage to hold them off for long, they will just burn you out. You should take what you need and get the hell out of here. I figure you have less than twenty-four hours before people begin showing up, more than likely less than twelve hours." Don nodded and I followed him back toward the hunting and gun area of the store. "What calibers do you need?" he ask. "First priority is 5.56 or .223 which ever you have in 65 grain, followed by 9mm jacketed hollow points, prefer the heaviest 9 mm jacketed hollow points you have that are not +P. I would love to pick up a Ruger .22/.45 with about 1000 rounds of CCI and three or four magazines for it if you have access to the guns," I said.

He paused and I could see him thinking it over, than his shoulders slumped and he nodded, "Sure why not, but I do want to make a copy of your credit card so I can charge your ass when the power comes back on." I laughed and said, "No problem, I can even give you my Texas drivers license as a

58

keepsake. But you know as well as I do that the power is not coming back on. But my licenses has all my current info on it and if I'm wrong and the lights come back on you can mail it back to me after you get paid for the stuff. Don nodded again and pointed to a row, "The 5.56 is down this row, I will get you a Ruger .22/.45 out of the safe. Anything else you want while I'm in there?" "Well now that you ask I would trade you a M9 Beretta 92 and two Sig 226 for a Glock G34 MOS if you have one in stock." "Let me see what I can do," Don said and gestured back to the ammo, "Just keep a count of what you're taking," as he headed into the back area.

I headed straight over to the M855 boxes. At 62 grains, the full metal jacket bullets would do well with the M4. I ripped open my ruck and pulled out the M4, slapping it together took all of ten seconds, after doing a quick ops check I laid the M4 on the shelf to my front. Next I pulled out my chest rig and strapped it on. I reached in and snagged one of the loose P-Mags and quickly ripped open one twenty round box and began filling the magazine, finishing the first twenty I added nine more rounds from another box. I stuffed the magazine into my M4 and chambered a round, feeling better and more comfortable than at any point since waking up that morning. Laying the M4 back down, I started packing boxes of ammo into the outside pouches of my ruck. After getting six boxes into each outer pouch of the ruck, I began stuffing rounds into each of the magazines on my chest rig. This took about ten minutes working like a madman. Twenty-eight rounds into each of the eight magazines. Pulling the last extra P-Mag from my ruck I stuffed the rounds into it as if my life would depend on it. Glancing up I saw Don standing about five feet away just staring at me. He looked from me to the small mountain of empty boxes around my feet.

"Sorry didn't mean to interrupt," he said, "you looked like a starving man at a buffet." "Not a bad analogy," I said, "I have felt naked since this happened with no ammo." Don lifted his hands and I saw he had three pistol cases in his hands. I was curious, as I had only asked about two weapons. Don quickly filled me in, "I have one Glock 34 MOS Gen 4 and one in Gen 5, didn't know which you would prefer and the Ruger .22 you ask for. You mentioned you had a Glock and figured you would prefer all the same Generation. Its here if you want them." I smiled, "Thank you, I would." I pulled out the two Sig's and the Beretta and handed them over with their magazines and said, "Just in case the lights do come back on, you might want to say you took those off some kids trying to break into the store during the blackout if anyone ever asks."

I took the cases from him and set them on the ground, first I popped open the Gen 4 and racked the slide open and checked the barrel. Clean as a whistle. Reaching into my ruck I pulled out one of my Glock magazines and ejected out the empty factory magazine. Double-checking the weapon was empty; I tried the trigger a couple of times. The factory trigger is ok in most Glocks, but I really do prefer the Zev Professional trigger. I would have to look and see if they carried Zev products. Slamming in one of the loaded magazines, I noticed there was still a little factory grease on the weapon. That would be fine until I had the time to give the new gun a cleaning. Pulling the slide to the rear, I racked a round into the chamber and laid it on the counter. I paused as I could hear Don a couple of rows over moving some boxes and muttering to himself. After listening for a few seconds I could not quite make out what he was saying but it sounded like he was not happy with or about something. I turned my attention to the second Glock pistol case. Opening the hard case I was greeted by a Gen 5 Glock 34 MOS that already had a RMR mounted on it. As I did with the other Glock, I completed a function check and shoved a loaded magazine into the mag well. About that time Don came around the corner with a pair of

Blackhawk drop holsters in his hands. It was a matching pair, one right handed and one left. I grimaced a little, wearing two guns was a little over kill but carrying a pack didn't leave a man many options for carrying a gun holster. Don just grinned and handed me the holsters. All I could do is grin back and nod my head. I noticed he had put on a pair of drop leg holsters and had the two Sig's I had given him. We were both like a couple of kids in a candy store. I thanked the stars that I had my suspenders on or the weight of the two guns would have to heavy for my pants to stay up. Taking my war belt off I secured it into the top flap of my ruck sack. Taking the two rigs it only took a minute to get the adjusted and I then shoved my Glock 17 into the holster on my right leg and followed that with shoving the G-34 with the RMR into my left leg holster. Was it over kill, sure, but I remembered something that Kipling had written, "A man can never have too much whiskey, too many books, or too much ammunition". I might not remember the exact quote word for word but his point is well taken. Settling the guns into place I walked over to the holster aisle and grabbed a set of suspenders for Don, he might not realize right now but he would thank me later.

Don walked back towards the rear stockroom and I turned my attention to the Ruger case on the counter. I frowned a little when I opened the case but decided that this would do. It was a Ruger .22/.45, but the color had thrown me for a few seconds. It was blue, not just "gun blued", but bright blue, but as I only needed it to kill small game it didn't really matter much. It was a six-inch barrel "lite" model with adjustable sights. I don't think the rabbits or squirrels would mind what color it was. Don had already found an Uncle Mike's soft nylon holster for it, along with a matching nylon magazine pouch and two spare magazines for the Ruger. I dropped the .22 into the holster and shoved the gun and magazine pouch into the top flap of my rucksack beside the spare Glock 34.

Don handed me six boxes of Federal 147 Grain, Hi-Shok 9mm. I stepped over to the magazine rack and snagged the only three Glock mags left on the shelf. Tearing open the magazine packages, I loaded them up with 17 rounds each and dropped them into the top flap also. I dumped the remaining rounds of 9mm into a 40-ounce plastic water bottle I had picked up earlier and secured that into an outside pouch of my ruck.

Turning to Don, "Sir, I don't know how to thank you for all your help," and offered my hand to the older man. Don stood there for a couple seconds and than took my hand and said, "Well actually I do need a small favor in return for all this." I didn't hesitate, "Sir if it is within my power to do, I really do owe you." With that he grinned and said, "Well first lets get you into some dry clothes and get a cup of hot coffee and we can discuss what I'm thinking about." I nodded and said, "Sounds good to me, just point out who you want killed because I have not had a cup all day," but what I was really thinking was I just wanted to finish loading up and get as much distance from this store as I could before the mobs arrived. But I did owe this guy and would need to do what I could for him.

True to his word after helping me find a pair of boots, a pair of Vasque GTX GoreTex waterproof hikers and a few pairs of my favorite Darn Tough boot socks, we were sitting in a couple of camp chairs holding what Don claimed to be a cup of coffee. Don had fired up one of the two burner Coleman camp stoves and put batteries into two LED camp lanterns. While I had been lacing up my new boots Don had gathered together several of the other items I had mentioned I still needed. As we talked I had basically dumped my rucksack out to repack. Don had offered and I gladly accepted to repack some of my ammo into MTM 100 round plastic boxes. This would greatly reduce the space needed for the ammo and protect the ammo better than the original cardboard boxes. Sitting and enjoying the coffee, I realized this was the first moment I had been able to sit and relax since waking up at 0500 this morning. After finishing up the coffee and the transfer of all of the 9mm rounds to the MTM boxes, I reached for the additional box Don had dropped off by my camp chair. My eyes widened when I opened the box, "Don, since when did Bass Pro begin carrying suppressors?" Don just look at me and shrugged. Pulling out the packing material, I closely examined the six-inch suppressor. Yes, this could come in handy. The suppressor was a Gemtech Mist-22 made for the Ruger .22/45. The Ruger using this suppressor, along with sub-sonic .22 rounds would make no more noise than an air rifle. Getting up from my chair, I walked over to the ammo section and began looking for sub-sonic rounds for the .22. Finally finding several boxes of Federal 40 grain sub-sonic, I grabbed these along with a couple of hundred round boxes of CCI hi-velocity Stingers. Returning to my chair, I snagged another cup of the so-called coffee from the camp store. Sitting down I dug the .22/45 magazines from the top flap of my ruck and loaded the two magazines, one with sub-sonic and one with CCI's. After completing the loading I packed the magazines, suppressor, and the remaining .22 rounds into the top flap.

Picking my coffee cup up and taking a sip I grimaced at the strong bitter taste. I turned at the sound of a laugh to see Don chuckling to himself as he watched me. "What's the matter Jarhead, can't handle real coffee?" I grimaced again and said, "I'll let you know the second I find a real cup of coffee." My next dilemma was picking though the assortment of Mountain House Freeze Dried meals. Finally deciding on sticking with what I knew I would eat, I picked out all the Lasagna, Chili Mac and Biscuits & Gravy bags I could find. Grabbing a stuff sack I carefully packed the Mountain House into the compression bag and cinched the bag down. I would save these for when nothing else was available. At this point it wasn't about the what it was, it was about the space and weight of each item.

Picking up my now empty daypack, I roamed the aisles to see what else I could find that I would need. Much to my surprise I found several steel traps and snare sets. Leaving the heavy steel traps I grabbed all the snare sets they had and one spool of wire. I smiled to myself; this really was a good sign. Now I needed to get some good cutting tools and water filters. Moving over to the knife section it only took me a few seconds to find and claim a new CRKT Ken Orion Foresight pocket folder. As far as I'm concerned this is one of the best all around folders and is a steal for the price, than laughed at myself, yes free was a pretty good price. While on the large size, if you can only have one knife, this is the one you want. Heavy duty, easy to sharpen and it holds a great edge. I also picked up a K-Bar for an all around utility knife, a Sven 15-inch folding camp saw and a Lansky Knife sharpener. Moving over to the water filters section, I picked up a new one hundred ounce Camel Bak, two in-line Sawyer Mini Water Filter Systems and one Katadyn Hiker Pro Water filter. Taking one of the in-line Sawyer Mini Water filters out of its packaging, I separated the filter and the backwash tools. The backwash tools I placed in a Ziploc baggy and stored in the top flap of the rucksack. Drawing my new CRKT pocket folder knife, I cut the drinking tube from my Camel Bak about six inches from the bladder. Inserting the in-line filter, I now had a means of directly filtering water from my Camel Bak. I would try and not do that but it was better to have the capability than to take the chance of picking up a bug from dirty water. For my primary water filter I picked up one of the new 2-liter Platypus Gravity Works filter and grabbed two 40-ounce stainless steel Klean canteens. These are great for boiling water in and are one of the few water containers that can be safely sanitized after having dirty water in.

Being satisfied with my water situation and leaving Don messing around fixing some food, I walked over to the gun counter and grabbed a can of CLP and a bore snake in each of the calibers I have. Unpacking the 9mm caliber bore snake, I ran the snake though each of my Glocks a couple of times for good measure and then wiped each down with CLP. I reminded myself that I should clean my M4 after things settle down tonight. Finding a small cleaning kit I added the bore snakes and CLP to the kit and sat it aside. I was feeling pretty good about things and was beginning to wonder about the favor Don had been talking about earlier. Picking up my cleaning kit, I walked over to the clothing section and selected a couple more pairs of Darn Tough boot socks, a good set of Redhead 3D camouflage, a Redhead Bone Dry CWS jacket, two pair of Merino long johns, and several pairs of ExOfficio underwear. Hauling all the stuff back to my ruck I stripped all the tags and packaging off of everything and stuffed the clothing into another waterproof stuff sack. Filling good about the equipment I had picked up to go along with the equipment I had traveled with, I sat and did another mental inventory of everything. Jumping up I strolled over to the camping section and grabbed a new Therm-a-rest sleeping pad. Just as I was finding a home for the sleeping pad on my ruck, Don called out to me, "Dave, get your butt back here and give me a hand with this stuff."

Chapter Five

I finished stuffing the clothing bag into the bottom of my pack and then stood and walked over to the area Don was standing at. He was standing behind the gun counter and had laid several boxes on top of the counter. Shining my headlamp on the boxes, "Do they work?" I blurted out. Don laughed, "Well Einstein, we won't know until we try them. Now make yourself useful and run over to the battery rack and get a bunch of double A and CR123's so we can find out if they work." Not arguing with the man, I stepped over to the battery rack and grabbed all the batteries I could hold and returned to the counter. Dropping the batteries onto the counter, I grabbed the nearest box and ripped it open. It was an Armasight PVS14-3 Gen 3 night vision device. I had seen these at Shot Show last year but could never dream of owning one as they ran around 3,500.00. This version could work as a stand alone monocular or could be used as a NVG riflescope. It came with its own mount and was as simple as tightening down on flattop of the M4. It also came with the battery adapter, which was great as it was a pain to carry enough CR123's, and I made a mental note to get grab a small solar charger and rechargeable double A's. Hopefully the store carried Anker Solar panels, which I have at home, but once again they are not going to do me much good there. Holding my breath I slide in the batteries screwed the cap on the battery compartment and hit the power button. To my amazement the device powered up. I looked over at Don and saw he was looking around the darkened store with the device he had put batteries in. Don met my eyes and said, "Lucky for you that I didn't have this a few hours ago." I nodded, "Ya, my wife would have more than a little pissed at you. She has always said that if anyone was going to get to shoot me that it would be her." Don laughed, "You had best load up on these batteries as it will be safer for us to move at night than during the daylight when all the crazies will be out." I paused and looked over at him, throwing him a question look, "Let's just get packed up and we can discuss what comes next after we are set. I want to be packed and ready to go before the golden horde arrives."

I carried the device back to the camping area and immediately loosened the ACOG on my M4 and quickly replaced it with the PVS14. Don watched and followed suit on his chosen AR. I said, "You need to find you a good sling for your rifle, I would recommend a two point sling but you pick what you're comfortable with." Don nodded and headed off to find his sling as I continued to get acquainted with my new toy. Bringing the M4 to my shoulder I quickly scanned the interior of the huge store. The difference between a Gen 1 or 2 compared to the Gen 3 night scope was amazing. Gone was the heavy green tint of everything and the need for an external light source. Of course the scope still had an infrared light but unless there was no ambient light there was no need for the light. Turning off the scope, I got up to find a case that would work for both my ACOG and the night scope, as I would be changing them back and forth each morning and each night.

While looking for a small hard sided case for the scopes, I grabbed a new headlamp, a Goal Zero battery charger which charges double and triple A batteries, two packs each of rechargeable double and triple A batteries, and an Anker 21 Watt Solar panel. The headlamp took triple A's while most of the other devices took double A's. While I was there I also grabbed a new Sure Fire and removed its packaging, you can never have to many lights. Placing batteries into the new Sure Fire, I double-checked that it worked and dropped it into my pocket. Returning to my ruck I found a home for all of the equipment. I hefted my ruck and frowned, the ruck was pushing the upper limits of what I wanted to carry. I would have to be very choosy about anything else I picked up.

Don was still behind the gun counter and was getting down a collection of shotguns. I looked over what he was getting down, mostly Remington Tactical 870's and Mossberg 500's. Without saying anything I walked over to the shotgun ammo and begun pulling boxes of the Hornady Coyote loads and the Federal rifled slugs. Returning to the counter I began opening the boxes of shotgun shells for loading the guns he had selected. "How do you want these loaded?" I ask. Don looked at me and said, "What would you recommend?" "I personally would load two rifled slugs and top the shotgun off with buckshot. That way if the buckshot doesn't get them before they get to cover then you have the slugs to deal with any cover they get to, " I said. "Sounds like a plan to me, " Don replied.

I began stuffing shells into the shotguns and once I had all the tubes full, I jacked one into the chamber of each and added one more shell to top off each of the guns. "So what favor do you have in mind," I ask. Don paused and said, "I need to get home to and I was hoping that we could travel together to my place and than you can head on to Texas from there." He could see the hesitation on my face and said, "I would understand if you don't want to do this, because it's just not me getting to my house, my grandson is a freshman at the University of Maryland, I am the only family he has up here, his parents are divorced and I have been looking after him for the last couple of years." "Do you know if he is going to stay in place or would he head up this way with all the trouble going on and the power out?" I ask. Don paused again thinking over my question, "I believe he would head this way, that why I decided to stay here and watch over the store. He would know that with the power out I would be staying here to make sure there were no break-ins. We have an apartment about a 1/2 mile from here that he might check first but would head over here once he saw I wasn't there."

"OK," I said, "After he gets here where are you planning to head to. I would recommend not staying here any longer than you have to. This place will be a mob magnet once people realize the shit has really hit the fan." "Oh, we have a hunting and fishing cabin out in the Blue Ridge that we will head to. It's not much but it does have its own well, a wood stove, and I have a couple of months of food stored there. We should be ok if we can kill a deer or two during the winter."

"OK," I said again. "OK?" said Don, surprised at my answer. "Yes," I said, "I'll help you and your grandson get out to your cabin. You helped me when you didn't have to, so why does it surprise you that I would help you?" Don smiled and said, "Well most folks these days only care about what's in it for them and I know you have a wife and young ones down in Texas and need to get home to them." "Well to be totally honest," I said, "that is the direction I'm going anyway and there is safety in numbers. It would be a little slower traveling in a group but I think the security of having three of us while we try and get out of the populated area would be better than just myself." "I appreciate it," Don stated, "while I know which end of a gun the bullet comes out of, I'm by no means an expert and we would really like to have someone that at least kind of knows something about moving though hostile areas with us." "Well," I said, "what I'd suggest we do right now, being that we are going to wait here for your grandson, is to get the rest of this place set up so we can defend it if we have to. Also after we do that, we need to make sure we have you and your grandson a loaded pack ready to go so we can get out of here fast if we have to." "Sure sounds like a plan to me," said Don.

Over the next two hours we were able to create several strong points inside the store. The exits from the store directly into the mall area had drop down metal gates that would be extremely difficult to breach. Grabbing a case of Taninite, I mixed three of containers together in accordance with the directions and poured the mixture into a one-gallon plastic drinking jug. Seeing that this only filled the one-gallon container part way, I continued to mix until I had all three of the gallon containers full of the Taninite. Taking a roll of duct tape with me I had Don open the gate into the mall high enough for me to slide under. Fake tree timbers bordered the entryway into the store and I duct taped two of the containers on the left and right sides of the entrance. Dragging a bench over to the entrance I stood on the bench and taped the third container to the exit sign hanging over the entrance. Double-checking that I could see all of the containers from inside the store we closed and locked the security gate. I was pretty sure that the containers would not sympathetically detonate when I would shoot one. Pretty sure, thinking that I would want to grab a pair of earmuffs. Of course after explaining to Don what I was doing he just about flipped out, but I convinced him that most (maybe) of the damage would be to the hallway. Fact is I had never played with Taninite but I have watched the guy on Demolition Ranch blow up all kinds of things with it.

The loading docks were secured from the inside with metal garage doors that again would be extremely difficult to breach. Not impossible, but difficult, and no one would be able to get in without a lot of noise. We staged weapons and ammo, along with a few bottles of water at each of the strong points. At each of the strong points we placed at least two shotguns and one high caliber rifle with plenty of ammunition for each weapon. While Don was moving guns and ammo to the identified strong points, I was rigging trip wires along likely avenues of approach if someone was able to gain access to the store. Most were rigged to noisemakers like bear bells to let us know if someone tripped over them. I also mixed up several more containers of Taninite and duct taped the containers above all the entry points and set several of them on top of displays visible from the upper offices where Don had almost shot me from my attempted entry. I placed a large Shoot and See target on each of the containers facing the upper offices. These would come as a very unpleasant for anyone near one when it went off. I also retrieved three sets of Howard Leight electronic earmuffs, three sets of eye pro, and three Midland two-way radios. I rigged up the radios with Midland headsets so we could all stay in contact within the store. I loaded them all up with double A batteries and set them all to the same privacy frequencies.

I walked over to where Don was packing up two of the Ascend Mountain Series backpacks. I handed him two of the radios, earmuffs, and eye pro. "Don, go ahead and put the radio and headset on. I would recommend always wearing the eye pro and hang the muffs around your neck. If we have to do any shooting in here it's going to get really loud, really fast. Really wish you carried the new Walker Game Ears. They are only the size of hearing aids but work just like the originals." Don nodded, "I couldn't agree more as my ears are still ringing from the one shot I took at you and that's been several hours ago. But just so you know, those new Walkers Game Ears are over on aisle eight." "That's good, do you want me to set you a pair up? We can only use one for right now because your radio ear bud has to go in one ear. I'll get them set up and grab all of the batteries I can find for them. They will be great to wear while we are on the road and at night standing guard duty. I think we pretty much have everything we can do finished up. You go on back up topside so if we do have visitors soon you will be back up where you were earlier. Do NOT shoot the Shoot and See targets over the main entrance and on the displays unless shit has gotten out of hand or there is a group of three or more clustered near the target," I explained. "Why?" ask Don. I laughed and said, "Lets just say you are not going to win store manager of the year from corporate if you shoot one or more of those targets. Under each of those targets is a half pound of Taninite and about a half pound of lead split shot mixed in. If you shoot one of them you might want to duck after you pull that trigger."

Don's eye grew large and he sputtered, "We can't set that stuff off in here, it will destroy all kinds of stuff." Attempting to be patient with him, I explained, "Don, if the people breaking in here are not deterred by a couple of warning shots what do you think they are going to do to you. Look I'm not saying we have to slaughter them but if it comes down to them or us, you need to shoot the damn targets or we need to get out of here and let them have this place." Don thought about that for a minute and nodded, "Lets get the rest of this stuff packed and get it moved back towards the exit point you picked. That way if we have to get out in a hurry we can." I agreed, "Sounds good to me, I already have my stuff staged back there. After that we need to get something to eat and some rest. Tomorrow is going to be a long day and always remember, rest is a weapon. I'll grab a couple cots and bags and get them set up behind the gun counter by the door to the back."

After getting the cots and sleeping bags set up, I used one of the pallet jacks to move several of the pallets of feed corn over to in front of the gun counter. While they might not stop much they were better than nothing. It was just after 0200 and Don had offered to take first watch for a couple of hours. I laid down and was out fast. My last thoughts were of my kids and wife. What were they doing, had her Mom and Dad made it down to the house? Were they safe?

It was almost 0500 when Don's voice sounded in my headset. I didn't realize I had not taken off my radio headset when I lay down. It took my a moment to remember where I was and then keyed the radio, "Will be right up." Don replied,

"Coffee is hot on the stove and the eggs have been setting for about ten minutes." I double clicked the send button to indicate I had heard and understood Don's last transmission and headed over to the bathroom in the back.

Quickly finishing my business in the bathroom, I hurried over to the stove and grabbed a cup of coffee and the bag of Mountain House eggs before heading to the upper office floor where Don was. He stood as I climbed the stairs and he handed me the night vision bino's, "You won't need these much longer, but they will still help out with the shadows for the next hour or so," Don said. "Thanks for breakfast," I muttered around a mouthful of eggs, "go get some sleep, I'll call if we have any visitors." With a wave of his hand, Don headed downstairs and quickly disappeared into the darkness. Taking another bite of the eggs, I raised the night vision bino's to my eyes and could clearly see Don sitting on his rack taking his boots off. I watched as he flopped down on his rack and didn't move.

As I had not seen the store from this vantage point I took my time getting familiar with the layout of the store and took note of all the Shoot and See targets. The platform I was standing on in front of the upper level office spaces was about 15 feet wide and ran about half the length of the store on the north side. The wall facing the store floor was high enough that it almost concealed the offices along the north wall. The platform gave a commanding view of the store with only an area directly behind the center display blocked from view. It was almost too bright already to use the night vision bino's if I looked towards the front of the store. While it wasn't bright to the naked eye, the light from the rising sun was almost to the point of overpowering the device. Putting down the bino's I picked up my M4 and switched out the night vision back to the ACOG. Placing the night vision scope into the small Pelican case, I placed the case near the top of the stairs so I could grab it if I had to vacate the upper platform in a hurry. With that done I decided to go ahead and make a round of the store and see what I could see out the front doors of the store and of course make sure I hadn't missed anything that could make my trip easier.

After ascending the stairs I walked carefully on the stamped concert floor so my boots would not squeak and making sure to watch out for all the trip wires I had put out earlier. Heading first towards the back of the store where the store led into the mall. Stopping in the shadows near the back exit, I stood and observed for a couple of minutes. Seeing no movement and hearing no noises, I turned and headed back into the main area of the store. As I walked back by the stairs I remembered my bag of eggs and cup of coffee upstairs. Making the detour to get my food I slung my M4 across my chest and began shoving eggs into my mouth as I moved slowly towards the front of the store. I am always surprised how good some of the Mountain House food is as I looked down and discovered I had finished off the 2.5 servings bag. Sitting the empty bag on a nearby shelf I took a sip of the strong black coffee Don had made. It was only lukewarm warm but it was strong enough to stand a spoon up in it.

Chapter Six

I had just gotten to the front store area when the silence was broken by a loud banging noise coming from the loading docks area. Turning and heading that way, I saw Don getting out of his cot and trying to get his boots back on. I ask him, "Do you want to handle this and I will stay out here or should we both go see who is knocking on our back door?" He gave me a puzzled look and I continued, "If it was me and I knew someone was in here guarding the place, I would attempt to draw your attention to either the front of the store or the back of the store and than enter where you were not looking. One of us should stay out here to cover the store front and the mall entrance, just in case." "Ok," said Don clearly understanding the why of it now, "I'll go check it out and will give you a call on the radio if I need any help." I nodded and headed back to cover the main floor of the store.

The banging noise stopped as soon as Don yelled to stop beating on his door that he was coming. After a few seconds I heard shouting coming from the back of the store and I turned to glance over my shoulder towards the back hallway. As I turned I caught movement in the shadows of the hallway which turned into a group of several individuals pouring out of the hallway. Dropping to one knee and bringing up my M4, I flipped the safety to three round burst and called out, "Freeze or die," in a loud command voice. As if by magic the young men froze in place just as Don's voice came into my earpiece, "Talon, my grandson and some of his friends are here," a very happy Don said. Don appeared from the hallway and looked around at the frozen boys, then looked over at me with my M4 shouldered. I saw him also freeze but relaxed a little when he saw me lower the muzzle of the M4. "Old man," I said, "don't do that to me again, these boys are lucky they were not carrying any weapons or we would have had a huge mess." Don laughed nervously and said to the boys, "Guys, this is Talon, I would suggest you listen to whatever he has to say and if he tells you to do something, just do it without questioning why." One of the boys ask, "Sir is it ok for us to move now?" I replied, "Yes, but for the time being please stay away from the rifles and shotguns laying on the counter. Most if not all of the guns you see are loaded and I don't want any of you messing with them until we can get you checked out on them." The boy looked at Don and Don nodded his head, "You boys head on over to the camping area and we will get some food fixed for you." The boys relaxed and moved off towards the camping area with the occasional glance over their shoulder at me. As the group moved off, Don grabbed one of the boys and stopped him from going with the small group. The boy, young man really, was a good-looking kid, about 6 feet tall with a lanky athletic build, and had the same light brown hair that Don did. It didn't take a rocket scientist to see the strong family resemblance.

Don approached sheepishly, "Sorry about that, I was so excited that Mat had gotten here that I didn't think about how it would look to you when the boys came in." "No problem this time, but in the future always let me know what is going on," I said rather more harshly than I meant to, so I added in a softer tone, "Really just communicate next time, every stranger outside is potentially an enemy who will not hesitate to kill you or Mat, or any of his friends." "Got it," said Don, "this is my grandson, Mat, Mat this is Talon." Good to meet you, Sir," said the young man and offered his hand. I shook his hand as I met his eyes. He didn't attempt to overpower me or play any games; just a good firm handshake and he met and held my gaze. I thought at the time, he would do. I can work with this kid.

76

After our introductions, Don began peppering Mat with questions about his trip up from the University of Maryland. I stopped him and said, "Hang on lets get with the whole group and get organized a little before we debrief Mat. It's going to take us a little longer to get out of here with all of these guys, so we need to get organized pretty fast." We all walked over to the group and Mat introduced everyone. There were a total of six of the boys counting Mat. All of them were sophomores and juniors and all were members of the Maryland Lacrosse team. After Mat introduced everyone I stepped forward, "Guys, I'm glad everyone made it up here ok, but we don't have much time to sit around and talk about what has happened, but I will try and answer all your question but right this minute we don't have the time. What I do need to know right now is which of you have any firearms training. I'm not talking about whether you have fired a gun before, but who has actually experience in handling a gun?" Two of the boys raised their hands along with Mat. I pointed at the first boy, who Mat had introduced as Ben. Ben was about 5'9" and had a solid build. He said, "I have been hunting with my father since I was 10 years old. I killed my first deer when I was twelve and every year we go turkey and duck hunting." "Ok Ben, I want you to take Don's radio, grab one of the shotguns over at the counter along with one of the loaded bandoliers and go watch the front of the store. Find a place where you can see everything but that allows you to not be seen by anyone messing around outside. Do not shoot unless someone is breaking into the store. Do you understand?" I instructed. He nodded and moved over to Don to take his radio. As he walked away I called after him, "Ben, all of those shotguns are loaded and have one in the chamber." Ben turned towards me and waved, acknowledging what I had said.

I pointed to the second boy who had dark hair and was about 6 feet tall. He stood when I pointed at him. The first thing I noticed about this boy was his green eyes and the very serious expression on his face. "Sir, I'm Jeff from Tennessee. I grew up hunting rabbits, squirrels, and deer. Mostly with a rifle but I know my way around a shotgun also." I nodded, "Go grab one of the shotguns, they are all loaded with one in the chamber, and a bandolier. Get a camp chair and go sit by the back hall door so you can see the loading dock area. We will get you a radio but for now just give us a yell if you see or hear anything." Jeff nodded and head back to the counter area. Turning to the rest of the group, I said, "The rest of you get something to eat and make sure you fix enough for Ben and Jeff. When you have it fixed let me know and I will take it to them. Stay in this area and don't roam around."

Motioning to Don and Mat, I headed over to the hand held radio's area. After Don and Mat caught up with me, I handed them each a couple of packages of the same kind of radios that Don and I had picked earlier. "Guys pull those out and get batteries into them and I will go get the headsets put together. Mat can fill us in on his trip while we are doing this," I said as I began cutting open the plastic packing from the radio headsets. Mat turned towards his grandfather and said, "Grandpa its crazy out there, I didn't think we were going to make it. People are losing their minds. A couple of us were at our dorm when the lights went out so we decided to head over to Ben's apartment, which is on the end of the campus. Most people had gone home over the long weekend and were not back yet. All of the other guys from the lacrosse team that had not gone home for the long weekend were hanging out at Ben's apartment. His girlfriend had flown home for the weekend. We were all getting ready to leave, as Ben had to leave to the airport to pick up his girlfriend. Her plane was the last flight of the night and was scheduled to land at BWI at 1245 AM. The power went out at 1230 AM, about 10 or 15 seconds after the lights went out the transformer on the pole down the street exploded. It scared the crap out of us. We had no idea what was going on. None of our phones were working, they all just went blank. The explosion from the transformer started a fire and before we knew it we were stranded because our cars would not start and we didn't want to go back inside because no police or fire trucks showed up. We tried to help out with garden hoses but there was almost no water pressure, after the second house caught on fire one of the older guys sent us to go house to house to get people out." His words came out with a rush and flood of emotion and as he talked he became more and more upset. I held up my hand, "It's ok, you guys did everything you could. On top of that you were able to get yourself and your friends out of there and safely here, so just take a deep breath."

I handed Mat a bottle of water and he took a couple of long pulls from it. Mat continued, "The first house I went to I could hear someone screaming for help before I could even knock on the door and I found an old lady kneeling down next to her husband yelling for help and repeating his name over and over. Before I could even check for breathing I knew he was dead, she told me later that they had been sitting and watching TV when the lights went out. She said she ask him to get up and get a flashlight but he didn't answer, so thinking he was asleep she got up and got a flashlight from the bedroom but it wouldn't work, so she went into the kitchen and got a candle. When she came back she saw him still sitting in his chair and there was blood coming out of his mouth. She figured he was having a heart attack and got him down on the floor and tried CPR. She said every time she pushed down on his chest that blood would come out of his mouth. I finally got her somewhat calmed down and she explained that her husband had just gotten a pace maker earlier this year. I got a blanket off of the sofa to cover him and got her to come outside. About ten minutes later her house caught on fire and burned completely down," explained Mat. He took a deep breath and continued, "One of the men explained that he thought we must had been hit with an EMP and told us the lights were not coming back on and we should try and get home if we could. As I'm the only one with family in the area near the university I told the group they should come with me. Also Ben wants to go to BWI to get his girlfriend."

I glanced at Don, then back to Mat and ask, "So what time was her plane scheduled to land?" "Around 12:30, I think he said, maybe 12:45, something like that," Mat replied. "Mat," I ask, "do you or any of your guys understand what an EMP is?" "Yes, we all understand basically what it is, why?" Mat ask. "Because this EMP was strong enough to knock every jet airliner out of the sky. I witnessed several crash within just a couple of minutes after the EMP went off. If Ben's girlfriend's airplane was flying at the time of the attack than it more than likely her airplane didn't make it." Mat's eyes got big and said, "We wondered what those large explosions were, we saw several huge fireballs on the horizon, but could not see any lights or hear any noise, just those huge fireballs, we must have seen a dozen or more within the first few minutes after the power went out, but didn't know what they were." I nodded, "Think about it, those airliners would have been cruising at around 45 or 50,000 feet when everything went dead. Everything is controlled with computers so at that point they just become a big hunk of metal and fell out of the sky. The chance of Ben's girlfriend's airplane making it in an hour early is remote. Not to sound cold but how long has Ben known this girl?" "They have been dating for over three years and just got an apartment together this summer, they were planning on getting married when they graduated next year," said Mat. I winced, "Well there is no use trying to talk him out of at least going to the airport and finding his girl. I know if it was my wife or one of my kids I would move heaven or earth to find them and nothing or no one would stop me."

I turned to Don, "So what's the plan?" Don turned to Mat, "So are these guys coming with us to the cabin?" Mat shrugged, "Grandpa I don't know, we didn't have much of a chance to talk on the way up here." I broke into the conversation, "Mat take this radio over to Jeff. Its already set on the correct frequency and turned on. Tell him to stay off the radio unless he has something to report. You also take one. Keep it on and with you all of the time. Then get something to eat. Make sure Jeff and Ben get something to eat also. Then we need to get everyone some basic gear put together. Don, I need you to get them started with a pack, sleeping bag, good boots, socks, stuff that will be warm for the coming winter. Make sure they all have water filters, a hundred oz Camel Bak, a couple stainless steel canteens and a Life Straw bottle. Issue each of them 50 buckshot and 50 slugs of 12 gauge. Add a few boxes of .223 and .308 to each, they are young and can handle the weight. Give every other one a camp stove and the others a cook pot. Make sure each has a fire starter, matches, and at least one lighter, more if you can find them. I will be over there to help in just a few minutes. We need to gather all the Mountain House we can carry. Try and get the same gear for each. Any questions?"

Mat said, "These guys are worn out, shouldn't we let them get some rest first?" I turned and looked him in the eyes, "Mat, we need to get ready to move before the people start getting here to loot this place. We have to at least get the basics packed up first, we might have to leave here in a hurry or we are going to have to kill a lot of people to keep what we have and I don't want to have to do that. I know they are tried but its better to be tried than to starve or freeze to death this winter. Lets get everyone moving so we can get these guys bedded down as soon as possible."

As Don and Mat moved off to begin laying out the gear, I walked over to the group of boys sitting around the camp stove Don had set up. They all turned to me as I walked up. "Good morning," I said, "My name is Talon. I believe all of you are aware of what has happened to our country. I know you're all tried but before you can get some rest we have a few things we need to do before you can get some rest. If we all work together we can get everything ready in about an hour and then you can get some rest. Right now isn't the time for a bunch of questions but I do want you to know what is going on. The reason we need to get packed up is that we might have to abandon this store at anytime. If Don or myself tells you to do something, don't ask why just do it. We will explain if there is time but things are going to get bad around here and worse as we begin traveling. Sometimes we will not have time to explain everything and life is going to get real interesting from here on out." The three young men looked up at me with a slightly stunned look. The young man on the right with blond hair asks, "I thought we were going to stay here until the power comes back on?" "No," I said, "the power is not going to come back on anytime soon, as in years. As soon as people realize that the power is not coming back on and no help is coming from the government than they are all going to head to places that have food and supplies, like here. A few days from now this store won't even be here. What the looters don't carry off someone will start a fire and this whole mall will burn to the ground. We do NOT want to be here when that happens." "So where are we going? I need to get home to Michigan to check on my parents," said one of the other two boys. All three looked at each other and each of them was nodding in agreement, than they all turned back to me. "I understand that each of you including Ben and Jeff have people you want to get to and you will, but first we have to get supplied and get out of the city. Any large city is going to be a

82

war zone within the next 48 hours. Don and Mat have a cabin in the Blue Ridge. We will make for that and then you can head on from there to your final destination. But we need to stick together until then; there is strength in numbers. But no one is going to force you to do anything. If you want to stay here let me know now so we don't waste our time. But if you are going with us I need for you to get up off your asses and go find four pairs of heavy boot socks, I would recommend Darn Tough socks, and then put on one pair of the boot socks and find you a good pair of winter hiking boots that fit. Do this as quickly as possible. Here is a radio and headset for each of you. To talk push this button on the side and hold it in while you talk. Release it when you are finished talking. Do NOT talk on the radio unless there is a problem or emergency. Always have your radio on and with you. If I call and tell you to drop whatever you're doing and get back here, do it without questioning me. Now go and get your socks and boots and get back here as quickly as you can," I said as I turned away and headed over towards Don and Mat.

Coming up on Don and Mat, I saw they had a good start on laying out the six packs and gear. I bent down and began stuffing sleeping bags into each of the packs. I glanced at Don, "Is your stuff all ready to go?" I ask. Don nodded, "I finished it up while you took a nap and its back there by yours. I do have a question, why the .308 ammo?" "I want to issue Ben and Jeff .308's. I figure to give Ben that S&W AR-10 .308 and Jeff one of those new DPMS in .308. In fact while you guys finish with the gear, I'll go over and get both of those set up for them. I want both of them to have both a day scope and a night scope. Mat what do you feel comfortable with?" I ask. "I would prefer as AR like yours but whatever you think is best," said Mat. I nodded and headed off towards the gun counter.

I stopped by and grabbed an armload of shotgun bandoliers. Walking over to the gun counter I looked over the selection of shotguns Don had laid out and loaded. I separated out the Mossberg 500's and 590's and a couple of Remington 870 tactical models. Laying a couple of bandoliers by each I then turned to go over to the riflescopes counter. Looking over the selections I picked out two Night force 5-25x56 for the .308 rifles. Carrying the scopes back over to the rifle counter I pulled down the rifles I had selected. As the tools were on the counter I went ahead and mounted the scopes. After getting them mounted I did a quick and rough sighting in with a bore sight. It would not be perfect but would do for now. Returning to the gun counter I looked over the inventory of pistols. I always knew what pistols I would pick out but I was hoping to see something that would inspire me to choose something else for them. You might not realize but I really do prefer 1911's in .45 caliber, but it takes muscle memory to safely operate one of these. After dwelling over the options, I knew that I needed to just get this done and move on. There was enough Sig Sauer's to equip each of the boys, but again, the Sig's needed training and we didn't have the time to do that. Sighing I moved down the counter to the Glock section. Sure enough, as I already knew, there were more than enough Glock 17's for all of them. Sliding open the case I began to remove six of the Glocks. After getting these placed on top of the counter, I ran over to the magazine row and pulled down all of the damn Maryland compliant 10 round Glock magazines they had. Dumping these into a shopping basket I took the magazines over to where the boys were sitting. Dropping the basket off, I said, "Come with me for just a couple seconds, each of you grab one of those shopping baskets." Giving me a puzzled look each of the boys got up and followed me over to one of the ammo shelves. I quickly located the rounds I wanted and begin piling 124-grain jacketed hollow points

Federal Premium Law Enforcement rounds into the baskets they were carrying. "Take these back over and begin loading up all the magazines. Each of the magazines should hold 10 rounds. Once you have all the magazines full, give me a call." More than slightly disgusted with only finding 10 round magazines for both the pistols and rifles; this was Maryland or used to be. At least there were enough drop-leg holsters for each of them.

About that time Don and Mat walked over to me. Don took one look at the AR I handed to Mat and held up his hand to stop me from launching into my carefully prepared rant about Maryland's bullshit laws about hi-capacity magazines. He turned and walked into the back. Mat and I exchanged looks and Mat shrugged his shoulders and said, "There is no telling with him." He was still looking over the rifle I had handed to him, handling it carefully and making sure the muzzle was pointed away from me, he cleared the rifle to make sure it was empty before putting it to his should and looking though the ACOG I had mounted on it. I nodded my approval as he laid the rifle back on the counter and began to examine the Glock 17 I had laid by the rifle. Don came out of the back carrying a tactical vest loaded down with six 30 round P-Mags. "Oh, you are so going to jail for that old man," I said as I grinned at him. Don grinned back and said to Mat, "Happy Birthday son, I was planning on giving this to you at the cabin, where by the way Mister Smart Ass they are legal." I grunted and said, "Save it for your lawyer, but I'm glad you did. Mat, get over to the ammo and load all of those magazines with 28 rounds. Use at least 65 grain .223 if you can find them. Do not use any of that Russian crap." I motioned to the Glock 17, "Are you comfortable with that?" "I've fired Grandpa's Glock 17 quite a bit so I feel pretty confident with it." "Good, how about any of the others?" I ask. Mat replied, "Ben and Jeff both shoot, I really don't know about the others, I know most of them have shot sporting clays as we have done that as a team. But as far as a pistol I just don't know." "Ok, fair enough, I want you to unload these six shotguns," motioning to the six shotguns laying on the counter, "Take the bandoliers over to the other three and have them load them up with half buckshot and half slugs. Make sure everyone has at least one box of #4's in his pack. How are we doing on room in the packs?" "Grandpa and I switched out a couple of the guys to the 5599 Ascent packs as they are big guys, but almost all of us are sitting around 45-50 pounds." Mat replied.

"Is that with or without water?" I asked. "That's with everyone's Camel Bak filled and most of them dropped several water bottles into their packs." "Alright, go make sure these guys get the shotgun bandoliers loaded up. Don't let them load any of the shotguns or pistols until I have a chance to go over the safety rules." I said.

Don came back with the five Glock 17's and the drop leg holsters, "Mat already has his," he said, "Figured we could give Jeff and Ben theirs but until we know more about the others experience with weapons, I figured we would hold on to theirs." Nodding my agreement, I reached out and took two of the rigs, "Don, I'm sorry I have been bossing everyone around, but I really have a bad feeling that this, the peace and quiet isn't going to last much longer. We need to be out of here by this evening. Hopefully we have that long, but regardless I want to be out of here before the crowds begin to gather outside of here. I really do not want to get into a running gun battle with these guys with us."

"It's not just the crowds I'm worried about," I continued to explain to Don, "The gangs in this area if what I'm really worried about. Primarily I'm worried about MS-13 and The Latin Kings." Don frowned, "I've heard of MS-13, its some Mexican drug gang, but I have never heard of The Latin Kings." "Actually MS-13 is mostly composed of guys from El

Salvador and are one of the largest and most brutal gangs in the US. They are very active here in Prince George's and Montgomery Counties. Normally they are easy to pick out because of their tattoos or by the blue and white Nike Cortez tennis shoes. Their motto is "kill, rape, control," and their favorite weapons are the knife and machetes. The Latin Kings are just as bad if not worse, their symbol is the 5-pointed star or a 5-pointed crown. Many of them wear a beaded necklace made up of black and gold beads. I don't remember the exact number of beads but I do remember that their enforcers and assassins wear one made up of all black beads. These are the guys I'm worried about showing up here for the guns and ammo."

Picking up two of the drop leg holsters with their Glocks, I headed towards Jeff position. "Jeff, strap this one," I said, handing him the holster setup, "I will go over the operation of the Glock once you have that adjusted." Jeff messed with the adjustments on the leg straps but finally got them tightened up. I showed him how to take up the slack and pulled out some duct tape to tape off the ends. "Ok, this is a Glock 17, it is a 9 mm that will hold up to 17 rounds, but as we are in the socialist state of Maryland, the store only has 10 round magazines. Once you chamber a round, the pistol is ready to fire. There is no safety other than your finger. Do not draw this pistol unless you are going to use it. Always keep it pointed in a safe direction when you draw it to clean it. Keep your finger out of the trigger guard, again unless you intend to shoot it. The holster will lock the pistol down until you press the release button. Any questions?" "No Sir, I'm familiar with the Glock action." Jeff replied. "Good, the mags are loaded, go ahead and chamber a round and holster your pistol." I instructed, watching Jeff closely as he drew the pistol from his holster and pulled out one of the magazines. He carefully pointed the pistol in a safe direction and locked the slide to the rear. After checking to make sure the barrel was clear, Jeff seated a magazine in the pistol, pulled back on the slide and let it go home on its own. Jeff holstered the pistol and looked at me for approval. I nodded and said, "Go drop off your shotgun on the gun counter and pick up that DPMS with the Night force scope. Find yourself a sling you like for it and then go find yourself a good set of bino's. After that go find some good waterproof boots and pick up several good pairs of boot socks, I already told the other guys but I would recommend the Darn Tough boot socks. We don't have a lot of time so get with it. Make sure you have at least three hundred rounds of .308 for the rifle. I already put a scope on it. Did you ever get anything to eat?"

"Yes Sir, one of the guys brought me over some food," Jeff replied. "Well get going and make sure you also pick out some winter stuff also, it's going to get cold before we know it." I said as Jeff turned to go. As he walked away I stepped into the nearby row of knives and grabbed several Gerber folding shovels and several mid-size knifes. I looked around the aisle for a Lansky Sharping Kit but didn't see one. Carrying the shovels and knifes over to the cooking area I saw the other three boys laying on cots and all of them were sleeping. As quiet as I could I laid down the shovel and knives. Taking the last pistol and holster I headed to the front of the store. Keying my radio, I pushed the transmit button, "Ben I heading your way with some gear." A couple seconds passed, "Roger that," came back Ben's reply. Rounding the aisle I could see Ben standing just inside where the clothes start from the front of the store. Walking up to the young man I handed him the pistol and holster. After observing him enough to see that he knew what he was doing I said, "After we talk I want you to do dump off that shotgun and pick up the AR-10 laying on the counter. Think you can handle that .308?" Ben just nodded and smiled, I continued, "I bore sighted the scope, so it should be good enough out to about 200 yards, beyond that I would not trust the bore sight. We will get it tighter when we get the chance. Also I want you to go get some winter clothing and boots get some good ones and several pairs of boot socks and long johns. Be quick about it, I don't know how much longer we have before we have to go. I know we need to talk about your girl, but for now just go get your stuff and get back here. Got it?" Ben nodded and headed off.

I headed over to stand by one of the Party Barges and took my bino's out of their pouch. I slowly scanned across the parking lot and was amazed that no one was visible in the parking lot. Well that won't last much longer I think, but when they do come it won't just be one or two at a time, it will be a lot of people who will not be happy that we were here first. They will be hungry and mad and I really don't want these boys to have to face that. Not yet anyway. So how in the hell were we going to move all these boys from here for a hundred miles away to the Blue Ridge? I'm thinking more and more about using bicycles. I needed to go discuss this option with Don. I could hear footsteps approaching and looked and saw Ben approaching. He appeared to be a little more energetic than when he left. "So what do you think," I said as I nodded to the S&W AR-10 he was carrying. He smiled wide and said, "Wow I always wanted one but could never afford one, it was love at first sight," and he grimaced as the words made him think about his girlfriend. "So Ben," I started, "I know your girlfriend was due to fly into BWI night before last. What time was she due in?" feigning that I did not know when she was due in. I saw tears well up in Ben's eyes and looked away so I would not shame him. Ben said, "I know her plane didn't make it. She was texting me on the plane Wi-Fi when the power went out. They hadn't even begun their descent into the airport so they were still a couple hundred miles out. I just didn't want to talk about it with the guys around." Inwardly I let out a mental sigh of relief, but at the same time I felt ashamed for thinking such a thought, but a trip to look for his girlfriend would have cost us at least two full days or more and would have taken us the opposite direction. I'm really hoping to have our little group to at least Harpers Ferry or beyond by that time. I reached out and put my hand on his shoulder, "Son, I know it isn't easy and I'm proud of the way you have handled it. I'm counting on you to hold it together as you are one of the few that knows how to handle a gun. And yes, it is going to come down to using our guns to get out of this area. I'm relying on you to help me get all of these guys to safety. You think you can do that?" "Yes Sir, I can do that," Ben said. "Ok, good. Now go and get some sleep. We need to move out of here by dark tonight," pointing in the direction of the sleeping area.

Taking one more quick scan of the parking lot, I walked back to the gun center area where Don and Mat were talking quietly. They both looked up as I approached, "So Don, is this doable? One, can we get all these guys to your cabin in one piece, two, do have enough supplies at the cabin that you and these six young men can make it though the winter?" Don thought for a moment before replying, "If we move before the panic really sets in I think we can make it to the cabin, as far as supplies, if we can get there and are able to kill a few deer or bear or find a head of beef I think we would be ok. I have about a years worth for two people but with 6 mouths to feed that is going to go quick."

"Here's what I'm thinking," I said, "There is a Sporting Goods store in this mall that has a shit load of mountain bikes that we can borrow to assist us in our little journey. It would be a lot faster and we should be able to clear most of the city by first light. That and if we could get a couple of those pull behind bike trailers we could take a lot more stuff. What do you think?" Mat's eyes lit up and he was nodding as was Don, "That my friend sound like a plan!"

Chapter Seven

After talking it over with Don, it was decided that Mat and I
would do a recon of the mall while Don, Ben, and Jeff would
go over firearm safety with the other three. We would all stay
on the radios, although I doubted they would work from very
far away. Yes I know, the packaging says "up to 30 miles",
but that is under perfect conditions and walls and metal
everywhere tend to significantly reduce their range. If Mat and
I ran into trouble we would fall back to the store where
everyone would be ready to go. Hopefully we would be able
to find the bikes we need at Modell's but if we could not we
would attempt to get the bikes from Wal-Mart. If we ended up
having to go to Wal-Mart we would all go at the same time as
the Wal-Mart was on the other side of the mall's casino and I
figured there would be some type of security element there.
Either way it would be much simpler if we could get what we
needed from inside the mall. We had tested the bolt cutters on
the inside grate for the store, so we knew we would be able to
breach the gate at Modell's in just a few minutes. I grabbed a
small daypack and stuffed it full of power bars and water
bottles for just in case. With Mat carrying the bolt cutters we
slid out from under the security gate that Don had unlocked. I
turned and whispered to Don, "Keep this unlocked unless you
see someone coming this way. If we need to get back in we
might be in a hurry." He smiled, "We will be here and
watching." I looked back sternly, "If we are not back by dark
stick to the plan. Head over to the park with all of our gear
and lay low. Mat and I will be there as soon as we can. If we
are not back by dawn, get these boys out of here and head
toward Harpers Ferry and we will catch up." I continued to

look at him until he nodded and with that I turned and headed down the mall corridor with Mat in tow.

We move down to the first cross-corridor and stop just short of the intersection. I move over to Mat and we both hunker down. "Mat as we move it will be in a leap frog fashion. Once I pass you, remember to keep a watch behind us. Keep your head on a swivel, do not watch me. If I begin shooting you wait until you have a target, if I retreat I will do so about 5 feet off the wall back to you. If there is shooting take a prone position until I get back to you, do not hug the wall that is just a good way to catch a bouncer." Mat gave me a puzzled look and I clarified, "Ricochet." And he nodded his understanding, "Give me cover fire if you have a target but be prepared to move back towards the store once I get to you. Stay off the radio unless you see or hear something. Got it?" I said. Mat's eyes where large but he nodded. "Good," I said and lightly slapped him on the shoulder, "When you pass me only go about 50 feet in front of me, but don't stop out in the open." Mat nodded to me once again.

I approached the corner and stopped just short of it to listen. Hearing no noise I took a quick peek around the corner. Nothing. I moved out to about halfway down the cross corridor. The sign over the intersection showed the food court to my right. I knew Modell's was to the left. It was so quiet it was eerie, so unnatural for this large of a structure. I know the Mall normally has security guards during the hours they are closed but don't know if any of them hung around. If they did and we ran into them would they be armed? That I did not know and was determined to see them before they saw us. I told myself to shut up and not to take council of my fears. There was no need to second-guess our plan. Either the guards were here or they were not, either armed or not. At this point we were committed to getting to Modell's and finding the bikes we needed.

Just as I was beginning to move, a loud crash of shattered glass broke the silence from the direction of the food court. There was a loud laugh that died away as someone commanded, "Quiet!" So at least two of them, probably more. I looked over at Mat and saw he had taken a prone position and facing the direction the sound had come from. I hissed at him to get his attention and when he looked back at me I motioned for him to head back the way we came. Mat immediately got up and took off back the way we came. I was pleased he moved quietly and that he stopped just short of the intersection. As I moved to catch up with Mat, I keyed my radio, "Don we are heading back in, ETA 30 seconds, be really quiet with the gate, we have visitors." I heard Don's double click of acknowledgement. I passed Mat and moved to the corner of the intersection. Glancing around the corner I saw no movement and motioned Mat to follow me. We moved towards the security gate just as it was rising Mat went down flat on the floor and rolled under the gate and I was just heading to the floor when I heard the sound of skate boards coming down the corridor we had just cleared. Knowing I would never make it before they rounded the corner, I stopped my movement to the floor and straightened before turning towards the corridor where the noise was coming from. Reaching up to the forearm of my M4 I pushed the connection button on my sling, unhooking the forward attachment, turning my sling into a single point where it could hang from the right side of the body. Standing in a relaxed manner I watched as a group of eight teenagers came to a stop about 20 feet from me. I immediately recognized several of the boys as the ones from yesterday in the parking lot. Without waiting for them to speak I said, "Good Morning, I hate to say it but the mall is closed today. You guys need to leave the area now." The boys all looked at their leader, a boy of about 16 or 17, medium build, with light brown hair. He hesitated but knew he had to say something in front of his little gang. "Who are you to tell us we can't be here." I stood relaxed and looked only at him, "I'm the guy that Mr. Colt appointed to make sure that guys like you don't trash the mall." The boy looked confused, "I don't know who Mr. Colt is and we are going to go where we want to."

"No," I replied letting a hardness creep into my voice. I took two steps toward him and said, "And tell all your friends that the next time I will not ask. Now turn around and leave the inside of this mall." The kid looked at me and sneered, " It's an awful big place for one old man to guard," but his voice trailed off as four shotguns barrels suddenly appeared though the security gate. "I suggest you leave now and don't come back," I stated. The other boys had already started backing up and their leader found himself all alone. I took two more steps towards him and said again, "Now." The boy turned away and took off after his friends. A few moments after disappearing around the corner the sound of more breaking glass could be heard, as the boys could not resist smashing more store windows on their way out. I turned back to the security gate and slid under the gate, "Well that was fun," I said standing up, "It is starting, we need to get moving away from the mall area. Are we all packed up?" Don finished locking the security gate and turned to me, "I believe we are. We might want to go over everything once more." "Ok, let's get everyone together with all their gear and do an equipment check. How did the weapons training go?" I ask. "As well as you might hope for, hopefully we would have to use any of this, but they understand how to use the stuff we gave them," Don said.

All the boys were gathered round the coffee pot area. I walked up and said, "Ok guys it is time to get this show on the road. Everyone go get your packs and let's make sure everyone is ready." After they all returned with their gear, I went over each to make sure it was adjusted to each of them.

A couple of them had some stuff tried to the outside of their packs. "Take all of that stuff on the outside of your packs and put it inside. We are going to go over some of the equipment. If you do not have an item I call out, you need to go get that item as fast as possible. We don't have much time so let's be as fast as we can be." After going over all the major items, several of the boys had to go get a couple of the items I insisted on. I made all of them go get and change into good camouflage. Most of them did not have gloves or a hat and I made sure they all had eye pro and hearing protection. "Get into the habit of wearing your eye pro and gloves all of the time and at least ear plug hanging on a lanyard around your neck. From here on out any small cuts could turn into something serious and if you damage your eyes there isn't much we can do for you. Now when we are moving keep about 5 meters between each of you. Stay off the radios unless you see something that is a danger to us. Don and Mat will bring up the rear. I will lead followed by Ben. Jeff you place yourself in the center of the column. If you absolutely have to stop than let me know. The front of the column will be 12 o'clock, so if I say there are hostiles at our 3 o'clock where would that be?" Pointing to one of the boys. He replied, "That would be on our right." "Correct," I said, "So if you spot anyone other than our group call it out. Everyone is to be considered hostile until they show otherwise. I know its a lot to take in and some of you still might not believe that it is going to be as bad as it is, but you will and if you want to survive you need to do what Don and I tell you, when we tell you without hesitation. I have spent my whole adult life in lawless places around the world. Things can and do happen fast. We don't have time to baby-sit you; we will treat you like the adults you are. One last thing, every time we stop you need to drink some water. Even if you don't think you need any, when the temperature drops and its cold you have to force

96

yourself to drink. The one thing you will not do is eat, you will eat when you are told to and only when you are told. The food we have has to last us. If you cannot or refuse to live up to our rules than you can go your own way. Any questions?" There was a general shaking of heads. "Alright, everyone grabs a bottle of water and drink it down right now." Pointing to a case of bottled water on the floor. "Last point," I said, "Our first objective is Harpers Ferry, if for any reason you become separated we will meet up on the southern side of the railroad bridge. From here we are going over to I-95 south to 29/200 and go west along 200 to just south of Gaithersburg. If we can find enough mountain bikes for all of us we will, but for now we are on foot. Any questions?"

One of the boys raised his hand, "Sir, Bobby, Jay, and I are all from the New England area. We would like to head that way if we could?" I looked at Don, who shrugged. "Son, I can only say if that's what you guys want then that's what you should do. I know there is nothing in the world that would stop me from heading toward my family and that is where I am heading. I wish you would go with us until everything has a chance to settle down but that's up to you." The three looked at each other than back at me, "Sir we need to get to our families, we are afraid if we go west with you guys we won't be able to get home before the weather turns cold." "I understand," I said, "but you need to understand that within a few days people will become desperate and the gear you have on will make you targets. There will be people out there that will kill you for what you have. You need to travel at night or off the roads, stay away from cities even if it takes you out of your way. Can any of you read a compass?" The boy that had been doing all the talking nodded, "Yes Sir, I know the basics." "Well go grab a couple of the ones you know how to use, one of you other guys run up to the front and grab 3 copies of a road atlas for the New England area. Try and find food along the way but only if you can do it safely. Always, Always filter your water. Set down your packs and take out all that shotgun ammo, except one of you. One of you should keep the shotgun and the other to should go grab a couple AR-15s. I'll come over and set them up with ACOGs for you. Everyone else take their shotgun and .308 ammo and spread load that. You guys use the extra space to add more Mountain House food."

Don motioned me off to the side, "Dave do you think this is a good idea?" "Don, if you were in their position what would you do?" I ask. He nodded, "Next item, what do I do with all of these guns? There are going to be lots of people in here real soon and a lot of these guns might end up in the wrong hands." I shook my head, "Yes some of them will be used by bad people but some of them will end up in good peoples hands allowing them to protect themselves and their families. We don't have time to worry about who ends up with what. The only other choice we have is to burn the place. But I'm against that as this store alone will allow a bunch of people from freezing to death over the next four or five months. But I won't stop you if that's what you want to do." "No you are right, it just worries me, " said Don. "Don, guns are just like any other tool, they can be used for good as well as evil. What people do with them is not up to you or me. I think the best thing to do is lock the racks so that the kids running around here can't just pick them up but the adults will figure out how to get to them. Now lets get a move on its almost 10 o'clock and I want to hit that Wal-Mart or Dicks for bicycles before dark." Don nodded and we both headed for the gun counter to help get the other boys set up.

After finishing with getting the boys set up to head northeast, I walked back and picked up my pack. Heavy, wow, I was not looking forward to carrying that. Dropping it back on the floor I moved over the ammo shelves and grabbed another couple boxes of 9mm Critical Defense for my Glocks. Returning to the rest of the group I stuffed the boxes into a side pouch on my pack. Unslinging my M4, I laid it on the table. Bending over I picked up my rucksack and shrugged into the arm straps, tightening them as I leaned forward. Straightening I snapped the waist belt and lightly bounced on by toes a couple of times to settle the pack. Picking up my M4, I turned to the group and said, "Well what are you waiting on, let's move." Everyone stood frozen for a couple seconds than everyone began moving at once. It took just a couple minutes before everyone had their rucks on and their weapons in hand. I turned to the three young men that would be leaving our group and struck out my hand, "Good Luck," I say as I shook each of their hands. After shaking hands with everyone, Bobby, Jay and Paul shouldered their packs and headed out the loading ramp door. I turned and began going over everyone else's gear to make sure we were not forgetting anything.

Everyone froze when we heard a shout from outside. Moving over to the service door with the small pane of safety glass, I observed a small crowd of about 12 to 14 men surrounding Bobby, Jay and Paul who were kneeling on the pavement. The three of our guys had their hands in the air. Keying my radio mic, I called, "Paul if you can hear me raise your right hand higher into the air." Watching out the small window I observed Paul raise his hand higher, keying my radio mic again, "When I tell you to, all of you hit the ground fast."

Turning to everyone, "Everyone drop your packs now, Don and Ben, go grab us all shotguns, Ben grab the Mossberg 930 for me and bring some extra buckshot rounds. Jeff, you and Mat get back inside and keep an eye on the front and back entrances, this might be some type of diversion to get inside the store. If anyone breaks in, don't hesitate to shoot the Tannerite if there is more than just a couple of them attempting to get in. Wait until they are inside and grouped together near one of the targets before shooting." Mat and Jeff took off back inside the store just as the other two came back in with the shotguns. Taking the 930 from Ben and grabbing a handful of 2 3/4 inch double 00 buck from the box Ben offered I quickly explained what we were going to do. "Ok, here how this is going to go down. I will go out the door first, they will want to talk, but we are going to take these guys down fast, I will take the leader out with my first shot, Ben you will be right behind me moving to my left, you begin taking the guys on the leaders left working your way back to the center, I will work to the right. Don you will come out to my right and begin shooting the guys beginning on the right working your way in to the center. Any questions?" Seeing nods all around, "Ok this is going to happen fast, don't freeze up, don't think, just from the look of them we are facing a local gang. Be careful not to shoot our guys laying on the ground."

I ran back over to the window and called out, "So what do you guys want?" Watching the crowd, a young man maybe 19 or 20 years of age, with a Spanish accent called back, "We want all of you out of the store, I promise you can leave unharmed, just leave all your weapons inside and walk away." Motioning to the rest of my guys, we lined up on the exit door, giving them a look I said, "Are you ready?" Again nods from the pale faces. Keying my mic, I said, "Paul hit the deck!" and I jerked open the door and took two quick strides forward, pushing off the shotgun safety as I stepped forward. The semi-auto Mossberg 930 was made for 3-gun matches and held nine rounds of 00 buckshot. Pulling the stock into my shoulder I squeezed off my first round at the young gang leader, the blast catching the man in the chest and head from about 25 feet. The nine .33 caliber pellets did not have time to spread at that range and dropped the gang leader like he had be pole axed. Moving my aim to the man standing to the former gang leader's left the man stood frozen with a look of horror on his face. My second round catching him before he could even begin to raise the pistol he had in his hand. By the time I had focused on my third target and pulled the trigger, my mind registered the third blast was much louder than my first and second shots had been. Moving my sight picture to my fourth target a large man armed with a rifle or shotgun was just raising the weapon to his shoulder when my round removed most of his head. Continuing to swing to my right I observed no more targets and quickly scanned back to my left. All of the gang members were down, most of them not moving but a couple of them were calling out for help. Reaching up and keying my mic, "Reload, everyone keep your eyes open, Don watch behind us, Ben watch the front corner of the store," I said as I shoved fresh rounds into my shotgun.

Keying my mic, "Paul are you guys ok." Watching I saw Paul raise his head and reach over to Jay, all three of them immediately got to their feet and headed back to the loading dock. "Everyone back inside, Ben you cover me from here." I moved down the stairs as everyone but Ben moved back into the storage area. Walking over to the two wounded gang members I didn't speak to either of them. One of the wounded gang members began cussing me in Spanish as I drew my Glock and silenced the gang banger by putting a single 9mm round into each of the men's heads. Quickly checking the others I found no more living gang members. Just as I turned to head back to loading dock I heard and felt a huge explosion from inside the store. Breaking into a run, I motioned Ben inside and I quickly followed him inside and secured the loading dock door.

As I ran for the main store area, I heard a fusillade of rifle shots. Slowing down long enough to exchange my shotgun for my M4, I turned to the group of young men following me. "Guys, go back to your rifles for this, as we move into the main store, keep below the gun counter. Don, take those three," pointing towards Paul, Jay, and Bobby, "Ben you are with me, when I call you on the radio, pop up and take down anyone that is not one of us." Leading the group we moved to the short hallway between the loading docks and the main store, I turned to group and motioned for them to stay low with my hand. Staying low myself I moved to the opening into the store, I motioned Don to take his guys along the gun counter to the left and motioned for Ben to follow me to the right. We moved to about the half way to the front before I motioned Ben to stay and I continued to move to the end of the counter. Glancing down the counter I saw that Don had his guys spread out towards the back of the store.

   Just as I was beginning to press the radio mic button a man towards the front doors of the store shouted, "We are going to kill all of you, that was my little brother out back that you assholes killed." Pressing the mic button, "Guys hold your fire until I tell you to, just everyone stay quiet and let's see if we can sucker these guys out into the open. Mat, are you and Jeff ok?" Mat immediately came back, "We are ok, but we found out that this upper floor will not stop bullets worth a crap." "Ok, just keep your heads down and keep moving after you fire a couple of shots." I said into my mic, "Be prepared to pop up and begin shooting the Taninite when I begin firing." Moving quickly though the hunting section to the boating area I stopped behind a large fishing boat. Taking a quick peek from around the boat I could see that someone had smashed the entrance doors. From what I could see about a dozen men had entered the store and where standing behind a large Hispanic man. Dropping the ACOGs green horseshoe onto the center of the man's chest I flipped the selector to burst and squeezed the trigger. The three rounds of 5.56 punched into the man's chest and dropped him into a lifeless heap. The men behind him froze in shock as their leader fell lifeless. Just than two containers of Taninite exploded in one roaring wave of

102

sound, blowing racks of clothes and men in all directions. Moving my M4 as rapidly as I could I took down three more before the shock wore off and the remaining men scrambled out the same way they had come in. Scoping the area I saw at least six bodies laying on the floor. Moving to the front of the boat I had been taking cover behind I stood and listened and watched for a couple of minutes. Seeing no more movement and not hearing anything, I called Mat and ask him if he could see any movement. Mat called back and said that he could not see anyone else inside the store. Telling him and Ben to keep a sharp watch out for any stay behinds, I moved towards the front of the store to make sure it was clear.

Moving cautiously I skirted the boats and moved to the same area I had broken into the store the night before. Using the crates of gasoline generators we had used to block the broken windows as cover I pulled out my bino's and began to scan the parking lot. It only took me a few seconds to find the group of gang members who had attempted to enter the store. They had re-grouped together behind a pickup truck parked about 100 feet from the front entrance. Grunting with the effort I was able to move the top crate a few inches to the side, however this was enough for me to get the muzzle of my M4 though the broken window. Not wanting to actually shoot anymore of them than I had too, I aimed in on the front tire of the truck they were behind and flipping my selector switch to single shot, squeezed off one single round. The tire exploded with more of a whimper than an explosion but it definitely got the idea across to the remaining gang members. They scattered like a covey of quail. Flipping the selector switch to burst I led a group of four gang members and put two bursts into a car they were heading to for cover. Using the remaining rounds of my magazine I chased the other members of the gang out of sight of my window.

Hoping the actions of the past few minutes would buy us some time, I quickly gathered everyone together over by the rifle counter. Glancing at the three young men in front of me, "You guys do realize we were very lucky just now. Next time that gang will not make the same mistake and will just shoot you on sight. You do understand that?" They all three nodded while at the same time looking scared to death. "Do you still want to head out on your own?" I ask. All three nodded again. I just nodded and told them good luck and to get moving. "I would recommend getting out of the mall area and finding somewhere to hole up until dark. If you want my opinion I would recommend you head for the railroad tracks to the northeast and hole up until dark than follow the railroad tracks north. But whatever you're going to do, do it now before those guys come back with friends." They once again said their good-byes and we all headed back to the loading docks area.

Cautiously I pop open the exit door by the loading docks. Easing it open I look and listen for a few seconds than slide out the door as Ben came into the doorway. I motion him to wait there and moved down the short flight of stairs off of the loading docks. Not seeing or hearing anything I move to the corner of the loading docks so I can see the far larger mall parking lot. Still seeing nothing, I keyed my radio and told the others to move out. We crossed the parking lot heading to the northeast towards the Hampton Inn. Moving as quickly as we could, we moved into the wooden area next to the hotel. I pointed at the three that were leaving us and then pointed in the direction of the railroad tracks. Having already said their good-byes they took off for the railroad tracks as if they were on fire. After their departure, it only took us about five minutes to reach the treelike bordering Highway 100. I raised my fist over my shoulder, signaling the others to stop in place. Looking back over my shoulder, I see that everyone had stopped in place and taken a knee. I made a mental note to go over hand and arm signals and radio procedures with everyone tonight when we stopped. Getting everyone's attention I pointed to where I wanted each of the group and then motioned Don to come over to me. I keyed the radio mic and let them all know that we would be here for only a couple minutes and to make any adjustments they needed to. I said to Don, "I want to watch the highway for a few minutes to see if anyone is out and about. If not I'm thinking we should get on the highway and move to that Dick's Sporting Goods store you told me about as fast as we can. What do you think?" Don nodded, "Ok with me, at my age I'm all for taking the easiest route we can." We settled down to watch the road in front of us, after a few minutes of observing nothing we picked up our gear and moved onto the shoulder of Highway 100 heading west.

Chapter Eight

After walking at a slow but steady pace for about 45 minutes, I walked off the road to the edge of the tree line. As we formed a small 360-degree perimeter, I ask, "How is everyone doing? Make sure you drink some water and take a piss if you need to. From now on when we are on the radio, I will be one, Ben two, Jeff three, Mat four, and Don five. That way we each know who is saying what. So if I call for a radio check, go in order, two roger, three roger and so on. Got it?" I get nods all around. "I figure we have covered a couple of miles. We should be coming up on Highway 1 soon and right after that, I-95. If we don't see groups of people we will stay on the shoulder and pass straight though the big interchange. In the near future we won't be able to do that as the overpasses will become choke points and will be too dangerous to cross. It will always be tempting to take the easiest route but think about it, where do deer hunters set up and wait for deer. At the intersection of deer trails. The same will go for the riffraff, they will set up on the interchanges to increase their odds of seeing all the travelers and then rob them."

After everyone had a chance to relieve himself and to drink some water, we took back to the road-heading west. Crossing over Highway 1 and then I-95, we stopped again. Mat asked, "Where is everyone?" Don replied, "I think everyone is waiting for the government to do something. Most people, even if they know it was an EMP are just hunkering down and waiting for the government to come fix everything." I agreed and said, "They will wait until the food and water is gone," I pointed to the south, "see that water tower over there. That is how the system works, pumps fill the large tank and the weight of the water is what creates the pressure that pushes it into the homes. Once that tank runs dry there will be no more running water. Oh, there is water there for those that know how to get it, but most people don't. Just like most will not think of draining their hot water heaters. Each of those holds 40 or 50 gallons of clean water. That and most people will let their frozen food go bad instead of eating it first." "But," Mat injected, "Won't the government help once they get the military and FEMA back up and running?" Don and I exchanged looks and I continued, "Not likely, most if not all of the military will have their hands full just taking care of their own. FEMA is made up of a small full time staff, but most are part time or volunteers that only come together in the event of a natural disaster. We are just lucky there are not nuclear facilities in this area. Most of them will be entering critical meltdown once the fuel for the back up generators runs out and the cooling pumps stop pumping the water to cool them. Some might, just might shut down safely, but some will not and once they go into meltdown it will create a deadly situation for anyone local. Our government has known for a long time how susceptible our power grid was and they did very little to fix it. I would say by tonight people will be beginning to get tried of waiting for help and almost all of the local grocery stores will be looted. We want to be out of the built up areas by tonight. If we can get some bikes at Dick's we should be able to make pretty good time tomorrow and at least get to Harpers Ferry by tomorrow night. Once we get to Dick's, Don and I will keep watch, as you guys are much more familiar with the bikes we need. Just get the best ones you can get the fastest. Be sure and get some tools and tire patches, chains, air pumps, and whatever else we might need to keep the bikes up and running. If there are any people at the store when we get there just follow my lead. Ben, you will be responsible for covering our rear if we are in the open, Jeff you concentrate on anyone carrying any type of long range weapon, such as a hunting rifle with a scope, the rest of us will handle anyone close to us. If the shooting starts do not hesitate, anyone with a gun pointed at us is the enemy. A kid with a .22 can kill you just as dead as an adult with a 12-gauge shotgun. Got it?"

After getting nods all around, I stood and motioned for everyone to get ready to move. So far everyone was holding up pretty well. We moved out and the next hour passed without seeing a single person. I turned us south once we reached Snowden River Parkway, not stopping for a break as we were within a couple of miles of our destination. Cutting though a couple of the residential areas we began to see signs of people, yet none came out to make contact with us. Any that were outside quickly went inside once they saw the weapons we carried, but one guy did call out to us and we stopped. I keyed my radio, "Don't bunch up, Ben keep a close eye on the road in front of us. Jeff you have our rear. Mat keep your head on a swivel. Don you are with me. Everyone call out if you see anything strange." After getting a roger over the radio from everyone, Don and I walked over to the guy. He was a middle-aged guy dressed in kaki trousers and a polo shirt, medium build and was fairly clean cut. He didn't appear to be bothered by our weapons. "How are you guys doing?" the man asks. "We are doing just fine," I replied, "How is everyone doing around here?" The guy looked us over and ask, "You guys cops or something?" I glanced over at Don and replied, "Something like that, have you guys had any problems?" "We haven't but someone needs to get here soon with some water, everyone is almost out since the water stopped yesterday. Some of us have some bottled water but that isn't going to last for long. Also someone needs to come pick up old man Evan's body. He dropped dead of a heart attack when the power went out, someone said that his pace maker stopped. His daughter found him the next morning but without phones we could not call anyone. I see you have

108

radios, can you call someone to come pick him up. He is already being to bloat and smell."

"Sir, you need to go ahead and bury him. I would recommend that if anyone has any lime that you all dig a grave at least four feet deep and wrap him in a blanket, cover his body with lime directly on top of him, cover him and place rocks or cinder blocks on top of the dirt to keep animals from digging him back up. No one is going to come and do it for you or to take the body away. As far as the water goes, get some of the guys together and go from house to house and drain everyone's hot water heaters, each of those will be holding 40 to 50 gallons of clean water. Any other water you collect you should treat it with plain bleach. Eight to ten drops per gallon," I stated. I motioned Don to follow and we turned away to leave. The man followed us, trying to get us to stop, "Hey aren't you guys going to help us?" the guy ask. I stopped and turned back to face him, "You are going to have to help yourself. No one is coming to help. Get your neighbors together and get a handle on your resources. Help one another. Again, no one is coming to help you, not now, not tomorrow, not from the government or the state. No one, get your act together or things are going to get really bad around here. Collect up all the bleach from all the houses, if anyone has a pool see if they have any pool shock. Regular bleach older than one year is probably no good. You can mix up fresh bleach from the pool shock. After you add bleach to water, shake it up and let it sit for an hour or so to make sure it has a chance to kill all the bad stuff. It won't taste great but its better then shitting your brains out till you die." I turned away again and began walking. The guy calls out after us, "So when can we expect help to come? We need food and water if this goes on much longer?" I just kept walking but could feel Don's eyes on me.

After reaching the end of the neighborhood, I dropped back to walk beside Don. Lowering my voice so only Don could hear, "Don, we can't stop and help everyone, you know that." Don started to say something but stopped himself, after pausing for a few seconds, he said, "I know we can't save everyone, but you have a lot of knowledge and skills that would help a lot of people survive. It just seems wrong not to help where we can." I didn't hesitate, "Don, none of those people in the neighborhood are going to survive this. I doubt any of them will make it to the 30-day mark. If someone within that community had the know how to organize them, they would already started getting their act together. Yes, I feel sorry for the kids but that is why we cannot stop and help. It would take days to organize them and then some of the people within the community itself would not want to contribute. What then? Kick them out, don't feed their kids. What about security? The neighborhood is undefendable without major work. I bet there isn't three firearms within that neighborhood and those are going to be a hunting rifle or a .380 someone has in their nightstand. No, these people are sheep waiting for the wolves to come to the slaughter and there is nothing you or I could do to stop it other then die with them. They will just sit here and wait to die. Within two or three days at the most waves of cholera is going to hit these communities as these people are already drinking contaminated water. The survivors of that will take what they can and start walking. They will have no idea where to go but they will know that they can't stay here. Most will head to Fort Meade thinking the government will help them. I know this sounds cold but it would not matter in the end if we stayed to help these people, we might buy them an additional two weeks or a month but in the end it would not matter. There just isn't enough food to keep this many people alive over the winter. If we stayed to help it would more likely be the death of us also. Are you willing to risk Mat's life on the off chance we can help the immediate situation. Because that what you would be doing. That is your decision to make, I'm heading west." Don met my eyes for about ten seconds before looking away and nodding. I heard him curse under his breath and I agreed, "yes it's a whole new fucked up world now."

It was almost 2 o'clock by the time we reached the shopping center that had the Dick's Sporting Goods store. We stopped in a small alcove of trees that provided a good view of the front of the store and the surrounding area. It was obvious that some looting had taken place. A health food store across the shopping center had its front window smashed out and various bottles and containers of product were scattered in front. Thinking waste not, want not, we would go there first. If we could pick up a few large containers of protein it would help stretch out our supplies. Calling everyone over to me, I said, "We are going to check out the store with the smashed out window first. Ben and Jeff will cover us from here and protect the gear. Mat, as soon as we are in I want you to grab as many of the protein bars as you can stuff into two shopping bags. Don't get picky, just grab all you can. Don, I want you to grab several of the large containers of Muscle Milk protein, try and get different flavors if you can. I'll be going after the vitamin packs to include vitamin C." Ben raised his hand, "Sir I hate those chocolate protein drinks, please grab any other favor." I smiled and said, "We will do the best we can. I want to be in and out within 5 minutes. Let's drink some water because I believe we should be able to refill at Dicks. We move out in three minutes." I pulled out my Klean Kanteen and took a long drink. Watching the others to make sure they were drinking I said, "If you see any sports drinks in there grab one or two but we don't have room to carry liquid that is not water. Grab it and drink it, but don't weigh yourself down with it. Understand?"

I stood from where I had been pulling several empty stuff sacks from my ruck. Everyone took up their positions and I nodded to Ben and Jeff. We all headed across the parking lot at a trot stopping at the corner of the health food store. Stacking up next to the building, I called into the building, "Anyone in there? This is the police, if you are in there call out now." Silence, I listened for about ten more seconds then moved inside thought the broken front doors. Without stopping I moved to the counter, which was located in the center of the store. Going low I ducked under the counter and stopped and listened again. Nothing. I popped up and did a quick 360 degrees of the store. Nodding to my team members, I motioned for them to get to it. As they began moving towards their objectives, I moved to the back storeroom door. Trying the handle I found it to be locked. I keyed my radio, "Mat change of plans. I need you to cover the storeroom door. If you see it move or hear something from that area, call it out." Mat immediately moved to cover the storeroom and I headed over to the vitamins. Taking one of the stuff sacks, I began grabbing multivitamins and a couple large bottles of vitamin C. Next I headed over to the protein bars and grabbed several boxes of Power Bars, ripping open the boxes and dumping them into the stuff sacks. After completing that task, I moved over to where Don was and at the same time pulled several heavy-duty gallon sized zip lock bags from my pocket. Opening one of the gallon sized protein canisters I opened the zip lock bag and dumped as much of the protein powder into the zip lock as it would hold. Repeating this until I was out of gallon zip locks, I double-checked to make sure I had at least two bags of something other then chocolate. Looking back at the shelf I grabbed a couple of shaker bottles, spinning off the tops and filling both of them with more Whey powder. After stuffing the shaker bottles into the stuff sacks, I turned keying my radio, "Are we ready," I ask. Receiving acknowledgements from Ben and Jeff, I got thumbs up from both Don and Mat. I nodded and turned to head back out the front door but froze as I heard the deadbolt from the storeroom turn. I gestured to Mat and Don to get behind the counter and raised my M4 to a ready position. The storeroom door cracked open about 1/2 an inch. I called out, "Freeze, this is the police. I want to see both of your hands out the door right now!" Talking a step to the left after I called out, just in case some one decided they wanted to shoot though the wall in the direction my voice. Two hands slid out of the darkened storeroom. Taking one more step to the left I said, "Ease the door open slowly and come out." The door opened as a young lady of about 20 eased out of the door. "Are you alone," I ask. She nodded, not really looking too scared just wary as is she was ready to leap back into her storeroom. She then saw the two other rifles pointed in her directions. "I work here," she said as if that would explain everything. "Miss, please step out of the door over to your right, Mat keep her covered, Don, if any shooting starts, empty a magazine though the wall to the right of the door." Reaching into my cargo pocket I pulled out several glow sticks, quickly breaking them I shook them for a couple seconds then tossed them into the storeroom, I followed the glow sticks with my M4 at the ready and had swept the room before the glow sticks came to a stop on the floor. The storeroom was about 20 feet by 30 feet with racks arranged along each wall and one down the middle of the room. It only took a glance to see that the room was empty of any other people. I let everyone know it was clear and that they could relax and return to watching for any other visitors outside. I walked back into the store and motioned for Mat to lower his rifle.

"Miss," I said, "This is not a good place to be. You need to get home as fast as you can." She was about 5'10" tall with an athletic build and blond hair, and very attractive. When I looked back up into her eyes, they were hard and flashing. "And just how would you suggest I get there. My apartment is in Silver Springs and none of the cars are working," she replied tartly. "Miss," I started again but she interrupted me. "My name is Elizabeth but most of my friends call me Beth, you can call me Elizabeth." I heard chuckles from all the guys. She looked over at them and gave them the middle finger. I openly laughed at this and looked over and saw Mat staring at her with his mouth hanging open. I walked over to him and whispered, "Close your mouth," I laughed, "Go find a bag and get more power bars." He turned to go but looked back over his shoulder. I pushed him in the general direction of the power bars and turned back to the girl.

"Miss, we are just passing though and saw the store broken into. We will be moving on in just a few minutes. If you are not aware of the current situation, we, the USA was hit with an EMP and nothing electrical is working. You need to come over to Dick's with us and we will help you get set up with a bike and some equipment so you can head home." "I know what an EMP is," she said, "Why in the world would I want to head into the city. It's going to be completely crazy down there. Plus I said that is where my apartment is, NOT where my home is. My family is in Kansas."

"Miss, Kansas is a long way from here, I know as I'm heading to Texas to my family, but isn't there somewhere else or somebody you know that is closer where you will be safe?" I ask. She looked at me and thought for a moment before replying, "No, not really, I just moved here after transferring to the University of Maryland. I got this job to pay the bills and I really don't know anyone around here." I looked around at Don and he shrugged. Mat spoke up and said, "She can come with us." I turned to him and glared, he sheepishly turned back to stuffing more bars into the gym bag he had found. Elizabeth jumped in, "And what makes you think I would want to go with you guys wherever the hell your going?" "Miss, we are leaving to go over to Dick's to rescue some mountain bikes. You can either stay here until the looters come back to finish the job or go with us. While I can't say what the looters will do with you, I can say that as long as you are with us no harm will come to you from any of us." She just glared at me as I walked over to my sacks and picked them up. All of the others took my cue and picked up their bags. Mat picked up the full gym bags and looked like he was going to say something to the girl, but he abruptly turned and headed out the door with the others. Mat stopped just inside the doors as all of us walked out and headed back across the parking lot. As I was crossing the parking lot I keyed my radio, "Mat we don't have time for this, let's move." Mat came back with, "Hang on for just a minute." Keying my radio again I said, "You have one minute." Looking over at Don, he just smiled and shrugged his shoulders. About 30 seconds passed when Mat appeared with the girl following also carrying another gym bag stuffed full of supplies. I keyed the radio, "Ok guys, stay sharp, pay attention to your surroundings, not the girl."

We moved across the small parking lot in front of the health store and across the road separating Dick's from the rest of the stores. A major brand discount store was beside Dick's but not attached. We moved between the two stores to the loading docks in back of the stores. "Ben, take the far corner, Jeff take this corner. Let me know if you see anyone," I said into the radio. Receiving "Roger that" from both, the rest of the group moved up the short flight of stairs to the loading dock. There were three-garage type roll up doors with no windows, and one metal fire door with a small 8 x 8 inch wire reinforced window in the upper half. Glancing at the door I walked past it to the loading ramp door. Rapping a knuckle lightly against one of the roll up doors I took a couple of steps to the side and shrugged out of my ruck. "You guys keep a sharp eye out," I said to Don and Mat. Beth said, "You guys are not cops." It was a statement, not a question. Glancing over to her, I said, "No, but my Father was a cop if that matters."

Taking out my Zombie Tools Traumahawk, I stood with my back to the roll up door and griped the handle. With a back handed motion I drove the hand ax into the light metal of the door. I inwardly winced thinking what I was doing with one of my favorite blades, but I knew that the damage to my ax would be little to none as the Traumahawk was almost indestructible. I worked the blade up and down and side to side a couple of times before pulling the blade out of the door. Turning and facing the doors I took three more swings of the Traumahawk, cutting an inverted V shape into the metal with each leg of the V about one foot long. Sheathing the blade, I pulled the tin snips out of the top of my ruck and began cutting across the wide mouth of the V shape. The metal of the door turned out to be tougher than I had estimated but it only took me a couple of minutes to get the V cut out of the door. Taking a look into the hole I had made I carefully reach into the hole. It only took me a second to locate the wire leading to the latches on each side of the door. I called Mat over the told him to get a hold of the door and help me to raise the door. He looked at me as if I had horns growing out of my head, but went ahead and worked his fingers under the door. Once he had a hold, I nodded to him and we both lifted. The door slid up smoothly. Withdrawing my hand as the door slid up, Mat and I raised the door to about chest height.

A quick look around revealed an empty loading bay, I stepped over and retrieved my ruck, "lets go inside, everyone in." I said into my radio mic. Everyone piled into the loading bay, followed last by Ben and Jeff. I lowered the door and reengaged the locking device and tripped the lock out device so no one could reach in the way I had to unlock the rolling door. Gathering everyone together I briefed them on what we

116

were going to do, "once we move into the main store, Mat, I want you and Beth to wait by the door leading into the main store. Stay there to cover us in case we run into trouble. Once we have cleared the store I will call you in. Don and I will take the lead. Ben, you have our left flank, Jeff, you have the right. If we run into trouble we will leap frog back here to Mat's position. Watch where you are firing and only fire if you have a clear target. It is not worth dying over a bicycle. Any question? Ok lets do this."

I led our little group into the main store, it only took a minute to make it over to the bike section. I called Mat and Beth over and told Mat to drop his gear and take Beth over to get outfitted with some gear of her own. Regardless of what she would do or go she needed better than some flip-flops and shorts. While Ben and Jeff worked on setting up our bikes, I had Don watch the front of the store. I roamed around to the camping section and picked up a female 3200 cubic inch pack and a good sleeping bag and pad. I threw in a small footprint tarp, a stainless steel cup, a Camel Bak bladder with a Sawyer water filter, a Lifestraw, and a 40 oz Klean canteen. Next I moved over to the backpacking food area and grabbed eight meals and stuffed them into the backpack. Heading back to the bike area I also stopped and grabbed her a Gerber fixed bladed knife, and a multi-tool, a fire steel and a couple packs of fire starters, a package of five Bic lighters, and some waterproof matches. Getting back over to the bike area, Mat and Beth were sitting on the floor putting laces in a new pair of hiking boots. Beth had changed into hiking pants and had on a new t-shirt and a long sleeve shirt unbuttoned and with the sleeves rolled up. I dumped the gear on the floor and walked over to my ruck. Removing all of the protein powder bags, I dug around until I came up with the Ruger .22/.45 and its three magazines. Digging some more I found two boxes of 100 each CCI Stingers. Walking back over to Beth, I squatted down in front of her. "Beth, have you ever handled one of these? Holding out the holstered Ruger. She reached over and took the holstered pistol carefully, looking at it closely. While doing this I observed she was careful not to point the holstered pistol at either Mat or myself. After a moment or two, she unsnapped the holster strap and pulled the pistol out of the holster. Keeping the pistol pointed in safe direction she released the magazine catch and removed the empty magazine. Lying the magazine down, she pulled back the bolt and carefully inspected the chamber. Releasing the bolt, she looked up, "My Dad has one of these, I've used it to shoot rabbits in Mom's garden." "Good enough for me," I said, "This is the only spare gun we have for now. This place doesn't carry any firearms."

"So have you had a chance to think about what you are going to do?" I ask her. Beth looked from me to Mat and said, "I guess for right now I'm going with you guys. If what Mat has told me is true than it is going to get bad out here and I want to get out of the city and head for home. I appreciate the invitation." I looked at her, "If you are coming with us than you need to understand that when we say to do something than you need to do it. No questions at the time, later when we have time you may ask why, that is not a suggestion. If you can't do that you need to go your own way. I will not have one of our group hurt or killed because you want to question a decision. Can you agree to that?" She looked at me, "Who are you guys anyway?" I put out my hand, " I am Talon, I'm a retired Marine and have spent my fair share in one hell hole or another. Don is a retired Navy Master at Arms, the rest of these young men are in college and we are all heading up to Don's cabin in the Blue Ridge. That is probably as far as any of us are going to get before the winter sets in, that is if we are lucky and get out of built up area around here. After that, when I can I'm headed down to my family in Texas, Ben and

Jeff are headed back to their folks out west. But more than likely we will all spend the winter at the cabin," I said, although I had no plans on hanging around for the winter to pass before heading out to get back to my family, I didn't want any of the group to worry or panic thinking I was going to leave them. "Ok," Beth said, "I can do that as long as you guys are the good guys." I smiled at her and said, "Ok then, get packed up we have a long way to go before it gets dark."

While I had been squatted down talking to Mat and Beth, I had noticed a picture on a display box across the aisle. Standing up and walking over to the display, I pickup up one of the flyers on the display. I took the flyer over to where Ben and Jeff were working on the bikes. Handing Jeff the flyer, I raised an eyebrow in question. Jeff shrugged and said, "Sure if we stay on roads or wide trails." "Its worth a try, it sure would make carrying supplies a whole lot easier, go ahead and put one on four of the bikes, don't put one on Don's or Beth's." Walking back over to the camping area I grabbed four duffel style waterproof bags. My first stop was to grab all of the camping toilet paper and wet wipes the store had and divided them into the four bags. My next stop was at the camping food, grabbing all of the freeze dried food they had, than over to the camp stoves and grabbed a couple of the Jet Boils along with several gas refills for each. Leaving the bags where they lay, I headed to the back of the store to check and see if they had any more freeze dried food.

Walking up and down the shelves in the back storage area I finally spotted a pallet of Mountain House boxes. Stacking up four of the boxes I headed back out front and emptied the boxes into the duffel bags. Standing back I looked at the half full bags, grabbing two of the bags I half carried half dragged the bags towards the front of the store. Arriving near the checkout, I stopped and began loading the bags with all of the beef jerky the store had, which turned out to be quite a lot. I also grabbed several handfuls of gum and a couple of large bags of Twizzlers. Moving over to the candy bars I finished filling the two bags with all of the candy and protein bars the racks held. Barely getting the zippers closed I again half carried half dragged the bags back to the bike area. Returning to the storage area I grabbed two more cases of Mountain House and finished filling the other two bags. Next I headed back and grabbed another water proof duffel and walked over to the clothing area. I stuffed this bag with a dozen X-Large terminal tops and bottoms, all of the Darn Tough socks they had in Large and X-Large, along with several pairs of medium for Beth, and finally six pairs of cold weather gloves and six wool stocking hats.

Keying the mike on my radio, I ask for everyone to check in, after getting an answer from everyone I said, "I want everyone to make sure they have a good Gore-Tex rain jacket. If you do not, stop whatever you're doing and go get one now. Do not get any bright colors or anything that will stand out. Do it now please, Talon Out." After dropping off the last bag I walked over and selected six medium size tarps, two coils of 120 climbing ropes along with six harnesses and a dozen carabineers and two climbing pulleys. Thinking to myself, as long as we have the room we might as well be prepared for anything. Never know when we would need a tarp or some rope. Grabbing another duffle I headed back to the bike area. Ben and Jeff had six bikes set up and were assembling the four bike carts. Dropping off the tarps and ropes by the carts I went over to my ruck and finished pulling out all of the protein powder and putting it into the duffel. Mat and Beth immediately did the same, placing all of the protein bars and powder from the vitamin store into the duffel. After they had finished, I told Mat to take the duffel around to everyone and have them empty their packs of the powder and bars.

Ben walked over to me, "You know these carts are going to be a gold plated bitch if we have to get off the road and going up those hills." I smiled, "That is why we are only taking four carts, we can switch off if someone needs some rest, but honestly most of the work is going to fall on you, Mat, and Ben as you guys are a lot younger and stronger than the rest of us." Ben nodded and walked back over to the bikes, but they were almost finished with the bikes and carts. I walked to the front of the store and found Don sitting in a camp chair with his M4 across his knees. "How's it going?" I ask. "Oh, about as well as you can expect. What with the world coming apart and resetting to the 1800's. I always thought I wanted to live in the Wild West but now that it is here I'm not so sure."

"We will be fine. We have a good team and have superior firepower to most of the people we are going to run into or up against I should say. We just need to stay alert and we should be fine. I do want to get out of here within the hour. You know this area better than I do, what route should we take to get us west of here and will take us though the least amount of built up area?" I ask. "I was just thinking on that very subject," Don said as he reached down and picked up a large laminated Rand McNally road atlas, "The way I see it we can cut down Snowden Parkway to Highway 32, go west a couple miles to pick up 29 South. Take 29 to 200 West. We can take 200 over towards Gaithersburg but drop off it south just before we get to the built up area. We can pick up 28 West and at that point I don't know. If we stay on 28 it takes us northwest until it meets 15 South to cross the Potomac or we can go on up to Harpers Ferry to cross. Either way is going to take us northwest but I just don't see that we have any choice because those are the only way to get across the river if we don't use I-495." Studying the map I did not see anyway around the problem either. I was hoping that we had at least another month before the weather became nasty. The bikes would vastly help us cover a lot more ground, that is if they did not get us all killed. Moving faster meant less security. We would have to be careful about getting strung out. At the end of the day it was a trade off of speed versus security. I believe right now we can risk the bikes. Once people begin panicking we might have to ditch them and take to the woods but for the next few days we needed to make as many miles as we could. I handed the atlas back to Don, "You ready to do some biking?" I ask, "When was the last time you were on a bike?" He surprised me, "Last week, Mat and I go mountain biking a couple of weekends a month," he replied and smiled, "Don't tell me a old Jarhead like you don't know how to ride a bike," he laughed. "Screw you old man," I shot back, "it might have been a couple of years since I rode a bike, but I'll manage. It is not today I'm worried about, its tomorrow." We both laughed, but than I headed over to the counter area and grabbed two large bottles of pain reliever. I'm going to need these I thought, and grabbed a couple of tubes of Ben Gay too.

    Returning to the bike area I gathered everyone to up. "Don will go over the general route of march in a minute. I just want to go over a few things. While the bikes will allow us to travel faster, they will also allow us to get into trouble faster. We will keep two people out front about a quarter mile ahead of the other four. If for any reason the two out front lose communications with the main body they are to stop immediately. If you still don't have comms after five minutes than you are to backtrack until you do get comms back or get back within visual range of the main group. If the forward two come under fire they are to take cover and wait until the rest of us have time to flank the attackers. If the forward two hear the main body come under attack, they are to double back and attempt to flank the attackers. Everyone understand? Good, we will keep the four bike trailers in the main group and switch out with the two others in the forward element. The

122

forward element will report back if they see anyone. If you come up to an overpass and see people, stop, do not approach them alone. Even if it is just a kid or a woman or they appear injured, do not approach them, people will use those types of ploys like kids to lure us in. Stop, report it and wait for the main body to catch up," I paused and made sure everyone was nodding, "Mat, did you and Beth get everything she needs?" Mat and Beth both nodded. "Did you pack all those double AA's?" Again nods, "Good, I hope you all realize that we are facing a completely different world out there right now than what you are used too. I know I have lived in this sort of environment for a long time. We cannot stop and feed every family we run into. The survival of our group is our first priority, if you reveal that we have food and water to strangers than you are basically saying that those people are more important than our group is. Because at that point we will not be able to extract ourselves without a fight. And if we end up in a fight it will be them or us. So think first before you offer anyone food or water. When we run into people, and we will, do not offer or let them know we have food and water. The way to cut off questions is the first thing you ask of anyone is do they know where we could get any food or water." I looked hard into each persons eyes, "Its easy to sit here and agree to a concept, but you will find out it is much harder when faced with some hungry children. But we can't feed the kids without feeding the adults. The first time one of you give food to a kid, mark my words, we will end up having to kill someone. Just remember I told you so. When we stop for the night we will have two people awake at all times. Everyone has night vision add on scopes for their M4's. Only turn them on if you hear something approaching the camp, otherwise use the night vision monocular, we do not have an endless supply of batteries for them. Also, do not point an M4 at me or anybody within our group. You point an M4 at me, I'm pointing mine at you and pulling the trigger. Keep that in mind. Back to the batteries, we will lay out the Goal Zero solar panels on the carts if the sun is out to recharge batteries during the day. I don't know if or how well that will work but we will give it a try. When you are on guard duty that is just what it is. Stay separate from the group and pay attention to any approaches to the camp, NOT what is going on in the camp. Stay off the radios, unless you spot something or someone approaching the camp. From here on out, most of the time we will be eating twice a day, breakfast and dinner when we stop. Most days we will try and stop for a brief rest around noon and eat a protein shake or power bar for lunch. Please try and not take extra power bars during the day. Within a few days your body will adjust and always remember we have what we have and it might have to last us for a long time. We will stop and scavenge when it is to our advantage. Anytime we stop, everyone goes into a 360-degree perimeter, please try and find some cover when we do this. Do I need to explain the difference between cover and concealment, good, if you have to use a car for cover try and stay behind the engine block and the wheels. Almost all rifle rounds from .223 and 7.62 and many pistol rounds will go right though a car or a bouncer will catch you if you're not behind the tire. If our enemy takes cover behind a car watch for his legs underneath the car and skip the rounds off the pavement into him."

   I made a mental note and continued, "we need to make sure we have a few empty duffel bags for when we stop to scavenge. When we stop to scavenge, everyone will set up in a defensive position and Don and I will enter any building to scavenge. If you have any questions now is the time to ask." No one had any questions, so Don went over the planned route for the day. After he was finished Ben went over the basic operations of the bikes. Ben had selected one of the bikes that the store had more than the six we needed. Ben and Jeff had

124

cherry picked several more of the same bikes for parts that we might need along the way. In addition, Ben and Jeff had found four Aosom Wanderer bike trailers. They appeared well made and study and would be packed with a couple of layers of supplies and still have room for each of our packs. Everyone had been instructed to always keep their bug out bags on their person along with one of the small camel baks back packs with water, batteries, snacks, and extra ammo. The trailers would make the ride much easier that is if we can stay on the bike trails. If not we would have to re-think the whole trailer idea.

As we packed up with Ben and Jeff supervising it was clear we all were overloaded. "We will have to keep the speed down with this much gear," Ben said. I nodded, "Especially going down some of these long hills, please make sure everyone has a good pair of sunglasses and one pair of clear riding goggles for night riding. I don't want anyone losing control because they got a bug in the eye." Ben nodded and moved off in the direction of the riding accessories. After a couple minutes, Ben came back and began handing out the riding goggles to everyone.

I looked around and it appeared that everyone was ready to get on the road. I keyed my radio mic, "Everyone give me a radio check." Mat had been able to find another radio and headset for Beth and she called in, "Beth here and ready to go." Earlier I had been pleasantly surprised when I had seen her picking out a compound bow. She already had it strapped to her trailer along with what looked like about 35 or 40 arrows in two quivers. I nodded at her when she saw me looking over the bow, "You'll do," I said, "That is if you really know how to use that," indicating the bow. She looked balefully at me and scoffed, "I got my first buck with a bow when I was 15, when did you get your first city boy?" I just laughed to myself and started pushing my bike towards the back of the store. Let her think what she wants, I was about as far away from being a city boy as you can get.

My earliest memories are of my family moving to the farm my Dad had brought in the summer of 1965. I was four going on five and was excited about moving to our own farm. I believe we had been living with my Mom's parents while they saved up to buy the farm. The farm was about eight miles from the nearest town. It wasn't much of a town but it was the county seat, population of 256 people and included the County Court House, Jail, School and one store with gas pumps out front. The farm we brought had been abandoned for more than 30 years and the only remaining buildings were an old one room school house (with no running water or electric ran to it) that had at one time been unprofessionally turned into a three room house and an old barn that was in fairly decent shape other than missing some tin sheets from the roof. They built the barns to last back than. The old school house was small, especially for a family of five. No running water, no indoor bathroom, no kitchen, and heated by a large pot belly stove made out of a 55 gal drum. It took my Father about a year, as he had a full time construction job, before we had an indoor bathroom and a working kitchen.

Thrusting those memories aside I turned to the task at hand. Everyone was ready to go, I walked over and unlocked the roll-up door, "Everyone ready? Don and Mat will lead out first until we get on the highway, until than they will stay about one hundred yards ahead of us. Beth, stuff that hair up under you hat, try and not advertise that you're young and pretty. Ben you will be first in line behind the front guard, let them know on the radio if they get too far ahead, I want them looking forward for any trouble not trying to watch us. Beth, you fall in behind Ben, keep about 5 to 10 yards between you and him, Jeff, you follow Beth, and I will bring up the rear. Stay off the radio unless you see danger. Use the clock method to indicate direction. The lead element will be 12 o'clock. Keep your eyes open and watch everything. Ben, you keep your eyes on the lead element, Beth, you keep your eyes to the right from 12 o'clock to 2:00. Jeff, you watch to the left from 12 o'clock to 10:00. I will cover the rest. Any questions?" Everyone just looked at me with impatient eyes.

I nodded and reached down and pulled the roll up door about three feet and squatted down to take a look. Seeing no movement, I finished pushing the door up, I motioned everyone to go and walked back to my bike and got on. Rolling the bike forward, I eased my bike and trailer down the ramp and we all fell into the order I had explained. Over the next few hundred yards there was some learning going on with the gears and the shifters but all in all we worked it out and the first hour went by uneventful. We actually made pretty good time down to Highway 32 and over to 29 South.

Stopping at the intersection of highway 32 and 29 for a water break. I walked over to Don and said, "Don I think it would be best if we stopped and made camp once we cross over the Rocky Gorge Reservoir. If I remember correctly that is all State Park and we should be ok off the road there. It will be 5:00 PM by the time we get there and we all are going on a couple hours sleep. That way we all can get some rest for a full day of riding tomorrow. What do you think?" "Sounds like a plan to me. I know I didn't get much sleep last night and I know the boys are wiped out, not that any of them are going to admit it," Don replied.

We were back on the road in ten minutes after everyone had time to grab a quick snack and drink some water. After an hour of weaving around the occasional stalled car we crossed over the bridge crossing the Rocky Gorge Reservoir. Once were all across and had passed all of the guardrails leading off the bridge, Don slowed down and coasted to a stop at the head of a dirt road leading off the highway to the west. There was a half inch thick cable across the road strung between two telephone pole size posts on either side of the dirt road. Don got off his bike and leaned it against one of the posts and walked over and picked up the cable, it had enough slack to allow the bikes to pass under it. Moving up to the front I got off my bike and pushed it under the cable and moved about 25 feet down the dirt road. I stopped and looked back over my shoulder, "Well are you all waiting for a written invitation or what. Let's get off the road and down into the timber before someone sees this circus," and turned back to walking my bike down the dirt road.

Chapter Nine

After walking about 300 yards down the road I began to see water though the trees. I parked my bike by a tree and turned to wait on the rest of the group. Ben arrived first and I told him to hold everyone at this location while I made a quick recon of the area. Slinging on my M4 I moved into the woods to the west for about 100 yards and stopped to listen. After standing for about five minutes in the shadow of a huge oak tree I moved north to where I could see the reservoir. Stopping I listened, hearing nothing I was again reminded of a couple of Twilight Zone episodes where someone woke up and everyone else was gone. The quiet was so complete. My thoughts turned to my kids, they were so young, they wouldn't remember how life was before the lights went out. Oh they will miss their iPad, boy will they, at least for a while but they will adjust and soon forget all about them. I have to get home and fast!

Completing my recon I return to the group and was pleased that they had settled into a 360 degree perimeter around the bicycles. No chatter on the radios, that is outstanding. I walk over to my bike and indicate that they should follow me. I move off the road/trail to the point where I had first stopped to listen. "Gather around," I said keeping my voice low, "Sound can carry a long ways, especially over the water. We need to keep the noise down as much as we can. I'm going to show you guys a few things while we still have daylight, which won't be for long but we will use what we have. Beth, get me a double handful of twigs no bigger than a pencil. Mat, get me a double handful of sticks no bigger than your index finger. Ben and Jeff, clear me off a five foot circle right here," pointing down to where I was standing. "Don, if you would stand watch while I'm showing these guys this. Thanks."

Turning to my bike trailer, I pulled my pack from the trailer and pulled on the straps to open the top of my pack. Opening up the drawstring I reached in and pulled out my bag that held my Solo stove. By the time I was back at the spot Ben and Jeff were done clearing off the forest floor in a five-foot circle and both Beth and Mat were back with the wood. I stepped back to my pack and grabbed my 40 oz stainless steel Klean water bottle and pulled a Bic lighter out of my outside pouch. Walking back over to the group I squatted and told Beth and Mat to lay the sticks down next to me. I opened the Solo bag and pulled out the Solo Pot. Lifting the lid I pulled the Solo stove out of the pot. Tipping the stove over the fire ring fell into my hand follow by a zip lock bag. Sitting the stove on the ground I picked up a few of the twigs Beth had gathered and broke them to a size that would fit into the stove. Picking up one of the twigs I opened the zip lock and stabbed one of the Vaseline impregnated cotton balls and set the zip lock behind me. Fishing the lighter out of my pocket I lit the cotton ball and dropped it into the stove. Picking up a handful of the twigs I began breaking them into the right size and dropping them into the stove on top of burning cotton ball. I next sorted though the finger size sticks, selected three and dropped those into the stove. I than sat the fire ring right side up on top of the stove. I rinsed the pot out with a little of my water, than filled the pot with about 24 ounces of water. Looking up I said, "And that is how you build a fire to heat water for coffee or as in this case for our Mountain House meal. Any questions?" Beth ask, "What are those things in the zip lock?" "These are about the best fire starters there are. But to answer your question, they are nothing more than Vaseline impregnated cotton balls. Just take a handful of cotton balls and about a tablespoon of Vaseline and squeeze it all together in a zip lock

130

and than you have your fire starters. It will take about seven minutes to bring that pot to a boil. The pot holds enough water for two Mountain House pouches. While we are waiting for the water to boil lets go set some fishing lines."

Walking back to my ruck, I pulled out two more small bags and my Platypus Water System. Turning to the group I said, "Grab your Water System, that is one of the first thing you must always do. Drink as much as you can, filter water and fill all your containers. Than you re-fill the filter bags so you can top off in the morning. Also I want everyone to fill their dirty water bags before we leave in the morning. That way if we stop tonight and there is no handy water we will have plenty. Jeff, grab Don's water kit while he stays here with the food." I handed Mat the slightly larger of the two bags and said, "Hold this for the next lesson." Taking the smaller of the two bags I headed towards the water, stopping by Don, "Don when that is boiling open two Mountain House bags and dump half the water into each bag. Seal each of the bags and squeeze them a couple of times to mix them up. Go ahead and add a few more sticks to the stove and set another pot of water on to boil. I'm going to show these guys how to set up a couple of YoYo fishing rigs and a couple of snares so in the future they can do it without us." Don nodded, "Can do, good idea to show them."

Walking down to the water I motioned for the group to fill their water systems and to hang them from a tree so the filtering process could take place. Standing and watching them fill their bags, I squatted next to the water and filled my own bag. Moving back to the trees I cut off a small branch, leaving about two inches of limb sticking out from the tree. Hanging my dirty water bag from the cut limb I laid my clean water bag on the backside of the tree in the shade.   As the others filled their water filtration bags, I said, "let's talk a little bit about our food situation, I once read a study that stated men should consume a minimum of 1,500 calories a day unless supervised by their doctors. Even at 1,500 calories a day a man conducting normal activity will lose weight. For a healthy adult male to maintain current body weight, most adult men will need to consume 2,000 to 3,000 calories a day. According to another study, I think it was out of the Mayo Clinic; a 160-pound person spends about 511 calories per hour while hiking with a pack at a moderate pace. That works out to burning about 4,088 calories over an eight-hour period of hiking (2.5 mph x 8 = 20 miles). I don't know about any of you but that sounds like a lot of calories to me. I am not a medical doctor, but I don't think anyone could survive or keep up that pace on taking in half the calories that you expend each day. This might work if all we needed to do was travel 250 miles. But multiplying that distance to 1400 miles, you have nowhere near the amount of calories to sustain your body let alone maintaining 20 miles a day. I will say that attempting to keep up a 20 mile a day pace is almost impossible if you are having to hunt, trap, and fish along the way. First you have no way to preserve the meat for any length of time and hunting, trapping, and fishing takes time not even counting the time to clean and cook your success. Additionally, we need to start immediately supplementing our food with game and edible plants. There are many rivers, lakes, and ponds in the Eastern United States. Water means animals and fish and with some knowledge and a little bit of luck we can easily supplement our supplies with fresh meat and edible plants. But all of this takes time. The key to the success of being a hunter/gather is that you get more calories from your hunting and gathering than you expend."

Next I moved back to the waters edge and stopped at one of the trees standing on the waters edge waiting for the rest of the group. After everyone was finished hanging their water bags and had rejoined the group, I squatted and opened the bag and pulled out a YoYo fishing reel and a small plastic box. Opening the box I selected a hook that already had a leader on it. Clipping the leader to the fishing line, I again reached in and pulled out a small jar of bait eggs. Moving over to the tree I flipped the 5/50 cord already attached to the reel over a low hanging branch. Catching the end as it wrapped around the branch, I clipped the small carabineer on the end of the cord back onto the YoYo reel. Tripping the reels catch I pulled off about 15 feet of line being careful not to tangle it. I tossed the bait hook out into the deeper water. Setting the catch on the YoYo reel, I proclaimed the task was complete. Ben said, "I have seen those on the Internet but have never seen one used. Do they really work?" "As well as anything. If a fish takes the bait it will trip the reel and snag him," I explained, "Lets go set a snare before it gets too dark." Walking along the edge of the woods I stopped at an opening into a blackberry patch. I pointed out the animal run and again squatted down near the mouth of the run. "Mat hand me that other bag." Taking the bag I reached in and pulled out a small animal snare, a support wire, my support wire driver and a cable extension. Unwrapping the snare I explained to them the basic of setting a typical snare. Extending the loop of the snare out to about six inches I laid it to the side. Picking up the support wire and driver I showed them how to place the support wire into the ground. Taking the snare I pushed the support wires end into the holder on the snare and adjusted the snare to about three inches off the ground. Fluffing up the grass around the snare I explained how it helps to channel the animal so they must pass though the snare. Attaching the extended cable I secured the cable to a small sapling nearby. "Class dismissed, so each night a couple of you will set out a couple of YoYo's if we are near water and several snares. This will teach all of you skills you are going to need and will allow us to augment our food supply. Once we get to the cabin in the mountains I will show you how to set a deer snare. Remember it is all about gaining more protein than the amount of energy expended to gain that protein. Any questions?" Beth again raised her hand, "Will the snare kill whatever animal gets in it?" "Not always," I replied, "If the animal tangles around a tree or bush, more than likely it will be dead. If it does not tangle, most of the time not. You will find most of the time when you snare a rabbit or squirrel they will be dead. A coon, most of the time he will be caught around the head and at least one leg. If you catch a coon around just the neck many times he will be able to pull the snare off with his paws. Be very careful approaching any animal in a snare. We will use Beth's .22 to shoot any thing caught larger than a rabbit or squirrel. Any animal will bite, do not take any chances. If as you approach the area where you set a snare and you cannot see the snare or a caught animal be very careful, circle around the area until you can see the snare. A live animal will sometimes hide and they will attack if you get within reach. Oh, and if by chance you see that the animal is a live skunk, please come and get me or shoot it from a distance. If you get within 10 or 15 feet of a live one you will get sprayed." Ben ask, "How successful is snaring?" "It depends on how much pressure is or has been on an area. If the area is not hunted a lot, chances are good. It is all about using the least amount of effort or energy to gain meat protein. If you walk five miles and only catch one rabbit you are at a net loss. You ended up spending more energy than you gained. Does that make sense? That is why we maximize our chances by using the YoYo reels and snares as we are using very little energy so anything we catch is a positive gain." There were head nods all around. "Lets head back, I'm sure Don has dinner ready by now. Get some food, clean weapons, and get some sleep," I said. Turning I began heading back towards camp, "As soon as we get back to camp, go ahead and get your snivel gear set up before it gets dark. Mat, you have

134

latrine duty tonight, its not a punishment, we will all take turns, dig a slit trench about 8 inches wide and 2 feet long and about a foot deep. Leave the shovel sticking in the dirt pile and tie a chem light to the shovel handle so everyone can find the trench. Anyone using it, and do use it if you need to go, use the shovel to cover any mess you make." Jeff said, "Just what exactly do you mean by snivel gear," getting chuckles from everyone. "What?" he said, "Like any of you knows what he's talking about either." "Settle down," I said attempting to not chuckle myself, "Your so called snivel gear is your sleeping and shelter gear. Your sleeping bag, poncho liner, could be your rain gear, just depends on the situation on what exactly it is. By the way, it was a good question. If at anytime I say something that you don't understand, ask. I tend to speak military most of the time, so if you don't understand, ask. It could be important." "Next question," Jeff said, "You referred to this snare as a small game snare, does that mean you have bigger ones?" "Good observation," I said, "Yes, I have a dozen coyote snares that can be used to snare larger animals such as deer. I wouldn't recommend attempting to use this size on a western mule deer, but on these white tails around here the coyote size snares should be able to hold them. Although it will more then likely destroy the snare. Always save the parts of the snares as I can make more from the parts." As I finished talking we arrived back at our campsite.

Not seeing Don immediately, I called on the radio, "Don where did you take off too?" Two guys I had never seen before stepped out from behind a large oak tree. One of them was a big guy and he was holding Don by the arm and waving around a large bladed knife. His buddy had Don's M4 and was pointing it in our general direction and both were grinning like they had won the lottery. The men were dressed as what most people would consider motorcycle gear. The big guy with the knife launched into a speech telling us what he was going to do

135

to Don if we didn't all drop our weapons, raise our hands and surrender.

Well last time I checked I'm not even part French, so like that was going to happen, like never I thought, I was standing slightly behind Mat and clearly saw that the guy with the M4 was unfamiliar with the weapon. The big guy holding Don wanted to talk as he was shouting all kinds of threats. Blah, Blah, Blah, I thought as I stepped forward and around Mat and palmed my Glock from my right hand drop leg holster bringing the Glock up into a good two handed position while pushing the Glock into the firing position. My first shot caught the idiot waving around the knife in mid-speech, his last by the way. The jacketed hollow point struck the big man dead center of his chest about six inches below his chin. The second round struck the big man about two inches lower and two inches to the left of the first shot. He dropped like he was struck by lighting with a surprised look on his face. I took another step forward and fired twice into the guy holding Don's M4. He was so surprised by my actions that he didn't even attempt to raise the weapon in his hands. I don't think he ever clearly saw me, he was too busy staring at his now dead friend with a confused look, disbelief that we wouldn't just do what they wanted. Both bullets took him center of the chest and he too dropped to the ground, dead before he hit the ground.

Hitting the mag release I dropped out the partially used magazine and automatically withdrew a new fully loaded magazine and shoved it into the Glock before holstering it. Walking over to Don and ask, "You ok?" He nodded, "They came up on me while I was fixing one of the Mountain House bags. I never heard them." It was than I saw he was bleeding from a cut on the back of his head, I pulled a bandana from my cargo pocket and hand it to Don, "Its clean, looks like you took a pretty good hit, hold this against that cut until we can take a closer look." I motioned for Mat to come over and told him to get a first aid kit from one of the trailers. Picking up my used mag from the ground, I moved over and checked both of the bodies making sure both were dead. Turning back to the group they were all still standing there staring at me. "Beth, go help Mat clean up that cut on Don's head. I'll be over there in a minute to take a look at it. Ben, Jeff, you guys get out your night vision scopes and get them on your rifles and than take up guard positions. These guys might not have been alone. One to the east and one to our south. Go out about 75 feet, no further. I'll be out in a few with your food. Let me know if you hear or see anything. Get moving."

That seemed to snap everyone out of their frozen state. Beth moved to help Mat with Don, while everyone kept stealing glances at the two dead guys. I ignored their looks and pulled out some loose rounds to reload the ejected magazine from my Glock; stuffing the rounds into the used magazine until it was full and replaced it into my vest. Walking back over to the two would be bad guys I turned out their pockets to see what they had. Mat glanced over at me, "What are you doing?" "Checking their pockets for loose change," I said. Mat's eyes widen and he stammered, "What?" "Sorry, bad joke haven't you ever seen the Princess Bride? I'm checking to see if they have anything indicating where they are from or where they were headed. I don't think we want to run into any of their friends," I said. The smaller guy that had been holding Don's M4 had a surprising amount of money in the first pocket I checked, I didn't take the time to count it but there had to be at least a couple grand, his other pockets had even more surprises. At first I thought they just rolls of coins, but when I pulled them out they were the plastic protective cases that coin collectors use for pure silver and gold coins. From the markings on the protective cases these guys must have hit a gold dealer or pawnshop recently. I didn't take the time to count the coins, but I did pat the guy down a little more carefully than I would have. Taking everything I had found on the first guy I moved over to the bigger second guy. Again another big wad of cash and several more protective cases of gold coins. I sat back on my heels and begin to think, surely these guys had more gear than just what they were wearing. I stood and began casting around looking for any backpacks or bags. Sure enough I found two mid size day packs stashed behind a large oak about 20 feet away. Judging from the weight of the two packs there was a lot more coins in the packs. Giving them the once over I pulled out a couple of baggies of weed and one of pills. Having no idea what I was looking at with the pills, I took the weed and the pills and carried them over to the slit trench. Dropping them into the pit I kicked dirt over them. I damn sure didn't want to explain how we came into possession of drugs. Taking the loose coins I took out of their pockets I dropped them into one of the bags and carried both bags over to the bikes. Catching Mat's eye as I walked past, I motioned him to follow me. Once he came over I said, "Take this bag and hide it under your equipment in your trailer. Just trust me, don't open it, just hide it, it might come in useful later on down the road." I could see that he wanted to ask what it was, but did as he was told without bitching about it. I took the second bag and did the same with it in my trailer.

Walking back over to the two dead men, I bent over picking up Don's M4 from the ground, I cleared the weapon and made it safe, checking to make sure the barrel was clear, just in case the idiot I shot had jammed the muzzle of the rifle into the ground when he fell. I next moved over to the knife guy and rolled him over. I spotted Don's Sig Sauer in the guy's waistband and pulled the pistol out. Dropping out the magazine, I racked the slide and caught the round as it was ejected. Again, checking the barrel to make sure it was clear, I thumbed the loose round back into the mag and reloaded the pistol. Walking back over to Don, I handed him his pistol, "That's loaded with one in the chamber," I said, than handed him his rifle, "The rifle does not have one in the chamber."

Don looked at me sheepishly, dropping the pistol into his drop leg holster, "Thanks," he said. "No big deal," I said, "I should be apologizing to you, from now on no one does anything alone, that was my mistake and it won't happen again." "Sorry I put you in the position of having to kill two men," Don said before I raised my hand to stop him. "No big deal, just probable saved someone down the road a lot of grief. A lot of these types of guys are going to be taking advantage of the situation now to act anyway they want and to take what they want. The only thing holding them in check was the fear of what would happen to them from the law if they were caught. With that fear gone now they thought they could do whatever they wanted. They wanted to see us cower in fear and beg but don't think for a minute that they would not have killed all of us, that is all of us except Beth."

Beth inhaled sharply at this. "Yes Beth, realize that the world has charged and it is worse for the females. Guys like this are scum and would torture and rape you before killing you after they got tried of playing with you." I was watching Beth's face and could see her looking between the bodies of the dead bikers and me. "Look, regardless of how it might look, it is never an easy thing taking another person's life. But in situations like this it was them or us. No amount of talking would have changed the outcome, other than to maybe get one of us hurt or killed. It really comes down to the difference between good and evil and I for one will never put myself in a position willing to surrender to the likes of these scum. And its not because they were bikers. I know a lot of guys that are hardcore bikers, but they would never prey upon the weak or helpless or jump someone like these guys did. Like I said they wanted to talk and intimidate us, to see fear of them, to some that is a huge high. I wasn't in a talking mood. Scum like these only understands force. If I had just disarmed them, than they would have done the same exact thing the first time they got the chance. No the world is better off without guys like this. Mat, let Beth handle Don's cut. Lets begin moving all the bikes about 50 yards north away from these guys." Mat got up and came over to me. "Mat, grab your rifle, don't ever go anywhere without your rifle, pistol and ammo vest. I know all of this has everyone a little off balance but all of you need to snap out of it," keying my handset I called Ben and Jeff, "Check In," I said. Ben came on, followed by Jeff, both reporting they had not heard or seen anything. Keying the radio again, "Come on back to camp, we are going to move a short distance away from here." After receiving an affirmative from them, Mat and I waited until the pair joined us.

"You guys go ahead and eat right quick, being Don already has the food prepared, after that we will move camp a short way so we won't be bother by the night time scavengers." "Should we bury them or something," ask Jeff. I looked at him and said, "No, why waste the time and effort. If it was one of our own, sure we would, trash like that, no. The animals will make short work of them. Speaking of chow, let's eat and get moved so we can get a good night's sleep. We have a lot of ground to cover tomorrow," as I moved over to the area where Don had been preparing the dehydrated meals. Picking up two of the Mountain House bags I turned and ask, "Ok, who wants lasagna?" Beth ask, "Who are you? In one day you rob a Bass Pro Store blind, a Vitamin Shop, a Dick's sporting goods store, teach us to build a fire, set fishing lines and snares, save Don and us by killing two homicidal bikers and are now serving us dinner like nothing out of the ordinary has happened. Who the hell are you?"

I paused for a couple of seconds looking at each of the group, "I'm just a guy that grew up in a different world than you know, along the way I picked up a few skills, a guy that I like to think is one of the good guys, well at least a slightly bad guy that does good things, a guy whose only mission in life right now is getting to Texas to be with and protect my wife and kids from the same type of scum I took care of tonight. By helping this group get out of the DC area, I'm helping myself. So that is who I am and that is all you need to know. Now let's eat before this gets cold. Ben, Jeff you guys take the Lasagna. Beth, Mat here is the beef stew, Don and I will share the Chili Mac. Everyone dig in and eat, but make sure everyone has their night vision on their M4s in case these idiots had friends within ear shot of the gunfire. Now snap out of whatever funk you are in and get your shit together." With my speech done, I handed out the bags of food and moved over next to Don. Fishing my CRKT spork out of my pouch on my chest rig I handed the bag to Don and said, "Eat up, how's your head feeling?" "Have a hell of a headache, but I think I'll live," he said. I got back up and moved over to my ruck and fished around in the top pouch to retrieve my headlamp. Flipping on the red lens light I dug around until I found my med bag. Finding it I carried it back over to Don and moved behind him. Seeing that Mat and Beth had done a fair job of cleaning up the cut on Don's head I pulled out a tube of Neosporin and applied a small dab to the cut. "I could put a couple of stitches in that if you want me to," I said. Don shook his head gingerly, "No I'll be ok." "Ok, let me wrap it up so you don't get anything in it tonight, we definitely don't want it to become infected." Handing him a couple of ranger tabs. Don looked at the large pills and raised his eyebrows. "Take them, its only 800 milligram Tylenol, be sure and drink plenty of water with those and eat some food or they might make your stomach upset. Now hold still while I finish bandaging this cut."

Pulling out a gauze pad I folded it in half and taped it down over the cut. "If you put your hat back on it will hold that bandage in place, at least until you go to bed. No guard duty for you tonight, just eat and get some rest."

After finishing up taking care of Don's cut, I took the remainder of the Mountain House Chili Mac from Don and sat down to eat. I hadn't realized how hungry I was until I began eating. It always surprises me how good some the freeze-dried foods are. Chili Mac has always been my favorite. Finishing the bag quickly, I stood and moved over to the trailer and grabbed the shovel. As quickly as I could I dug a hole about one foot deep next to the area we had the Solo stove set up. "Everyone finish up and put all of your trash in this hole. Last one to finish covers the hole over so no one will step into it and break an ankle." Dropping my empty bag into the hole, I gingerly touched the Solo stove to see if it was still hot. Finding it had already cooled, I picked it up and shook out the ashes and repacked the stove into its bag. Carrying the bag over to my ruck I repacked the bag into its proper place inside my ruck. Cinching down the straps on my ruck, I made sure it was still securely in the trailer and moved over to my bike. Pushing the bike I began moving though the trees to the east. After about 75 yards I ran into a wall of black berry bushes. While normally I don't like to set up close to briar patches, tonight we would make an exception for one night. Snakes like briar patches because rabbits and other small animals like the briar patches. But it would have to do for tonight as it was almost completely dark and with no moon this time of the month it was going to get pitch dark very quickly. As everyone strayed in I told them to get bedded down and that I would take the first watch, I would wake Beth and Mat for the next watch and in turn they would wake Ben and Jeff. Ben would wake me at 0400 for the last watch.

Slinging on my M4 I checked to make sure the night vision scope was securely mounted and working. I made a quick check of the area and saw that everyone but Don was already in his or her sleeping bags. Moving over to Don, I squatted down next to him. "How's the head feeling?" I ask. "Its ok, throbbing a little but I'll be ok by morning. Bye the way, I didn't get a chance earlier to say thanks for taking care of those two morons. They were telling me the whole time just what they were going to do with us and how happy they were to finally get their hands on some weapons. They said they had been down in Richmond and were heading back when the EMP hit. They were heading back to their home in Laurel when their motorcycles just quit running. They saw us turn off the highway and followed us. They knew we had at least one girl with us and the things they were saying they were going to do to her were horrible. What's really bothering me is they were able to sneak up on me. What if they had killed a couple of these kids? I just feel stupid letting them get the drop on me like that."

"Don't beat yourself up, I should never have left only one person alone. From now on we stick to the two-person rule for everything. Now try and get some sleep. Do you want me to set up your hammock real quick?" "No, I'll be ok just with my sleeping bag tonight. But thanks again." Don said as he began spreading out his bag. I stood and moved a few feet away and waited until he had crawled inside the bag. All of them were going to be sore and cranky tomorrow. I made a mental note to stop sooner tomorrow night so everyone would have time to set up their hammocks.

Moving about 25 yards back towards the south; I found a tree to sit against that gave me a good view of the area. Bringing up my M-4 I slowly scanned the area. An owl began softly hooting nearby but it was the only sound from the woods. Sitting and listening to the night sounds I thought about how this event had changed the world so much for the young members of our little group. Well they will adapt and do it quickly or it could become a huge liability. If the group as a whole doesn't adapt to this new world, I will have to leave them and go on my own. Wow, that is cynical I thought, they are a good bunch of kids but they are not my kids. My kids are 1400 miles away and need me there with them not shepherding a bunch of strays. But I had given my word to Don that I would give him a hand in exchange for the weapons and equipment. By now my wife would have opened the Emergence Folder. She had made fun of me when I told her about it, but after she got mad about a couple of my SHTF purchases I had kept any future purchases off the books. She did not know about the cases of number 10 cans of Mountain House stored under the stairs or the large cache of ammo stored in the master bedroom closet. As she always had me get the suitcases out of the false floor in our master closet for any family vacation, she did not know I had lined the back wall with ammo cans. Inside the Emergence Folder were spare keys to the safes, as I'm sure the electronic locks were fried from the EMP and detailed instruction on what to do. She had been so mad when I had ordered two bathtub BOBs. Waste of money she had said, I agreed with her it was a waste of money at the time, but not now. I would always wait until she was at work and the nanny had the kids at gymnastics before pulling everything out of the closet and storing the new purchases and than putting everything back. The ammo was a little more complicated. I would have to wait until the house was empty, break out the ammo, repack into MTM boxes and ammo cans, pull out all the suitcases, stack the ammo cans against the back wall and replace the suitcases. I just really, really hope we never have a fire; the local fire department is not going to be happy if that ever happens, not to mention the insurance company. Well I guess I don't have to worry about the

144

insurance company anymore. Have I mentioned that my wife if very hardheaded, brilliant, well educated, hardheaded, ok you get the picture. Anyway, I wasn't going to win that argument but at least now they had plenty of beans and bullets, but I did need to get home as fast as I can.

Glancing at my watch I see I still have another hour before I wake up Beth and Mat, I decide to make a short patrol of the area. Moving slowly, using my night vision scope ever few paces I move down to the shoreline near where we set the YoYo fishing reel. Reaching out I feel for the line feeding out of the reel. Sure enough the line is taunt and vibrating. Pulling my gloves from the pouch on my vest I pull them on. Taking the taunt line in my hands I slowing pull the line in as the reel takes in the slack. Getting the fish into the shallows I briefly turn on my headlamp to see what it was before pulling it out of the water. The red light of my headlamp revealed a very nice channel catfish in about the 4-5 pound range. I pulled it up onto the bank and stepped on it to hold it still while grabbed it by its lower jaw. Using my Gerber tool I reached in and removed the hook. Making a small slit in its lower jar I snap in a small carabineer with about ten feet of 550 cord. Tossing the catfish back into the water I tied the line to a small nearby tree. Hopefully a coon would not come along and steal my catfish. I would build a fire in the early morning to get some coals going in order to cook it for breakfast.

Moving on with my walk around the camp I went by and pulled my snare off the game trail. No use trying to catch something when we had plenty and I didn't want to take the time of having to skin and cook something when we already had one nice catfish for the morning lesson. Coiling up the snare I shoved it into my cargo pocket. The rest of my walk around the camp area was uneventful. The night remained quiet other than an occasional light wind rustling in the trees or the distance hooting of an owl on the hunt.

Around midnight I woke Beth and Mat and got them situated on either end of the camp in good locations. Telling them to call me on the radio if they heard or saw anything and to wake Ben and Jeff and to show them where to sit. I than went over of my ruck and pulled out my Warbonnet hammock. It took me all of two minutes to string up the hammock, thanking god once again for Dutchware for making it so easy and quick to set up a hammock. Sitting in my hammock, I stripped off my vest and drop leg holsters, laying my vest on the ground under my hammock, I laid my M4 on top of the vest than covering the rifle with my jacket. I went back over to my ruck and fished around and pulled out my poncho liner and inflatable pillow. Sitting in the hammock again I drew one of the Glocks from its holster and placed it on the hammocks bookshelf, pulled off my boots and lay down in the hammock. Zipping the mosquito net closed I then blew up my pillow and rolled my poncho liner around me.

The next thing I knew I was startled awake by a small pine cove hitting the netting of my hammock. Looking around I saw a small red light about 5 feet away pointing into my face. "I'm awake," I said. Jeff's voice came out of the dark as the light disappeared. "I didn't know how to wake you and figured it was best to toss something at you first," Jeff said. "No problem," I replied, "Rest assured that if I ever shoot you it won't be by accident." Jeff laughed and in a low voice, "Ben and I were talking, if you could, can you work with us on some of our shooting skills. Both Ben and I have hunted for years, but neither of us knew what to do today and we would like to know how to handle situations like yesterday if it happens again." "Jeff, we can all work on how we need to react to different situations. It is really not about the actual shooting we need to work on, it is how to react to a given situation without having to think about it. Yesterday those idiots wanted to talk when in fact it was time for action, not talk. There might be situations where we might have to buy time with talking but most of the time if the situation calls for action, than execute the action with brutal force and speed. Yes, being able to hit your target when you do shoot is important but training yourself to react to where it is muscle memory takes time. But we can work on it," I said. Sitting up I unzipped my netting and swung my legs out of the hammock. Reaching down I grabbed my boots and shook both of them out. Always best to make sure no creepy crawlers took up resident in your boots. Pulling them on, I laced up my boots and stuck my Glock back into its leg rig and slid my jacket back on. Shrugging into my ammo vest I was ready for a new day. Slinging on my M4, I headed down towards the water to get and clean the catfish. Looking back at Jeff I said, "Go ahead and built a fire in the same place we used the stove last night, I will need a good bank of coals to cook the catfish we caught last night." Jeff nodded and headed out to start the fire.

Stopping by the slit trench, I quickly relieved myself and kicked some dirt into the trench. Morning routine done, I headed down to the water and began removing the YoYo fishing reel from the tree. Stowing the reel in a pocket after cleaning off the hook, I found the catfish was still alive and kicking where I had left him. Carrying the fish over to a fairly large downed tree I brushed off the tree truck and laid the fish on the log. Not really trying to be quiet, I noticed Mat sticking his head out of his sleeping bag in the early morning light. I called, "Morning sunshine, time to get your happy ass out of bed and get moving. Once you're up, get up and help Jeff with the fire and get some water on the stove for coffee. I'll have this fish ready in a couple minutes to throw on the fire. Oh, and wake up sleeping beauty over there while you're at it." I could hear him grumbling that it was too cold and he needed just five more minutes of sleep. "Get your ass out of that sleeping bag or I'm going to drag you down to the water and roll you in," I said, "Now get your big boy panties on and get up." I could hear him talking to Jeff but could not make out what they were talking about. I made a mental note to break out my Walker Hunters earplugs before we got on the road today. Even wearing just one it really increased a person's ability to hear things way before you normally could. I did hear Jeff call out to Mat asking him if he wanted a cup of coffee. Mat replied with, "Hell yes, thanks." Glancing back over my shoulder I saw Jeff appear near Mat's sleeping bag and Mat holding out his cup to Jeff. Jeff took the cup and disappeared back into the trees, appearing a few seconds later with Mat's cup, but he stopped short of Mat's sleeping bag by about 15 feet and set the cup on a rock. Mat called out, "Hey man, hand me my cup!" Jeff just laughed and told him to get up and get it himself. Mat climbed out of his bag slowly and pulled on his boots. Standing he shivered as he only had on a t-shirt and running shorts. Walking quickly over to his cup, he began cussing Ben when he picked it up. "You asshole," he yelled, as I could hear both Ben and Jeff laughing now. Ben yelled back, "Get your butt dressed and help me gather some firewood and we can make some coffee."

Laughing quietly to myself I turned back to cleaning the catfish. After scoring the fish around the head, tail and backbone I pulled the outer skin off with my Gerber tool. Removing the head and fins, than gutting the fish I moved back down to the waters edge to clean up my tools and to wash off the fish. I got Beth's attention and ask her to get out my stuff sack marked cooking supplies from my ruck. Once she had, I had her get one of the tin foil cooking bag out, as I was rinsing off the fish with clean water from my canteen. After she had the bag open I dropped the fish into it and washed my hands off. I have always hated having fish slime on my hands. Drying off my hands I took the tin foil bag with the fish and added salt and pepper to the bag. I next took out a small bottle

148

of cooking oil and squeezed a small amount into the bag. Rolling the top of the bag down, I put away all the cooking supplies and walked up the small hill to the campfire. The fire was going good by this time and the guys also had the Solo stove going heating up water for coffee.

Moving over to the fire, I picked up a stick and gently moved the fire over a few inches leaving some of the glowing coals on the uncovered part. I laid the tin foil bag down on the coals and than pulled the fire back over the top of the bag. "That should be ready in about 15 or 20 minutes," I declared to the group. Walking over to my ruck I pulled my cup out and a zip lock bag of Starbucks instant individual coffee packets. Going back to the group I opened the bag and pulled one out and passed the bag around the group. Dumping the instant coffee into my cup I poured it about 2/3 full with the hot water from the Solo stove. "You guys eat up, fix one pouch of breakfast food for each of you. While you're at it, please fix me one too, I'm going to take a walk back up to the road for a few minutes and see if there is anyone traveling this early. Everyone stay here and try and keep the noise down. And Mat, please wake up Don if he is not already awake. After you eat go ahead and pack everything up."

Chapter Ten

Taking my coffee I moved slowly back towards the highway. The sun was up enough now that I didn't need the night vision and stopped by a large tree and removed the device. Swapping the night vision for my ACOG, I stored it in its pouch and dropped it into the pocket of my chest rig. I stood quietly by the large tree and listened for several minutes. I could hear a slight noise coming from camp and a laugh broke the morning silence a couple of times. Not hearing or seeing anything, I moved until I could see the highway. From this vantage point I could see all of the bridge and the road leading south until it crested out of sight. There were several dead cars scattered along the highway, but nothing moved. I leaned against a tree for about 5 minutes watching and listening before turning back to the campsite.

Walking back to the group by the fire, my presence stopped whatever conversation they all were having. Don was seated with his back to a tree and he nodded in my direction as I walked up. Mat handed me a bag of biscuits and gravy. "Thanks," I said, these just happen to be another of my favorite Mountain House meals. Everyone was looking at me so I started laying out the plans for the day. "Before we leave here today I want everyone to test fire their weapons, both rifle and pistol, and to make sure the scope we have on them are at least sighted in. They should all be close as we did bore sight the long guns," I began, "We will need to be quick about it and have everything packed and ready to go. No telling who will come looking to see what the hell is going on. I was somewhat surprised no one came to look after the shooting last night. We need to cover some ground today; I would really like to be west of the major built up areas today. Things are going to get really bad, really fast once everyone realizes no one is coming to help. After you finish eating and get cleaned up, get everything packed and ready to go. Any questions?"

Don came over with his coffee and sat down next to me while I dug into the biscuits and gravy, I ask him how his head was doing. "I'm ok, head still hurts a little but mostly just to the touch, but I'm ok." I nodded, "If it gets worse today, or you start having double vision, please let me know immediately. You could have a slight concussion and we can deal with that, but if you push it and wreck your bike and get another hard hit it could be trouble. So just let me know and we will take a break. Did you get any sleep last night?" I ask. "Not bad, head was throbbing for a while but the stuff you gave me helped and I was able to sleep most of the night," Don replied. Patting the older man on the shoulder, I stood and walked over to the trash hole someone had dug. Tossing in my bag I turned and headed over to my hammock. I deflated my pillow and stowed away that and my poncho liner. Quickly I unhooked one end of my hammock and stuffed it into the double-ended stuff sack, closed that end and finished stuffing the rest of the hammock into the other end. The entire process took less than a minute. Finishing I turned back to the fire and saw everyone had been watching me. I heard someone mummer, that's not fair, and I laughed. "Hey, I can't help it if you guys were not prepared. You all have hammocks with you and tonight I will make sure we stop early enough that you have time to set yours up. I know they are not like mine but they are better than the ground."

Going over to my ruck, I pulled off my chest rig, I than striped off my fleece and put it away in my ruck. Putting my chest rig back on I next dug around and found a box of lens cleaning single use packages, pulling one out I cleaned all of my optics. Putting away the box of lens cleaning paper, I dug out my toothbrush and toothpaste. Making quick work of my dental needs I packed away the brush and toothpaste. My morning routine complete, I tightened down the straps on my ruck and made sure it was secure in my trailer. Seeing Mat over by his bike I ask him to pull out the pack of Shoot-n-See targets I had made him pack. After he found them and passed them to me, I walked off 25 yards and attached two of the targets to a large oak tree, repeating this on two other oaks nearby.

Returning to the fire, I pulled the foil pack from the coals and opened the pouch. Checking to make sure the fish was fully cooked I got everyone to gather round and turned the pouch over to them. Don had already had his fill from the Mountain House meal so he declined the fish and left the four teenagers to deal with the fish. It didn't take the four long to polish off the catfish, Jeff was still picking small bits out of the pouch when I took the pouch from him and tossed it into the trash pit. Jeff frowned at this but I said, "You will live, get cleaned up and get ready to go." He smiled and headed down towards the water. I called after him, "Maybe tonight you will set out more than one YoYo reel." Walking away as Jeff was swearing he would set more reels the next time, I grabbed the shovel and filled in the trash hole. Carrying the shovel back over to my bike trailer I secured it and grabbed the canvas bucket that was in the trailer. Walking down to the water I scooped up a bucket and walked back to the fire. Stopping on the uphill side of the fire I poured the water onto the fire. Catching Ben's eye I motioned to him to take the bucket and get another bucket of water.

After the fire was out and all of the equipment secured, I had everyone get their bikes lined up in the formation we would be traveling in today. Gathering everyone together I went over what we were going to do, "Ok everyone, now that we are finished up and ready to go, we are going to test fire our weapons and make sure they are sighted in. I want to be out of

152

here in no more than 30 minutes. I do not want to have to explain to anyone why there are two dead bodies over there. We are going to do this by the numbers. Ben and Jeff, go ahead and push your bikes up to the edge of the trees and watch out for anyone traveling on the road, if you see anyone radio me. Once you get up there, let me know if it is clear. Just radio, Clear or if you see anyone just say Stop and the number of people you see. Got it?" Both of them nodded and grabbed their bikes and began pushing them back up towards the road.

"Alright, Don and I will go first than Mat and Beth. Beth you can fire my M4 just to get familiar with it. We will get you one the first chance we have. Ok lets do this. Everyone will aim for the center of their target. Make sure the caps are off your scopes so I can adjust without you having to get up." I said. Pulling out my bino's, I laid down, put on my Peltors hearing muffs. Checking to make sure the line was clear, I sighted in with my ACOG and flipped my safety to the fire position. Taking a deep breath, I slowly let half of it out. Gently squeezing the trigger I fired off my first round, followed by a second and third. Flipping my safety on, I picked up my bino's and check my grouping. All three rounds had struck the target in a one-inch group about 2.5 inches below the bullseye. Seeing this I thought that whomever had sighted this rifle in had done so for about 300 yards. I wanted it sighted in at about 200 yards. Taking my Gerber tools straight screwdriver I moved the elevation up by 4 clicks. Taking sight again I fired off three more rounds and saw my group had moved up by about half an inch. Knowing that was about right I double-checked that my rifle was on safe and stood up. Unclipping the sling I motioned Beth to come to me. "Make sure you aim at the center of the target. As you will see my groups are a little lower than the bullseye. At this range that is where the round should be hitting the targets. I can explain more later if you have any questions." She indicated she didn't and took the M4 and got down into a prone position.

The entire process took longer than I wanted but we finally got everyone sighted in and to my surprise Beth turned out to be a fairly decent shot and was not afraid at all of the M4 even if it was her first time firing one. After Don, Mat, and Beth had fired, I sent them up to take Ben and Jeff's position. While they were pushing their bikes up the hill I fired one magazine out of each of my Glocks and fine-tuned my RMR's. After finishing up I had everyone reload their magazines and we all headed up the hill. With everyone gathered by the cable, I pushed up the cable and everyone pushed their bikes back up onto the road. After checking the highway with my bino's and not seeing anyone in sight, we got mounted up and checked our gear. I conducted a radio check and we headed out.

Highway 29 ran into Highway 200 about four miles south of where we had stopped for the night. Other than a few cars and semi trucks stalled on the road we saw no people until we neared the intersection of 29 and 200. Don called on the radio, "Talon we have a situation here," Don and Mat were about 300 meters to our front and had stopped about a 1/4 mile from the intersection. "There is a mob of people at a store just off the east side of the road ahead," Don radioed. I pushed my transmit button, "Are they blocking the way we want to go?" "No, I don't think so but we have seen several people crossing the interstate going or coming from the store. From where we are we can see a bunch of people in the parking lot," Don stated. Punching my radio again, "Hold fast we will come up and we will go though as a group," I said. I turned to everyone, "Ok we will all close up with Don and Mat. Once we are all together, I will take the lead, followed by Ben and Jeff, than Mat and Beth, with Don right behind Mat and Beth. If there is any trouble do NOT stop, keep going, I will handle any problems. If I have to stop, keep going and make the turn on Highway 200, go for about one mile and stop if it is safe, if it is not safe go another mile. I will catch up. Wait for thirty minutes, if I'm not there by then, than I won't be coming, so stick to the plan and go on."

Pulling up to Don and Mat, I nodded at them, "All right, everyone stays together, again keep going no matter what happens. Do not stop if I do, just keep going." I pull out my bino's and take a quick scan of the area. From our position I can see several people standing by the guardrail on the west side of the road. As I watch a couple of people, looked to be in their 30's, make a run from over the guard rail to the east. The group by the guardrail on the west chased after them. I realize what is going on and quickly put away my bino's. "Lets go, let's get up to about 25 mph and go right by these guys, let me get out about 50 yards in front. Again NO ONE stops but me," I growled. Checking for everyone's head nod, I pushed off and began pedaling hard. It only took me less than two minutes and I got to the gang standing in the road over the bodies of the couple I had seen in my bino's. A glance at the bodies told me I was too late to do anything for them. Two of the four were gathering up the groceries lying scattered on the pavement. At the sound of my brakes, they all turned towards me. I looked and saw many of the items scattered around were diapers and baby formula.

All four of the young men were armed with aluminum baseball bats and were around 16 to 18 years old. I had stopped about 20 feet away and as they turned to me they saw the oncoming other bicycles. One of the oldest of the group began to move as if to block the road but stopped when he saw my M4 come up to a ready position. "Morning Gentlemen, just what the fuck do you think you're doing?" I ask in a causal tone. The biggest of the four, about 5'10" and had the stocky build of a high school football player respond, "We are keeping people from stealing all of our grocery's. My Dad told us to stop anyone that was taking stuff from the stores. If its any of your business." The other three were watching the kid doing the talking and kept looking from him to me, or I should say my M4. The talker turned to the other kids and motioned for them to block the road. They started to move but stopped again when I said stop. The leader of the group barked, "Fuck you man, nobody tells us what to do!" I could hear the bikes getting closer behind me, "All of you down on the pavement NOW!" I shouted. Two of the gang began to get down but the leader of the group took another step towards the center of the pavement. Bringing the rifle up I placed the green horseshoe reticle on the gang leaders lower leg and triggered off one round. At that close range the 5.56 65 grain bullet punched straight though the would be toughs leg. Moving my rifle to the other standing gang member, he had better sense and quickly moved to the ground.

Our group of riders sped by taking quick looks at what was going on before pedaling harder to get by the mess. Right about then the pain of the leg wound hit him as his cusses turned into screams of pain. Looking at him I said, "You might want to get someone to look at that before long." As I dropped my M4 on its sling and pushed my bike off and began pedaling as hard as I could. Glancing back over into the parking lot I could see a large group of men heading from the store towards me. Pedaling hard I was about 200 yards away when at least a couple of that group opened fire on me with what sounded like deer rifles. This motivated me to pedal even harder and soon I was out of sight and the firing stopped.

I caught up with my group after about 15 minutes, waiting for me at the top of the first hill on Highway 200. No one ask any questions and I left it at that. "Lets make some distance," is all I said and motioned for Don to lead again. We rode that way for about another 30 minutes and had just crossed another bridge and climbed a long hill overlooking the valley we had just crossed. Several cars had stalled near the top of the hill and had been left sitting where they stopped. The vantage point gave us a clear view almost all of the way back to the 200 Intersection. I keyed my mic and told everyone to stop for a water break and to stretch. Coasting to a stop at the crest of the hill, I leaned my bike against the guardrail. Calling out to Ben and Jeff, "Hey you guys make sure you keep an eye on the road heading west. I don't want anyone to sneak up on us." Taking out my bino's I scanned the road behind us, noting that the road behind us was empty, for now anyway. I was just having that feeling you get before something bad is about to happen and I wanted to get as much distance between those people and us. I just couldn't help but think that if the father of that kid was the type to order his teenage son to beat people with baseball bats, then he was the type to want revenge for me shooting his worthless son. I said as much to the rest of the group. "We might have trouble coming up behind us. I get the feeling that the individual that has taken over that area back there isn't the type to put up with someone challenging his authority. The question is do we run and deal with it when they catch up to us or do we deal with it now?" I ask. "What did happen back there?" ask Don, "we heard one shot." "The kid said his Dad told him and his friends to stop anyone from stealing food. That translated into the kid and his friends beating people to death with baseball bats. I don't know if you saw but that man and women only had bags of baby food and diapers and that kid and his friends beat them to death on the orders from his Father." Beth step up and joined the conversation, "Maybe they were just trying to keep the supplies from being looted for the larger community, you could have just scared them off."

I looked at her for several seconds, "I learned a long time ago that anyone who would do something like that is an animal. I really should have put him down like a rabid dog. If they were only protecting the stores for the community, tell me why they attempted to stop us on the road. It was obvious we had nothing to do with the stores or their community. I probably condemned several people, more than likely women, to a brutal death or rape at that kids hands. He had no hesitation or remorse about what they had done to that man and woman. He is trash and a killer and my only regret is not putting a bullet in his head and not his leg. He is no different from a Somali clansman." This last statement caused a puzzled look from the group. "Look, have any of you ever seen any of the CARE commercials on TV late at night. You know the ones asking for money to save the starving children?" There were a few head nods. "Did any of you ever see a male between the ages of 15-40 years of age in any of these camps with the starving kids. No, I guarantee you didn't, and the reason you didn't is all the fighting age males are in town sitting on their asses drinking tea and chewing Khat, waiting for the next food shipments to roll though so they can hijack it. None of those men are starving to death, plus those men own hundreds of camels and livestock, but you're kidding yourself if they would kill one of those valuable animals to feed starving women and kids and old people. They are worthless pieces of shit, lower than a rabid dog if you ask me. That so called kid back there falls into the category. A complete worthless piece of shit." Not waiting for a reply I again turn and scanned the highway back to the East.

Sure enough there was a group of men on bikes about a mile off and coming our way fast. "Enough talk, a group of 15 to 20 riders are coming our way fast. We are not going to outrun them with all this gear and the trailers," I stop talking as Don shook his head in agreement and the rest joined Don in nodding. Don spoke up, "We are all in this together and I for one do not like the idea of splitting up if that is what you're

158

thinking." I shrugged, "Ok, thanks, but you all need to realize that to stick with me will mean that we will more than likely have to kill some or all of those men." Jeff and Ben had rejoined the group and were scoping out the oncoming group. They both looked at me and Jeff ask, "What is the plan?" I answered quickly, "We need to move down to those cars that are stalled on this end of the bridge. Let's move while we still have time." Grabbing my bike and getting it turned around, it took us less than a minute to get to the west end of the bridge.

The bridge was about a quarter of a mile long and would keep any of the oncoming riders from flanking us. I reminded everyone to stay behind the wheel of the vehicles. There were five stalled vehicles within 100 yards of the west end of the bridge with the closest being about 50 yards from the end. I keyed my mic, "When the shooting starts they will attempt to take cover behind that closest vehicle. Jeff I want you to make it really uncomfortable for them. Take up a prone position over by that van and shoot under the vehicle at their feet. If they run away let them go. If I can take out their leader they will more than likely retreat. Ben, after I open up you take out anyone that has a weapon with a scope on it. I'll try and talk to these guys but I don't think it's going to do any good."

The group of men were bunched up and had slowed as they neared the east end of the bridge. They had obviously seen us take up positions at the end of the bridge. "That is far enough," I yelled, "what do you want?" A large man stepped off his bike and let it fall to the ground. He unslung a shotgun off his back and took a couple of steps forward. "I want the son of a bitch that shot my son back there," he screamed. "You need to take your men back to town," I said, "your son is lucky I didn't kill him after seeing him beat two people to death with a baseball bat. If you push this there are going to be a lot more leaving wife and girlfriends without someone to protect them." This only angered the large man, "We are not leaving until I kill you for shooting my son!"

I keyed my mic, "I tried, Ben you take the guy with the deer rifle standing behind the guy doing the talking, Jeff, you take the long haired guy to his left. Don, start on the right and work your way to the center, Mat, take the left." Turning I look at Beth, her eyes were wide but she had her .22/45 in her hands. "Stay down and watch my back," I said to her and she nodded. "Last chance, take you guys home, go now, there is no reason these other guys have to die." Keying my mic, "Stand by, if he moves towards me I going to take him down. Everyone stay under cover because most of them will empty their guns at us in just a few seconds." Just then the big guy broke into a run for the car between him and me. My M4 came up from the ready position and I put a three round burst into center mass before dropping down behind the front tire of the car I was standing behind. There was a thundering barrage of pellets and rifle bullets punching into the cars we were all behind. Giving it a few seconds and waiting for the volley to die off, I keyed my mic, "NOW, NOW, NOW!" I said into the mic.

Hooking my leg into the wheel well I pulled my M4 into my shoulder and swung around the front of the car and began servicing the men on the bridge as if they were targets on the range. I don't think most of them even saw me as the only part of me that was exposed was my rifle and part of my shoulder. I gently squeezed the trigger once per target and moved on to the next. My M4 spitting three rounds of 5.56 with each pull. Most of the men we were facing were armed with shotguns, but a few of them obviously had deer rifles judging from the thump of the heavier bullets hitting the car. They had split into three distinct groups. There was a small group moving along both guardrails and the main group attempting to hide behind the closest stalled car. I had concentrated on the main group. The first guy I took had been about 30 something and had the look of a runner, long and lean, distantly it registered that he had a Ruger 10/22 in his hands as my rounds took him from around his belly button to mid chest. They obliged me by coming around that stalled vehicle in ones and twos, again most never even spotting me. After taking down another three, I glanced over at the group along the guard rail on my right, as I ejected my magazine and slammed in a full one, releasing the bolt and pulling it back into my shoulder. By the time I got the magazine seated the fight was over. I could see a couple of guys running back across the bridge towards town but I let them go. Enough I thought, as I turned to Beth. "You ok?" I ask, she was still holding her .22/45 but was looking away from me towards the back of the vehicle we had taken cover behind.

It was then that I noticed the bolt of the pistol was locked back on her pistol. Leaning around her I looked and saw a pair of boots sticking out from around the corner of the vehicle. I reached out and touched her on the shoulder and she jumped and screamed, then after seeing it was me she broke down and starting crying. I stepped up beside her to see who it was she had shot, I was surprised to see the big guy that had been doing all the talking. He was lying on his back not moving but with a slight movement of his chest told me he was not dead, yet that is, with the ten rapidly expanding red spots on his t-shirt it was clear that Beth had emptied the .22 semi auto dead center of his chest. Beside him was the shotgun he had been carrying and I observed that the stock was splintered. It appeared the burst of rounds I had fired at him had hit stock and receiver of the shotgun he was carrying, but the force of the impact had knocked him down but otherwise had left him unhurt. Somehow he had made it to our vehicle and was coming around to catch me from behind. A cold chill pasted over me, if Beth had not been there he would have had me cold.

Stepping around Beth, I nudged the shotgun further away from the man with the toe of my boot. I leaned over him and patted him down making sure he did not have any other weapons. Picking up his shotgun I saw it was a tactical model Remington 870. Attempting to work the slide, a round was ejected but would not chamber the next round due to the damage. Placing the weapon on safe, I picked up the ejected round and slide it into my chest rig. Laying the shotgun on the trunk of the car I told Mat to make sure and throw it over the side of the bridge before we left. It was worthless and I didn't want someone to pick it up and attempt to fire it after it had been damaged. "Help me," the man gasped. Ignoring him I keyed my mic, "Everyone check in," I said and waited until everyone did. Don's voice came into my earpiece, "Mat and I are good to go." Jeff was next, "We are good over here, both of us caught a couple pellets from all those shotguns but we are ok." "Roger that," I called back, "stay sharp until I check all of these guys out. Mat you move down here and stay with Beth, Don go over and check on Jeff and Ben." About ten seconds later, Mat came trotting over, slowing down after seeing Beth crying. "Take care of her, she is upset she had to shoot this idiot, reassure her she had no choice, he would have killed both her and me if she had not shot him," I said and moved back to the shot man at the back of the car. Apparently he had taken all 10 rounds of .22 in his lungs and upper chest. The man struggled to breath and again began begging for help. I squatted down next to him, "I wonder if the two people you had your son beat to death begged for help?" I said staring directly into the dying man eyes, holding his stare of hate until he took one more ragged breath and panic entered his eyes. I smiled and waved my hand as if to say good-bye. His chest stopped and he was gone. Good riddance I thought.

Standing I moved out onto the bridge to check on the other bodies laying every which way on the bridge. After checking

162

them, a couple were still alive but none of them would last for more than a few minutes. I collected up a couple of the weapons they were carrying that we could use. Carrying those back to the trunk of the car I returned and began collecting magazines and ammo. One of the guns I definitely wanted to keep was a DP-12. I hated to add the weight but it might come in handy and to tell the truth I had always wanted one but could not justify the cost and it is a massive gun, I definitely would not want to hump it. As a defensive weapon it was awesome, not so much if you had to carry it everywhere. Carrying it back it made my M4 feel like a popgun. I also collected one Bushmaster AR-15 and several 20 round magazines and five pistols all in 9 mm. I had stripped off a nice leg rig with an M&P 9 mm from one of the bodies. Beth would get the Bushmaster and M&P rig. Moving to the next stalled vehicle on the bridge, I found several bodies. Ben and Jeff had really done a number on that vehicle with their .308s. The big rounds had pretty much riddled the vehicle and the individuals hiding behind it. Figured it was best if neither of them got an up close look at their handy work I called back and told everyone to stay where they were. Overall the bridge battle was a positive gain for us because of the gain in weapons, ammo, and equipment. At least for the short term, we really had no idea how the rest of the town would react and we needed to get a move on before the remaining town people could gather and come after us.

Walking back I dropped off the pistol and leg rig with Beth and told Ben and Jeff to gather up the other weapons, ammo, and equipment and to get it packed. Ben was busy making fun of Jeff for getting shot in the ear. Going over to Jeff, he pulled the bandage away for long enough for me to get a look, I too chuckled, "Keep pressure on that until it stops bleeding. It looks like it will be painful for a couple days, but you will live." Turning to Ben I told him to go get a tampon from my

163

med kit in the top pouch on my ruck. Grinning evilly, Ben took off.   Once he had returned I took it and cut it down until it would fit in the 9 mm sized hole in Jeff's ear. Taking out an alcohol wipe I ripped it open and wiped the wound down front and back. Pulling out another alcohol wipe I ripped it open and pushed the cut down tampon into the small packet. Working it around and squeezing it until it became soaked with alcohol I pulled it out and motioned for Jeff to drop his hand. Jeff was softly cussing as he pulled the bandage away from his ear. "Suck it up Buttercup, this is going to hurt you a hell of a lot more than it is me. Here bite on this," I said holding up my leather wallet, "there is nothing in it but some cash and it was made of soft calf skin. Nothing in it to hurt your teeth and this might sting just a little." Taking the tampon I grabbed Jeff's ear and rammed the tampon though the hole, of course this resulted in no small amount of cussing and hopping around by Jeff while we all laughed. After he stopped jumping around I distracted him with handing him the DP-12 and taking back my wallet. I told him he could not swap it for his .308, but that he could stand watch at night with it.

Heading over to where Don was sitting, Don ask, "How did we do?" "We did pretty well. Nothing major broken that would slow us down. I do want to get moving again and get past Rockville before dark today. We will stick to the plan and pick up 28 down to River Road. New rule, we don't get involved, we blow though and we don't stop to help unless we really need to. We can't stop ever 5 miles and have a gun battle. You ready to move out?" I replied. Don nodded and stood, walking over to his bike. I keyed my mic, "Ok, enough sitting around, let's get loaded up and get back on the road." Walking over to Beth and Mat, I said, "Thank you Beth for taking out that guy back there, he would have had me dead to right if you had not stopped him. I know nothing I can say will

164

make you feel better, but Thanks." Beth nodded but was clearly still upset, but she had strapped on the leg rig and had her new rifle in her hands. I nodded my approval as I saw her adjusted the sling of the rifle and she turned and headed to her bike. Keying my mic again, "All right, mount up and let's move out."

Chapter Eleven

"Lets stop at the top of this hill for a water break," I said into my radio mic. I had just tried to drink from my Camel Bak water bladder and after a short spurt of water it had come up dry. We had pushed hard since the incident at the bridge this morning and had made good time. It was almost 3:00 PM and if our luck continued we would make it to the canal towpath before dark. If I was correct, we were only a couple of miles from where we wanted to get off the highway and get onto Shady Grove to head southwest toward the old Chesapeake and Ohio Canal Towpath. We had all agreed the old towpath would lessen our chances of running into large groups of starving people. Catching up with the rest of our group I stopped and leaned my bike against the guardrail. After taking a few seconds to stretch I went to my ruck and pulled out my Klean stainless steel water bottle. Taking a long drink, I looked over at the rest of the group. They were taking turns drinking from Jeff's Camel Bak tube. I walked over, "What is going on?" I asked. Jeff just smiled and said, "Everyone else is out of water and I was just sharing mine." I smiled back; well maybe smile is not the correct turn of word, grimaced would be more accurate, "Everyone gather around, this is a good learning point." Once everyone had gathered, "We made a mistake this morning of not refilling all of our water containers. I know I had everyone refill their dirty water bags, and I know everyone has a full clean water bag, but I didn't make sure everyone also had re-filled their Camel Baks and all of their canteens. We cannot afford to be running out of water while we are on the road. The second mistake was no one self identified that they were out of water in their Camel Bak. And last but not least, one of us made the mistake of not drinking enough during the day. We definitely cannot afford for one of us to go down from heat exhaustion or heat stroke. I know that all of you are in great shape, well excluding me, but we sure cannot afford for someone to become dehydrated. From now on I will be checking to make sure everyone is drinking and to stop and replenish our water before we are all out. Also that no one immediately had to run over to the shoulder of the road and pee tells me none of you are drinking enough."

Jeff just looked at his feet sheepishly, looking up and catching my eyes on him, he quickly nodded. I continued, "I know everyone has heard the old saying about three." Seeing several puzzled looks, I explained, "The saying goes something like this, I can survive three weeks without food, I can survive three days without water [if I'm doing nothing but sitting in the shade], three hours without shelter, three minutes without air, and three seconds without a defensive weapon. But doing what we are doing you can dehydrate in just a matter of hours, no matter how good of shape you are in. From now on we will stop at least once an hour and you will drink during that stop. If you do not need to pee every two or three hours than you are not drinking enough," looking at each of them in turn until they nodded their understanding. "Don, how is your head?" I ask. He replied, "I wouldn't gripe if you could spare a couple more of those horse pills you gave me this morning." I nodded, "No problem, but please eat a granola bar or something before you take more. These things can really do a number on an empty stomach." Walking back to my ruck, I pulled out my med pack and retrieved the pain meds for Don. Passing by Mat and Beth, I asked Beth how she was doing. She flashed me a brief smile and said, "I'm ok, not something I want to do everyday. But I'll be ok." "Nobody but a psychopath ever get used to taking another person's life. But you do understand that he would have killed the both of us and never given it a second thought don't you?" I ask. She nodded and took a deep breath, "I hope I don't have to again but I do understand and know that he would have killed us given the chance. I just keep seeing the crazy look he had in his eyes and the joy he showed when he saw you with your back to him. I don't think he ever saw the pistol I was holding. Than he would not go down so I just kept pulling the trigger until the gun was empty. He still just stood there for what seemed like forever with a surprised look on his face before he fell over." She shuddered as she recalled the moment. "Well, again, thanks for saving my life. I for one am glad you were there. I never saw him and have no idea how he got by all of us." She brightened up a little at the praise in front of everyone. Until than no one but maybe Mat had known what had happened. Everyone came over and either hugged her or in Jeff and Ben's case gave her a high five. By the time they were done she was laughing and pretty much back to her old self. Jeff was teasing her and telling her she could borrow his DP-12 if she needed to. She told him where he could carry his DP-12 and I knew than that she was going to be ok. After that I walked over to Don and gave him the pain meds. "You ok to do a couple more hours of riding after we refill the Camel Baks?" I ask, "We will stop again the first chance we can to re-fill all of our water containers and bags, that is if we can find a place where there isn't a bunch of people. I really want to get past all of this built up area if we can."

   After getting everyone's Camel Baks re-filled, we all mounted back up and pushed off. After a few minutes of riding we came to the overpass we had been watching for. As there was no exit ramp onto Shady Grove Road from the highway, we stopped on the far side of the overpass to push our bikes down the embankment. The overpass had the typical chain link fence surrounding all Maryland overpasses, still have not figured out why that is, I assume this is to discourage

168

people from doing exactly what we are doing but it shouldn't slow us down for long. We all stopped and dismounted. "Ben, Jeff, and Mat, take up position to watch for any unwanted visitors. Let me know if you see anyone approaching." I say to the group, "Don, Beth, and I will handle the fence. This should only take a couple minutes." I walked over to Ben's trailer and pulled out the bolt cutters. Motioning for Don and Beth to follow me, I walked down the embankment to the fence. Stopping when I came to the fence I looked over the terrain and saw we shouldn't have any trouble navigating down the bank and onto the road below. "Beth, keep a sharp eye out while Don and I get us a hole cut." With Don holding onto the fence I began snipping the chain link from the bottom. While the individual wires were easy to cut, there were a bunch of them. About half way though I was wishing I had grabbed a smaller set of cutters, as these were getting heavy. Ignoring the burning in my forearms I pushed though and finished cutting a door within the fence about five feet tall and four feet wide. I took a small carabineer off my vest and used it to clip open the cut door. Leaving Don and Beth at the fence I climbed back up the embankment to the road. "Mat," I called, "grab Don's bike and take it down through the hole. I'll grab Beth's and do the same. Jeff take your bike and trailer down now. Ben, Mat and I will be right back." We caught up with Jeff and helped him get his bike and trailer past the hole. I told him to hold up at the bottom and sent Beth on down with him. Mat and I headed back up the hill to get our bikes and Ben. Ben was ready to go and took off pushing his bike as soon as we reached the top again. Grabbing our bikes we followed after Ben and again had to help boost the trailer through the hole. After we all passed though the hole Don unhooked the carabineer and let the fence spring back into place. Grabbing his bike he joined us in pushing our bikes down the embankment to the shoulder of the road.

Jeff came up on the radio, "We have a group of 15 to 20 people moving our way from the overpass. I don't see any weapons. Mostly adults, but some kids too." I keyed the mic, "Ok lets move, no need to wait and see what they want. Let's just move on." Everyone was already on their bikes and moving when the people began yelling at us to stop. Some were begging for water or food, while others were just demanding for us to stop. Making sure we were clear I glanced back and saw most of them heading back towards the underpass. I saw they had blocked the road under the highway with stalled vehicles. Good thing we had come down on the west side of the overpass and that they had not spotted us until it was too late to catch us. I made a mental note to carefully scout the next overpass or choke point. Just a couple of minutes slower and we would have had a real mess on our hands. Keying my mic, "Don, take the lead, keep your eye out for a gas station, 7-11, any place that should have water that doesn't have a crowd of people that we can get in and out of fast. When we stop, everyone pair up and cover the area. I will clear the building. Let me know immediately if any of you see anyone approaching. Acknowledge please." Everyone sounded off to the positive.

The road we were on was passing though residential areas, but the quiet was eerie and making everyone jumpy, including me. Two or three times I thought I saw curtains move in houses but at the pace we were moving I couldn't tell if it was movement or just my imagine. Don slowed down after a mile or so and stopped at a major intersection, his voice came over the radio, "Talon, there is an Exxon Quick Stop here, do we want to check it out?" "Roger that," I replied, "coming up now." I coasted my bike to a stop next to Don and he pointed to the right at a building mostly hid behind a small grove of trees. "Keep everyone here, but keep a sharp eye out," I said. Stepping off my bike, I slid my M4 back around to my front and moved over to the tree line. Skirting the side of the building, I peeked around the corner and saw no one near the store. There were a few people by a McDonalds about 200 yards away but no one closer. Could we get what we needed and go before a crowd gathered? I hesitated than moved around the corner and attempted to see inside. It didn't appear to have been looted, yet anyway. I heard a noise above me and froze. A male voice said, "We are closed, please leave now." The voice was calm but the tone left little doubt that it was not a request. Not moving I said, "Sorry we were just needing some water, we will move on. Don't guess you would be of a mind to do any trading?" The voice responded, "What do you have in mind?" "We have some spare rifles and handguns we recently picked up, like new, most have only been dropped once. We would be willing to part with some in exchange for some water, Gatorade, batteries, Bic lighters, some snacks." I said. "You have any shotguns or any 12 gauge shotgun shells?" the voice ask. Thinking about the DP-12 we had picked up, I dismissed mentioning it as Jeff had fallen in love with that damn thing. "We might be able to spare a few rounds of 00 buckshot, but we don't have any spare shotguns. We do have a Remington 700 in .270 with about 30 rounds and a Glock 19 with 2 spare magazines we could trade." After a minute of silence the voice said, "What would you want for trade." I did some quick math, "12 bottles of Gatorade, red or green, 6 packs of triple A's, 6 Bic lighters, 4 cases of water, and 12 candy bars, Milky Way or Hersey Chocolate bars." The man barked a laugh, "That's a lot of water, I can do two cases of water, the batteries, lighters, Gatorade, and candy bars. With the water not running I might be here for a while." I replied, "If you will throw in a couple bags of powdered donuts we have a deal." "Done," the voice said, "bring the rifle and pistol to the backdoor so I can take a look at them.

Don't try any funny stuff, just leave them by the door and back away."

I keyed my mic, "Don, get everyone into the trees. Send Mat down here with that .270 and all of its ammo, 20 rounds of .12 gauge 00 buck and one Glock 19 with 2 spare magazines. Make sure the mags are loaded. The owner is here and is willing to do a little trading. Keep everyone else with the bikes and let me know if anyone approaches our group." A few seconds later Don came on the radio and said Mat was on his way. I walked back along the building and met Mat coming out of the trees. Taking the rifle, pistol and ammo from him, I told him to hang tight but to stay behind the building until I called him. Taking the rifle and pistol over to the back door I laid them both on the ground after checking to make sure both were unloaded. Hanging onto the ammo I backed away from the door. It was a metal security door with no outside handle but it did have a small five-inch by five-inch wire reinforced window in the upper part of the steel door. The interior was dark and I could not detect any movement inside the building, but knew I was being watched.

Hearing the deadbolt unlock, I was a little surprised that the man inside would expose himself. He could have been anywhere between 65 and 80, short grey hair with a suntanned face and arms. I couldn't tell how tall he was but got the impression he could not have been over 5'5" or 5'6". He quickly snatched up the .270 and the Glock and the door shut again behind him. I heard the dead bolt go home a couple seconds after the door fully closed. The man called out a few seconds later, "I take it I will get the shotgun shells and ammo after you get your things." "Yes," I said, "I will leave the shotgun shells and ammo as agreed on by the back door after we get our trade goods." Hearing the door unlock again, the man's head popped out and he said, "Send that young man in here to carry out the water and other drinks, have him leave his

172

guns outside please." Looking over at Mat, I nodded and Mat unslung his rifle and leaned it against a tree, drawing his pistol he laid it beside the rifle. After glancing at me, he walked to the back door and disappeared inside the building. The old man must have had the stuff gathered at the back door as the door never closed all the way before Mat re-appeared with his arms full with the cases of water and a couple sacks on top. Taking the bags from Mat, he set the water cases down and returned to the door. Again re-appearing a couple of seconds later with another case of water and a couple more bags. Grabbing one of the bags I emptied it into another bag and dropped the .270 rounds, shotgun shells and the Glock mags into the bag. Walking over to the door the old man opened it a crack and I handed him the bag. "If I were you I'd get the hell away from here as soon as you can. You know the folks over there across the road are going to come over here before long." I said. The old man looked at me and said, "This is my place and I'm not going to let anyone take a damn thing from me or let anyone loot my place. The government will have the electric back on before long and the cops will deal with all of these low life's." I nodded, not willing to waste the time attempting to convince him the electric would not be coming back on. "Thanks for the square trade, good luck old timer." And with that I turned to help Mat carry our goods back to the group.

Carrying the supplies back to the group, I said, "Everyone get your Camel Baks and water bottles filled up, I want everyone to drink one of these Gatorades now. Get filled up, I want to be back on the road and out of here in 3 minutes. There are way too many people roaming around here." Grabbing one of the red Gatorades I unscrewed the cap and chugged about half of it down. Sitting it down next to my bike, I grabbed the top of my ruck and loosened the straps to get at my Camel Bak. Walking back over to the water cases I grabbed six of the bottles and returned to my ruck. Unscrewing the Camel Bak, I dumped all six bottles into the water bladder and screwed it shut, securing the top of my rucksack. I next shrugged out of my vest and quickly did the same with the Camel Bak in the back of my vest. Putting my vest back on I moved around the group making sure they each had topped off their water bladders and canteens. As I moved among the group I handed out candy bars, lighters and batteries. Walking back to my bike I took the opportunity to rip open one of the Milky Way bars and devoured it in two bites, washing it down with the remaining red Gatorade. Tossing the empty bottle away, I got a dirty look from Beth. I shrugged my shoulders, "We don't have the time to spare to find a trash can right now and we are not going to carry around trash with us. I'm just a big a believer of Do No Harm as the next person but the world has changed and we need to get back to moving. Right now we are ahead of the Golden Horde but if we keep stopping they will catch up with us and than we will be in big trouble." Seeing blank stares from the group, I explained, "Before anyone asks, the Golden Horde, is the surge of people that will flee the inner city once it becomes so bad or fires force them out of the built up areas. This will only become worse when the people in areas like this," gesturing around me to the town houses, "all of these people will get swept up into the horde or they will die in place attempting to protect their homes and families." Ben raised his hand, "But won't the police and National Guard stop the rioting and fires well before it gets that bad?" "The police and national guard will be too busy protecting their own families and their own supplies to worry about any neighborhoods other than their own." I replied, "Ok, enough questions for right now, we can talk more tonight when we stop to rest. Let's mount up and get moving, if we can get to where I'm thinking within the next couple of hours, we can relax a little and get some real chow

174

and rest. After we cross 270 we will only have 4 or 5 miles to go. We are not stopping unless the road is blocked. Let's move out."

Mounting our bikes we headed south on Shady Grove, dodging the occasional stalled car or truck. Several of the trucks had already been looted and the contents were all scattered on the roadway. We crossed under Highway 270 after about ten minutes of riding and did not encounter any more problems. Shortly after crossing under 270, Don came up on the radio, "Talon we have a large crowd at the shopping center up ahead." I keyed my mic, "Are they blocking the road?" "No, doesn't look like it." Don replied. "Push on by, everyone pick up the pace, let's get by this as quick as we can," I said. We all redoubled our efforts and from what I could now see as we rode past, was a large crowd busy looting a Giant Grocery Store. It looked as if there were at least 200 people going or coming from the store and there were at least three fistfights going on in the parking lot. Most of the crowd was ignoring the men fighting and quickly moved around the men and into the shattered storefront. We were lucky that the front and loading docks were not facing the road we were riding on. All of the people were busy with either trying to grab what they could or were watching the fights. As far as I could tell no one even noticed us riding by. "Keep going on this road," I transmitted, "hopefully the communities between here and the river have not closed the road. We are coming up on some high dollar neighborhoods. Don, if you see a road block, stop immediately." "Roger that," Don radioed back.

Thinking back, I don't know if we were just lucky, or we got out in time before people began closing off their roads though their neighborhoods, but we didn't run into any problems. About 15 minutes later we hit River Road and I let myself relax just a little. Turning west we arrived at the water treatment plant after another ten minutes. "Go to the first road on the left pass the water treatment plant," I told Don on the radio. I didn't know if there was anyone at the treatment plant and I didn't want to just pull up to the front entrance if there were. Turning on to the access road just past the treatment plant, we rode down the gravel rode for a couple hundred yards. "Everyone hold up," I radioed. Catching up with everyone, I spoke to the gathered group, "Get the bikes off the road and into the trees over there," pointing to the south side of the gravel road, "get security out and wait until Ben and I get back. We will do a quick recon of the area and will be back in just a few minutes. Call us on the radio if you see or hear anyone nearby." Getting our bikes off the road and into the trees, Ben and I headed past the truck dumping area and cut though the woods towards the small footbridge leading over to the Chesapeake and Ohio Canal Towpath. I motioned Ben to stop and for him to take up an overwatch position while I checked out the area. Pausing at the edge of the tree line, I took out my bino's and did a quick once over of the area. Not seeing anyone I returned my focus to the equipment shed about 50 yards to my north. Again motioning to Ben, I let him know I was going to check out the building. After scanning the area once more and not seeing anyone, I stood and walked to the southeastern corner of the building. I walked normally as not to appear to be sneaking around because I didn't want anyone to panic if they spotted me. Upon reaching the corner of the building I looked around the corner. The building was about 50 feet by 70 feet and enclosed on three sides with the east side open. A small enclosed office was located in the front middle of the building. Still not seeing anyone I crossed the open bays to the small office. Peeking in the windows revealed no one. Circling around the office I saw two small tractors with mowing decks attached parked in the northern two bays of the building. Walking past those I looked around the corner towards the main part of the water treatment plant compound.

Standing there for about five minutes, I heard and saw nothing to indicate anyone was on the compound. Keying my radio, "Don, I'm going to send Ben back to guide the rest of you over to this equipment shed. Leave my bike and move everyone over here and get out a couple of people on security. I'm going to finish checking out the area and will swing over and get my bike and equipment." "Copy that," Don replied.

I moved to the edge of the service road that led into the main compound of the waste treatment plant. Stopping just south of the main compound I paused and listened for any sign of activity. After a couple of minutes I moved into the main compound though the open gate. The compound appeared to be empty and reminded me of a movie set from Twilight Zone. I still was not used to the unnatural quiet or should I say the natural quiet our world had taken on. Moving slowly I moved to the corner of the main pump house building. Glancing around the corner I saw two large pools of a dark colored dried liquid. Moving closer my stomach tightened, blood. I debated on whether to call and let everyone know there had been trouble here but decided not to. Everyone was tried and there was no reason to get everyone upset about something that they could do nothing about. Due to the dryness of the blood, whatever had happened here had been several hours if not a day ago. Easing to the main door I tested the doorknob, finding that it turned easily in my hand. Pulling open the door just enough to let me in I moved to the left of the door with my M4 in the ready position. I stood and listened for a couple minutes but detected no movement of any kind. Inching along the wall and keeping my head on a swivel I moved to the first office. The smell hit me before my eyes adjusted to the dim late afternoon lit shining though the windows. I didn't bother to count all the bodies but it appeared to 8 to 10 bodies, all were dressed in coveralls and all had been shot multiple times with a small caliber handgun or carbine.

Seeing how the men had been lined up against the wall and made to kneel before they had been shot at close range indicated an execution. This was no random act. Stepping out of the office I move down the corridor to what appeared to be the control room for the water treatment plant. Entering the control room with my M4 in the ready position the first thing I saw was the complete destruction of the room. Every computer and workstation was destroyed, yet not just smashed. Who ever had done this was not just out randomly destroying; there was a organized look to the destruction. Taking a closer look I saw that the hard drives had been removed from each of the workstations before each of the machines motherboard had been smashed. Even each of the monitors had been destroyed in the same way. This was a planned operation with an objective. Continuing to look around the office a saw a huge map of the District on the wall. It was really a monitor instead of a paper map. If the power had been on it would have been showing the flow rates and status of all the pumping station throughout the District of Columbia. Even without a PHD in hydrology I could tell that this was the main treatment plant to supply water to the District. Slightly horrified I realized the District was without potable water and there would be no water pressure for fighting any fires. This was worse than I thought it was going to be, someone had planned this. We had been lucky to get out when we did. I can only imagine how bad it was downtown D.C. If the fires were not already out of control they would be sometime in the next 24 hours, but the worst thing is, nobody is going to realize it before it is too late. Realizing I had been daydreaming, I turned and headed back to the main entrance of the building. Nothing I could do here and I just eased back out the way I came in careful not to step in any blood spots or the dried pools in front of the building.

Moving back towards my group I stopped by the exit gate of the compound and stood and watched and listened again for any sounds. My thoughts turned to my family, as skilled as my wife is, the one issue I have always worried about was with the size of Houston came the same threat we were now facing with the possible Golden Horde I had told the group about. It didn't matter how many bullets or guns you had, one or two people could not stop a crowd of hungry desperate people with nothing to lose that was moving though your neighborhood. Human locust that leave nothing of value and have very little to no regard for life or property. I keep telling myself that our house is far enough off any main roads that it is unlikely people fleeing downtown Houston would venture that far off the main highway. There are no stores or major built up areas that would attract the mob but it still worries me. People that have lost everything are capable of anything if they think you have something that can help them.

So far I had traveled maybe 30 miles from where I started. That was about ten miles a day, which meant I might make it home in six or seven months. I will have to do a lot better than that and pick up the pace. Our food supplies at home were good for 90 to 120 days but water would become a problem after about 60 days. I had to pick up my pace. Once across the Appalachian Mountains I was hoping to be able to travel by river over to the Mississippi and down it to around Baton Rouge. That should cut a lot of the time off my trip as it would allow me to make 30-50 miles a day, especially once I make the Mississippi as the current really moves along. Not easy, but much better time than I could make on foot or bike. Of course that brings up the point about the bikes. While the bikes allow us to make much better time and to carry more weight. They are a security problem as they will be very noisy on the gravel towpath and they allow us to ride right into trouble before we even know there is any problem. I will have to discuss it with the group tonight.

Still not hearing or seeing any sign of people I moved back to the Southwest and though the woods to the service road. Locating my bike I pushed it over to the maintenance shed to join the group. When I got within sight of the shed I radioed the group and let them know I was coming in. Pushing my bike into the shed I leaned it against the south wall with the rest of the bikes. Don and Beth already have on some water to heat. Mat had dug out everyone's water bags and already had them hung from the wall filtering. I dug into my ruck and pull out my own Solo stove and headed over to a spot near them. Unslinging my M4 I sat and begun unpacking my stove and water pot. "So how is everyone holding up?" I ask. "Oh, pretty good I think," Don said, "although I'm looking forward to getting some sleep tonight." "Be sure and have someone help you change that bandage on your head before you go to sleep tonight. There is one thing we all need to talk about," I said as Mat joined the three of us, "its about using the bikes. Once we are on the tow road beginning tomorrow we are going to have to be very careful. The tires on the gravel will be very loud and we could ride straight into a dangerous situation before we even realize there is a danger. I'm not saying we should ditch the bikes but with each day passing people are going to be getting more and more desperate, just saying at some point we might have to, hopefully we won't start running into people on the tow path." I stood and walked outside to grab a handful of twigs and small sticks for my stove. Returning back inside the shed I built a fire in my stove with another of the Vaseline soaked cotton balls. Sitting my water pot on the stove I continued, "Tomorrow will be day four of this and from this point on people will really be beginning to panic. There will still be a large percentage of people in denial; wishing and hoping the government will swoop in and save the day, putting everything back to normal. But there will also be those who will step up and seize power of everything that they can. Some will be good people with good intentions, others will be bad people with bad intentions," I paused while checking my water, "even those with good intentions could cause us problems. Hell, anyone that has read "One Second After" or "Lucifer's Hammer" will have already shut down their town or communities and won't allow outsiders in." Seeing blank looks on everyone's faces I explained, "Those are two books widely read within the prepper communities, one is about an EMP event and the other about a meteor striking earth. That is not to mention the crazies and hardcore gangs and criminals. We definitely want to avoid those if at all possible. There is nothing worse than someone that truly believes in a cause. Either will kill us in a heartbeat if they perceive us as a threat. And I will say it again, Beth, you need to dial down as much as you possible can with your looks." With that statement, anger jumped into Beth's eyes, I held up my hand palm down in a patting motion, "Hang on it's not a slight on womanhood, but you are not to go anywhere alone. Most of the 'bad element' would kill any of the guys and never think anything about it, you on the other hand, one look at you and well there are worse things than death. So during the day when we are traveling, please, no tight shirts and if you can hide as much of your hair under your stocking cap." Beth was still visible angry and she started to say something several times but ended up just sitting and glaring at me. I could understand her being mad at the situation but hopefully she would think it though and not be mad at me. "Beth, if you draw attention to yourself than you are not only putting yourself in danger, but all of us also. As any of us would do whatever it takes to protect you, you have to realize that you are a beautiful young lady, and I agree it is not right that you should have to hide that fact, but if it keeps us out of one firefight or keeps one of us from having to shoot som once, than isn't it worth it?" Beth held my graze for heartbeats, than her shoulders slumped and she nodded, "Your right, I don't want any one of you guys to get hurt or have to shoot someone because of me. I will make sure and dial it back as much as possible. Although right now I would kill for a hot shower." I smiled, "Well normally I would say go jump into the river and wash up but as we are at a major water treatment plant, a un-operational plant, I would not recommend the river right here. Tomorrow upriver we will stop early enough for all of us to take a dip in the river."

My water was boiling, so I ripped open my Mountain House bag of Chili Mac and dug around in it until I found the oxygen absorber packet, pulled it out and dumped the boiling water into the pouch. Sealing the bag I turned it over several times to make sure everything was mixed together and set it aside to rehydrate. I thought again of how lucky we had been so far, between being able to stock up before leaving to being able to find the mountain bikes and trailers. Not to mention that the Mountain House meals actually tasted pretty good. I let my mind relax and drift to wondering how my wife and kids were actually doing right now. By this time my wife would have gotten out the SHTF binder out of our gun safe. She always teased me about spending so much time on that "damn binder". She refused to have anything to do with it, but I know her and she would have gone to the safe by now and gotten it out. Chapter one of the binder would give her an overview of the binder and by now she would know about the stored food packed in the storage closet under the stairs. The five gallon buckets and cases of number 10 cans had been hid behind some of our Christmas decorations. It had been fairly easy to do, as I had moved most of the decorations out to the garage when I put in the new shelving in the garages. As I had always dealt with the decorations (at least the pulling out and putting away), she was none the wiser. I left just enough of the bins of decorations in the closet to build a wall to hide the rest

`2

of the gear behind. As I have said before, my wife is one of the smartest people I know but we don't always agree on the need or depth of prepping that is (or was) needed beyond 3-5 days of stuff. She had given me no end of grief when I ordered two bathroom tub reservoirs. She would have been mad as hell if she ever discovered the stored food, well until now. I doubt very much that she is mad at me about that right now. I had tested it on the kids and they all liked the Mountain House meals, well at least most of them. They really liked the Chili Mac, Lasagna, and Beef Stroganoff, and of course all of the breakfast meals. Oh, my wife might still be mad at me but she would get over it once she saw this wasn't just another power outage. So the food and the ammo might have, would have really got her blood boiling, but again she would quickly realize the need for it. That's not to mention the four short-barreled AR15s or SBR's that I had built from parts and stored in the gun safe. The SBR LWRC 5.56 I had built for her to go along with her Sig M11 pistol. I might have forgotten to mention them to her also. She is short, about 5'3" and while she is in good shape and could handle a full size M4, most of her experience was with an SBR, so that's what I put away for her. Both the SBR and the M11 were the weapons she was trained on and had deployed with on her three tours in Afghanistan.

Giving myself a mental shake, I snapped out of my daydreaming and refilled my Solo pot with more water for a cup of coffee and some spare to clean up with. Before putting the pot back on the stove I checked the fire and added a few more pieces of wood to the stove to keep it going to heat the water. "What were you so deep in thought about," ask Beth, "that was the first time I think I have really seen you smiling since we met?" I looked over and she met my eyes, "I was just thinking about my wife and kids," I said. I could tell she would like to ask more questions, but she was a smart one and realized that I would have said more if I had wanted to share any more of my thoughts. After a few seconds she nodded and turned away and began a conversation with Mat. I walked over to the wall with all of the water bags and began pulling the now empty dirty water bags. Gathering all of the empty dirty water bags, I grabbed my M4 and headed down towards the river. Mat and Beth got up and took the bags from me and stated they would handle the water detail. I approved as both picked up their rifles as they headed down to the canal to fill the bags.

Seeing that my water was getting hot again, I radioed Jeff and Ben to let them know Mat and Beth were going down to the water and to ask them what they wanted to eat. Both wanted beef stew so I walked over to the trailer with the open case of Mountain House and dug around until I found two beef stews. Adding hot water to both packages, I refilled by water pot, stood and grabbed my M4 and slung it at the low ready, picked up the two meals and headed out to find Jeff and Ben. Chatting with both of the guys to make sure they were ok to stand first watch I dropped off their food and headed back to the shed. Getting back to the shed I told Mat and Beth to get some sleep as they had the 2200 to 0200 shift. Neither looked too happy about it but they both nodded and got up to get their snivel gear. Don had already rolled out his sleeping bag on the floor in the corner and was softly snoring. I pulled my rucksack from my trailer and headed to the far back of the shed. Dropping my ruck in the corner I dug out my Warbonnet hammock. The metal building we were in had metal support beams about every eight feet, perfect for hanging my hammock. Taking all of 30 seconds I had my hammock set up, slide in my sleeping pad between the double layers and turned to pull out my sleeping bag as padding and my blow up pillow. Hey, I learned a long time ago not to practice being miserable. My first Warbonnet had been a single layer, and it was a great hammock for warm weather or for inside sleeping. But the only draw back to sleeping in a hammock or hanging as it is called by the hammock community, is that in cooler weather a hammock can get cold really quick. Warbonnets answer to this was to create a double layer hammock that you could slide a ground-sleeping pad between the layers. This keeps your body heat trapped and the double layer keeps the sleeping pad from sliding around. After getting my gear set the way I wanted it, I walked back over to my stove and added the remaining hot water to my coffee. Returning to my hammock I sat down in it and sighed. It felt so good just to sit and relax while I finished my coffee. Sitting my cup down, I pulled my boots off, got one more radio check with Jeff and Ben, curled up with my M4 and closed my eyes.

Chapter Twelve

I must have been more tried than I thought, it seemed that I
had just closed my eyes to when Mat woke me by shaking my
hammock support strap. "Its time for your watch," Mat
whispered, "I have on water if you want a hot cup of coffee."
Sitting up and swinging my legs out of my hammock I nodded
and muttered thanks to Mat. I felt like shit, no other way to
put it, I had not been on a bike in years and I could feel every
muscle in my legs and my lower back and butt was screaming
in protest. The early morning air had a slight chill to it and did
nothing to improve my mood. Reaching down I grabbed my
boots and shook them out. Old habits die-hard, it only takes
once to finding an unwelcome visitor in one of your boots.
After getting my boots on I rummaged though my ruck for my
Ziploc baggie of coffee singles. Really wish they had had
these when I was in the grunts, so much better than instant
coffee and you could get two cups from each one when in a
pinch. Finding the coffee I grabbed my cup and my canteen
and headed over to the cooking area. After filling my cup, I
refilled the pot and added a couple of small pieces of wood to
the stove to keep the fire going. I then headed out of the shed
to man my post. Don was already waiting outside and nodded
to me as I walked up. Raising his own cup of coffee he blew
on the hot coffee raising a small cloud of steam. "Winter will
be here before we know it," he said. I nodded in agreement,
"Hopefully we can make it to your place in another 3 or 4
days," I said, "I really need to get though West Virginia before
the cold season arrives." Don gave me a long look and ask,
"So you have decided to try the river to get south?" "I think
so, it will be faster and I think safer in the long run, especially
traveling alone. Also I will be able to travel longer each day if

I stick to the water," I replied. I could tell Don had something on his mind, he had been unusually quiet all evening. "Go ahead and say whatever you're thinking Don," I said. He jumped a little at my tone, and then stood looking at the ground like a little boy caught doing something wrong before speaking. "I was just thinking it might be best if you waited until spring to try and cross over the mountains. I could really use the help with these kids though the winter and if you are caught in an early winter storm in those mountains, no amount of skill or knowledge is going to help." He would not look me in the eyes when he finished his statement. "Don, you know I would stick around and help if I could, but I have my family I have to get back too. My family needs me there now, not in the spring. I have to get over to the Ohio before the first snow hits. You will be fine, these guys are all smart and in good shape. As long as they don't do something stupid you all will be fine." "I'm just worried," Don said, "I'm a city boy with a few hunting skills, sure some of them have grown up hunting and fishing but when there is 3 feet of snow on the ground that isn't going to do us much good," he mused. "We can discuss it again once we get to the cabin and I will help you lay out a plan for the coming winter. We should be able to scavenge a little between here and the cabin, plus you said you have a good amount of supplies laid in already," I answered, "lets get out to our posts and like I said we can do some planning once we get to the cabin. I promise I won't leave until we have a good plan in place for you guys. Ok?" Don nodded and smiled before turning and headed out to replace Beth on guard. I finished my coffee and sat my cup by the stove and headed out to relieve Mat.

After getting Mat headed in for some sleep I sat motionless for several minutes letting my eyes and ears adjust to the sights and sounds of the early morning. It was still very dark, but with the slight grayness that comes right before the raising sun.

I dug around in my vest until I found the Walker Hunter Ears I had grabbed from Bass Pro. I thumbed on my small light attached to my vest and found the on control for the small earpieces. Gently pushing them into my ears I was pleasantly surprised, I could actually hear Mat and Beth talking over by the stoves. Playing with the volume I finally got them turned down so I could concentrate on the sounds of the woods coming awake. These are really good at pinpointing what direction sounds are coming from. After a few minutes I raised my M4 and did a scan of the area. The night vision adapter worked really well and I was glad we had them. Hopefully the idiots that launched or set off the EMP would not do it again. I had seen several scenarios that one EMP would be set off and 12 to 24 hours later, they would set off another in an attempt to catch those devices the first EMP missed. Now isn't that a pleasant thought. But than again, that's what I would have done if I had set off the first one, I thought. Well, hopefully it won't happen again, I would really hate to lose the advance equipment we had now.

The night slowly turned into day without any manmade sounds interfering with the new dawn. The temperature dropped a couple of degrees right as the darkness was turning into the pre-dawn gray making it feel colder than it was. Taking one more scan of the area, I unscrewed my night vision off of my top rail and shoved it away in my pouch on my chest rig and replaced the ACOG on the M4. While it was not cold enough for frost yet it sure felt close and it wouldn't be too long, probably within a couple of months before we did have frost in the mountains we were heading for. Pulling a cleaning rag out of my pouch I wiped the gathered moisture off of my M4 and made a mental note to have everyone clean their weapons before we took off this morning. Might as well get them used to doing this everyday. After a few days it will be routine and I won't have to force them to make the time. I had gotten onto Mat a couple of days ago when I saw him hose down his bolt carrier group with a can of WD-40. A little oil goes a long way with an M4/AR-15 type system. It's ok to use a little more in a piston driven system, but on these direct impingement systems you are just asking for trouble. The excess oil collects the carbon like a magnet collects iron fillings.

I checked my watch again and saw it was 0530, still about an hour before the sun was fully up. We needed to be moving as soon as it was light enough to see the towpath. My radio came to life as Don called, "Talon have you seen the sky line back to the East?" Looking over my shoulder eastward, my view was blocked by the trees, I keyed my radio and let Don know I was heading his way. Passing by the vehicle shed I ducked in and saw that all four of the others were already up and fixing breakfast. Walking up to the group, "Make sure everyone cleans all of their weapons as soon as you finish breakfast. Go light on the CLP but wipe them down and be sure and run a bore snake down each of them," I said and waited for an acknowledgement from each. None of them looked overjoyed but they all at least nodded. "While you're at it, make sure each of you drink at least one of the Gatorades. Enjoy them while they last, it could be a while before we have anything other than water," I added, as I headed out of the shed to meet with Don down by the canal.

Looking south towards the river I could see it was going to be a clear day but that thought was cut off as more and more of the eastern skyline opened up to my view as I approached the river. I had imagined Don had observed the smoke coming from the fires and wanted me to see it, but I was not prepared for the image I was seeing. Everything to our east and northeast were rolling clouds of purplish black dense smoke that reflected the red glow of fires. My God, I thought, there hasn't been a fire like that since World War II. There was no doubt that the city was caught up in the next best thing to a firestorm. I had seen old footage of "Operation Gomorrah" during World War II and the cloud formations I had seen on the footage and these clouds looked exactly like the ones from the WWII footage. In reality I doubted it really was a fire tornado but it did appear it was close and regardless if it was or not the fires were ripping the built up area of DC apart. I knew that most people anywhere near the fire were dead, most would die from carbon monoxide poisoning as the fires would suck up all of the oxygen. Don's voice snapped me back to the moment. "What do you think?" he ask. "I think we need to get the hell out of here, and fast. There is going to be a massive wave of people fleeing west from that and I don't want us to get caught up in it," I said. "But what is it, I've never seen anything like that," said Don gesturing towards the mass of swirling black and purple clouds to the East. "It's close to being a firestorm, the only real firestorms that I know of were the cities of Hamburg, Dresden and Tokyo the Allies created from massive bombings in WWII. I doubt that this is a full-blown firestorm, but it is close and could burn for days and will until it runs out of fuel. For a real firestorm to take place it would require almost calm conditions and plenty of fuel. Concrete buildings do not burn hot enough to produce the heat required for a real firestorm. But like I said it will push all the survivors in front of it. That wave of people will have nothing and will be like locust. We need to get everyone packed and get moving before the panic sets in. People will naturally head for water and we are traveling along the biggest source of water around here. So let's get them packed up and moving." I explained as I turned and headed back to the shed.

Walking into the shed, all four of the kids, guess I really shouldn't call them kids but that was the way I saw them at this point, were cleaning their weapons. Without stopping I said, "Get it packed up, we need to be moving 5 minutes ago.

Fires have completely engulfed DC and it's going to be driving all the survivors our way. We need to move and move as fast and as far as we can." There were a few seconds of stunned silence, and then everyone began moving at once and began packing their gear. I went over to my gear and rolled my snivel gear up and stuffed it back into its compression sacks. Un-hooking my hammock I stuffed it and the strappings back into their bags. I next went over and grabbed my Solo stove, dumping the ashes out and quickly put it away inside the water pot and stored them in their bag. Dropping all of the bags into my ruck I secured the ruck straps and carried it over to my trailer and secured the ruck in the trailer. After double-checking that all of my gear was accounted for and secured I pushed my bike outside the shed and leaned it against the side of the shed. Ben and Jeff followed me out and said that Mat and Beth were almost finished packing up. Don was already packed and was again down by the footbridge watching the clouds. We all stood there watching Don watching the sky until Mat and Beth finally got packed and came out to join the rest of the group. I nodded at the group and began pushing my bike towards where Don was.

Once we were all together at the footbridge, I could see the fear in their eyes as they kept glancing at the swirling clouds to our east. "I know it looks bad and it is, the fires create a thermal updraft that pulls all of the hot air up which creates a low pressure event that pulls in the cold air. It's like a siphon and it just keeps feeding itself as long as there is fuel. Everyone give me a quick radio check and lets get on the road. I would really like to get across the river today. Hopefully the ferry is still running west of here, if not we will have to continue up to one of the bridges." After a quick radio check, Don and I led off followed by Mat and Beth, with Ben and Jeff bringing up the rear. The canal towpath for the most part is just a narrow strip of land with the river on the South side of the path and the canal on the North side. We walked our bikes across the footbridge and down the switch back to the canal path. The path itself is a well maintained bike path covered with crushed rock but should be fairly easy pedaling. I keyed my mic, "Lets gather up for a couple minutes and go over a few things." Once everyone had gather close by I began going over how we would react to a couple different threats. "We need to keep about 50 or 60 feet between each of us. Sing out if you see or hear anything I need to know about. It should be about 25 miles to the Great Falls Ferry, we will take a break every 30 minutes or so. If the lead rider spots a group of people ahead, they should radio it in and turn back to the main group. We will all stop and form a perimeter if the terrain offers us some cover and decide how to deal with the situation. If we run up on a group camping next to the trail, blow by them and let us know they are there. Do not point your weapons at anyone; this is the fastest way to start a firefight in the world. Be at the ready and if anyone points a weapon at you do not hesitate to open fire, do not wait until they fire at you. That's just a good way to get killed real quick. Remember be polite, be firm, and have a plan to kill everyone you meet. Ok lets get moving. Any questions?"

The towpath was well maintained and the bikes made easy work of lightly graveled surface. Much as I feared the noise of our passing over the gravel was loud but there wasn't anything we could do about it. Everyone was quiet and I caught more than one of the kids glancing over their shoulders to look at the dark mass of clouds to our east. As much as I hated it my mind kept going back to my family. Was Houston experiencing the same problems with fire? More than likely every big city in the effected areas was experiencing problems with fire and mobs of desperate people. Hell, I didn't even know for sure that Houston had been affected by the EMP. I made a mental note to break out the emergency radio tonight

192

and see if we could pick up any news on the shortwave bands. Although the chances of any downtown Houston fires reaching the Woodlands was almost impossible, mobs could be going neighborhood to neighborhood raiding the high income areas just because they could. After about 30 minutes I began looking for a good place to stop and refill all of our water dirty water bags from the river and to refill all of our containers with the clean water. Catching Don's attention we stopped by a small clearing that gently led down to the water on the river side of the trail. After gathering everyone and having them pull all of their water bladders and canteens I had Jeff and Ben provide overwatch while the rest of us pulled out our clean water bags and refill everything. This didn't take long as we had hung up the bags last night and as always the gravity filters worked like a charm. Once we got across the river I would have to have everyone break out their mechanical filters and learn how to us them. I had made sure all of them had the same type to reduce the need for different types of replacement filters. Before the gravity filters came out I had used the Katadyn Hiker Pro for years, they could be a little awkward to use at first, but after you figured out how to use them they were reliable and lasted forever. Of course they were a pain in the ass with having to backwash them and you had to be careful not to allow the feeder tube to come in contact with the filter end. It only takes a couple of drops of unfiltered water to end your trip, forever. Pick up the wrong bacteria (cholera), or amoeba (dysentery), or protozoa (giardia), by drinking contaminated water or absorbing through a scratch or cut and you will be down for the count without the proper medical treatment. The last thing we needed was for someone in our party to pick up a parasite. With that in mind I needed to make sure everyone added a few drops of bleach to their water bladders. Better safe than sorry.

It took us almost 30 minutes to get everyone topped off with water and to refill the dirty water bags. If we could we needed to make sure and do this each night so we wouldn't lose the time we could be traveling each day. As everyone worked I had talked to them and warned them of all the problems we would be facing concerning water and how important it was to be extra careful when it came to filtering and treating their water. Most Americas have no idea how fortunate they are (or were), to have the infrastructure of water and electricity. The number of people that would die from water borne illness was too great to imagine right now. Four-fifths of all illnesses in developing countries are caused by water-borne diseases, with diarrhea being the leading cause of death among children. But they would either learn or die, most would die. I know that sounds cold but the truth is the truth. Within the next few days we would begin to see cholera outbreaks and that would hit the young and the old the hardest. For the past several decades there have been less than ten reported cases of cholera inside the United States per year and most of these were picked up while traveling outside the States. After the Haiti outbreak in 2010, worldwide cholera cases jumped 85%. Most large-scale outbreaks are most often caused by fecal contamination of water supplies or food. If treated, most often its nothing but mild diarrhea, but left untreated it can cause profuse diarrhea and vomiting, followed by circulatory collapse and shock. If left untreated death tolls of 25% to 50% are not unheard of, mostly from dehydration. That's not to mention salmonella, hepatitis, or cryptosporidium. All of these are much easier to prevent than to treat after the fact. But most people have no idea how to treat water and will end up drinking contaminated water. Symptoms can begin to show within hours but most typically begin to show in two to three days. Of course this will lead to panic and make anyone with "safe" water a target. I'm sure more than one person will be killed over a bottle of water or someone's Life Straw. These idiots won't know enough about surviving to save themselves with just a few drops of bleach but will kill to take what they perceive is "clean" water. Hell most won't even know that they can just boil water (well most water) and make it safe to drink. But that would mean they knew enough on how to build a fire to boil water. Don't get me started on the grasshoppers and the ants.

Ben and Jeff took the lead as they were pulling the heavier gear and I was hoping we wouldn't have to stop again for at least one hour. If we could average even five miles per hour we should make it to the Great Falls Ferry location by noon. I hadn't said anything to the others but I had my doubts about if it was still running. It might be if the operator was also a good mechanic and as long as the ferry engine didn't have much in the way of electronics. While I'm not an expert on ferryboats, I do know a couple of things about engines having spent my junior and senior years attending technical school for automobile mechanics. I'm pretty sure the ferryboat at the Great Falls Ferry was actually a tow cable boat if I remember correctly. And if that was true, then more than likely if was powered by a diesel engine and was several if not twenty years old. The EMP might or might not of fried the electrical system. But if the ferry was not running we would either have to borrow a boat to get across or have to go up to the bridge on Highway 15 to cross over. I really didn't want to do that as that would take us back into several built up areas that I would just as soon avoid.

We were making good time and the level ground made for easy pedaling. Everyone voted to push on after the one-hour mark and I agreed but insisted that we stop after two hours so everyone could stretch out and get some water. Everyone was in high sprits with the distance we had covered and I was really happy that we were not running into any people on the trail. Hopefully our luck would hold out but we couldn't plan on that and I really needed everyone to stay alert and not be lulled into a false sense of security. We would at some point run into people. If we could get across the river and though the small towns on the way to Don's cabin before the towns began to shut down any outsiders from passing though, if, if, if. I hated to held hostage to chance. It would not take long for people to realize help was not coming from the State or National level and they could not afford to feed everyone passing though, nor could they take in the people fleeing the big cities because that also would deplete their meager resources. Although I would think most people would be heading south instead of west or north because of the cold weather. Once winter truly hits anyone caught on the open road would be in trouble.

I walked around our small group and briefly spoke with each member, one to make sure they were drinking some water and two to remind them to stay alert. As I approached Beth and Mat, I could tell they were having a heated conversation. As I got closer, Beth stood and said something to Mat and stomped off towards her bike. "Trouble in paradise?" I asked Mat as I squatted down beside him. Mat frowned at me, "Yeah, she's mad at me. We were talking and she was complaining about how we, especially you were so fast to shoot first and never give people a chance to explain why they were doing something. She is saying that she might leave our group when we get to the next town and was trying to get me to agree to leave with her. I tried to explain to her that things are different now and just ask her what else could we have done, both at the river or at that town. She said we should have just talked to both and worked out our differences instead of us, really she means you, just shooting them. And of course she blames all of us for her having to shoot that man back there. She is just having problems dealing with it all." "How

196

do you feel about it?" I ask. Mat glanced at me, "I know you didn't have a choice, those guys would have killed Grandpa in a heartbeat if you hadn't shot them and probably all of us, well except Beth. Also we didn't start that fight back there at that town. So I think she is just having a hard time dealing with it all." I nodded, "When we stop for the night I will talk to her. Just give her some space to work though all of it, she's a smart girl and will come around." Patting him on the shoulder I stood and headed back over towards the bikes. Passing Ben I said, "Ben I want you to switch places with Mat for the next leg, is that ok with you?" Before Ben could answer, Beth jumped in, "Ben can change with me, I would like to take point for a while." I looked from Ben to Beth. "Ok," I said, "just stay alert and stop and call out if you see anyone." Beth nodded and hurried over to her bike. "Lets get this show on the road, we should be able to make the ferry crossing within the next hour or so," I said as I walked over to my own bike. Mounting our bikes, we took off with Beth and Jeff in the lead, followed by Don and myself and picking up the rear was Ben and Mat. I knew that Mat wasn't happy with Beth being alone with Jeff but they were all big boys and girls and needed to work these things out among themselves.

Chapter Thirteen

About an hour and fifteen minutes from our break, Jeff called in our next checkpoint saying he had the old bridge near the ferry crossing in sight. I called back on the radio telling them to hold up at the bridge for the rest of us to catch up. As I stopped my transmission I heard Jeff yelling at Beth to stop over the radio. I cussed as the next thing I heard was a flurry of gun shots followed by the rapid fire of a heavier rifle which I knew had to be Jeff's .308. A panicked Jeff came on the radio, "I'm hit, fuck, fuck, fuck, they grabbed Beth, don't know if she was hit or not, I'm down by the old bridge, hurry." The transmission stopped again and another volley of shots rang out followed again by the distinctive booming of Jeff's AR-10. I motioned to the other three to gather on me. "Switch to channel 23," I said getting nods, "ok, we need to get to Jeff so we are going straight in. If I remember correctly there should be cover at that old bridge. When we get there dump your bikes behind the old brick works, Mat you take a position to make sure no one is flanking us from the West, stay low and behind cover, shoot anyone with a weapon that is moving towards us, Ben and Don, you guys take a position to cover us from the South. I will take care of Jeff, got it?" After getting nods we pushed off and covered the final 300 yards in just a couple minutes. I again cussed myself for letting Beth and Jeff get that far ahead of us.

Arriving at the old bridge I immediately spotted Jeff. Jumping off our bikes and unslinging our weapons everyone moved to take up their appointed positions. Moving over to Jeff I immediately knew he had been hit hard. Pointing at Ben I motioned him to me and we both moved up to beside Jeff. Jeff had taken cover next to the old bridge, but was lying face

down on top of his rifle. Rolling Jeff onto his back, I was
shocked to see how pale he was. "Where are you hit?" I ask,
not that I really needed to ask from the massive bloodstain low
on his left side. Not waiting for an answer I pulled my medic
shears out of my vest and began cutting away his shirt. "Ah
shit that was my favorite shirt," groaned Jeff. Ben gave a half
laugh half cry, "Don't worry about the shirt you asshole, just
keep breathing." I glanced over at Ben and nodded for him to
keep talking to Jeff, "Keep talking to him, we can't let him slip
into shock," I said. As soon as the wound was exposed I
ripped open a large combat dressing and placed it over the
wound and instructed Ben to put pressure on it. Ripping open
another dressing I switched places with Ben and rolled Jeff
onto his right side, applying the second dressing to the exit
wound on his back. Keeping my hand on the dressing until we
rolled him onto his back where his body weight would keep
the second dressing in place. Moving back to my trailer I
quickly pulled open my ruck and removed nitrile gloves, a
small bottle of Betadine, several female pads, a tampon, two
packs of blood clot and my last two large combat dressings and
hurried back to Jeff. Pulling the gloves on as fast as I could, I
flicked open my pocket knife and nicked open the plastic
wrapper on the tampon. Pulling off the wrapper I poured
Betadine over the tampon and motioned for Ben to lift the
dressing and as he did I stuffed the tampon as gently as I could
into the bullet entry hole until there was only about a quarter of
an inch still sticking out of the wound. Telling Ben to toss the
now soaked dressing I handed him the female pads and told
him to again maintain pressure on the wound. Opening both of
the blood clotting dressings, I once again had Ben roll Jeff
onto his right side. Working as quickly as I could I pulled the
blood soaked dressing off the exit wound and pressed the
blood clotting dressings into the ragged exit wound. Taking
the last large combat dressing I had I covered the blood

clotting material as best as I could with the combat dressing. Easing Jeff back to the ground, Ben said, "Hey buddy, I always said that mouth of yours was going to get you into trouble." I reached over and grabbed Jeff's jacket off his trailer and used it to cover him with. Next I grabbed a loose stuff sack full of food and used this to elevate Jeff's legs against the shock I knew Jeff was falling into.

"Jeff can you tell us what happened?" I ask. In a painful whisper Jeff said, "We came up to here and we had stopped so I could call in the checkpoint, that was when Beth spotted some people over by that blue building, she took off before I could stop her and I went after her. I was about half way to them when she got to them and I could hear them laughing and shouting in what sounded like Arabic to me, that was when they just started shooting at me. I returned their fire and was able to get back to my bike here by the bridge. I really don't know when I was hit, it all happened so fast. I think I hit at least one of them but I didn't see what happened to Beth after all the shooting started. I'm sorry I screwed up." "Jeff you did fine, now just rest. I'll take care of this," I said. Ben started to say something than I realized that Ben had stopped talking to Jeff, I looked up and saw the tears steaming down Ben's face. Ben looked back at me, "Do something, you know all this shit so fix him, do whatever it takes!" he begged. "He's gone," I said, "Ben, we did everything we could, there was just too much damage." "I'm going to kill all those bastards!" screamed Ben. Looking back at Jeff, I saw his blank staring eyes and I reached out and gently closed them. Patting Jeff on the chest I whispered, "I swear I will pile the bodies of these bastard up to rot at your feet my friend."

Ben reached for his rifle and began to stand up. Reaching out I grabbed Ben by the arm and pulled him back down below the wall around the bridge. "Stop and think before you act. Getting yourself killed is not going to bring Jeff back," I said.

Reaching over to Jeff again, I began pulling Jeff's .308 magazines out of his chest rig. Telling Ben to stay with Jeff and to keep an eye to our west, I gathered the mags and picked up Jeff's DPMS.

Duck walking over to beside Don I ask, "See anything?" Don looked at me, "A lot of movement in the windows but nothing outside, how is Jeff?" I shook my head and saw the tears begin to form in Don's eyes. "Not good, he lost too much blood and there was too much internal damage. We did all we could do, that is except killing all of these bastards that did this to him. Jeff told us that these guys were speaking Arabic. That doesn't make sense. The ferry is ran by an older guy and his wife." Picking up the DPMS I began scoping the building. The building was an old farm style two story made out of cinderblock painted a light blue, with the front door being centered on the east side flanked by evenly spaced double hung windows. The second floor had three evenly spaced double hung windows. It was not a large building measuring about 60 feet long by 30 feet wide. There were four white rental vans parked in front of the building. As I was watching the building I saw movement in one of the second story middle windows. I zoomed the scope on the .308 to maximum power and saw a man dressed in what looked to be coveralls like the type painters or car mechanics wear standing in the window and talking to someone in the same room. The man turned towards the window and leaned out of it, "Hey," he yelled in heavily accented English, "this is what you are going to go. Drop all of your weapons and gear and begin walking back to where ever you came from or we are going to do some really unpleasant things to your friend here. You hear me!"

Still zoomed in I centered the crosshairs on the bridge of the man's nose and ever so gently stroked the trigger of the .308. The 168 grain bullet covered the distance in an instant and punched straight though the assholes brain housing group and

201

struck the man standing behind him in the base of the throat. The man who had been doing the talking fell forward and tumbled out the window to land directly in front of one of the parked vans. The man inside the second story wasn't so lucky, we could clearly hear him screaming. My only thought was I hope the motherfucker suffers. Turning to Don I said, "Don, I need you to get over to those trees, do not expose yourself and do not shoot unless they make a break towards you. If they do make a break, shoot them all. Do not hesitate. Find a good place with cover where you can see but don't let them see you. Can you do that?" Don nodded and I could see he was ready. I continued, "I'm going to send Mat over to our west to make sure they can't go that way. Get moving, take your time, let me know when you're in position." Turning to Mat I motioned him over to me and explained what I wanted him to do and sent him on his way with instructions to radio me when he got into position.

Crawling back over to Ben, I squatted beside him. When he did not respond to my presence I reached out and touched his shoulder. "Ben, I know it is tough losing a friend this way, been there, done that and it always sucks and always will. But there is nothing we can do except kill these assholes that did this to your friend. I need you to focus and do exactly what I say. Get your grief and temper under control and lets take these bastards out for Jeff." Ben took a long shuddering breath, "I'll try," he said. I nodded, "Ok, here is what we are going to do, when I tell you to start shooting, begin shooting up their vans, because what we want them to do is get really pissed and do something stupid. Try and not shoot the gas tanks until I tell you to, mostly just a couple round half way up in the cargo areas and a couple into the cab. Just shoot one van each time I tell you too. If they come out and try and move the vans, shoot them. If one of them get inside one of the vans riddle it full of holes. If not, only shoot when I tell you too,

202

four rounds, each van. Got it?" Ben nodded and turned and picked up his rifle and extended the bipod legs. "Get a good prone position here at the end of the bridge. Be careful not to expose yourself too much," I instructed.

The new leader of the group in the building yelled out that he wanted to talk but I ignored him for the time being. His accent was Middle Eastern too, not sure from where yet but definitely Middle Eastern. I kept wanting to think Arabic but something was not quite right about it. After both Mat and Don reported in that they were in place, the new leader showed up in the window but this time he was holding Beth in front of him as a shield. Looking though the scope I grinned, asshole I could still take you but you wanted to play so let's play. Beth screamed as the guy pulled her by her ponytail. The new leader yelled, "I not screw around anymore, you guys drop everything and walk away now or we kill the infidel whore!" I looked over at Ben, "Get ready, but don't shoot until I tell you too." I snugged up behind the DPMS Nightforce scope was dialed to 16 power and at the 100 yard range the guy's head just about filled the scope, yup either Iraqi or Iranian from the look of this guy. Backing off the zoom a little I could see a little more detail, yup I thought, definitely Iranian seeing the open collar of the guys coverall and seeing the gold chain around his neck. I carefully settled the crosshairs on the bridge of his nose and gently applied pressure to the big rifle's trigger. The guy's head pretty much exploded the same as the first guys from the 168-grain hollow point match grade bullet. His body continued to stand for a second or two before it got the message that it was dead. Utter silence crept in for several seconds with nothing but the sound of the one round echoing into the distance. Then a chorus of Farsi, I'll assume cussing, erupted from the building. Beth was once again jerked back from the window disappearing from sight. Turning my radio back to the original channel I pressed the transmit key, "So

which one of you camel fucking, Khamenei sucking assholes
want to take over negotiations next? Get your next pick of a
leader on the radio now. You have ten seconds." I turned to
Ben, "Get ready," I said, counting down ten seconds.
Reaching ten, I nodded at Ben and he triggered off four
rounds. I had been hoping they were watching, but they failed
to notice the .308's punch straight though the panel vans sides
and from the sound of it into something solid inside the second
van. An idea formed and I ask Ben, "You think you could
throw one of those exploding target cans as far as those vans?"
I ask. Ben grinned and said, "I could from over there where
Don is." "Go grab three cans of that stuff, don't mix it until
you get over there and throw them in among those vans or the
side of the building," I said.

My radio came to life and another Iranian accented voice
spoke, "Who are you guys?" An idea popped into my head
when I again heard that accent. Pressing the mic key, "I am
one pissed off individual right now. As your late leaders found
out. First you come into our country and attack our water
plant, killing all of the workers there and now you have
grabbed one of my friends. I don't have time to deal with
idiots like you. You will release the girl or we will begin
shooting up your vans one every thirty seconds until you do
and then I will kill everyone of you no good son of a bitches if
one hair on her head is harmed. This is not a negotiation. You
have thirty seconds to release her." Now I have to admit, the
string of curse words and name calling that followed was
impressive, but Lee Emery could have done better, not to
speak ill of the dead, but he still owes me over 300.00 dollars
for the last bar bill he struck me with. Ben was back from his
mission and had resumed his position behind his rifle. After
about a minute I nodded again to Ben and said, "Ben, put a full
mag into those vans, make sure you shoot out all of the glass
so they will hear it please." Ben began firing round after round

down range, striking each of the vans in turn. This time we had their attention judging from the chorus of cussing coming from the house. Their commander came back on the radio with panic in his voice, "Stop, do not shoot the vans, you will kill everyone if you continue to shoot the vans."

As I watched the building I saw a window on the second floor slid up a few inches. Turning to Ben I said, "Ben I do believe our friends are about to return fire, get completely behind some cover over there. Move over to your right about seven or eight feet, wait until I tell you to, then pop back out and shoot another couple of rounds into the first van, do not stay exposed, there is a sniper set up on the second story." Ben nodded and scooted back and to his right taking cover behind the stone wall of the low bridge. Just as Ben moved back, there was a furry of shots fired from the houses second story. I zoomed my scope up to max and sure enough the muzzle of a rifle came back out as the individual finished changing magazines. Aiming a couple of inches above the muzzle I squeezed off two rounds hoping to catch both the rifle and the shooter with the rounds. My rounds were again followed by much yelling and cursing in Farsi. Turning from the rifle I said to Ben, "Ben, go ahead and shoot another please." This was followed by a few seconds of silence then the boom of Ben's rifle filled the air. I grinned, but it turned to a frown as another howl of protest came from the building. I began to wonder just what in the hell they had in the vans that they were so worried about. All of the vans were fairly new, so I knew none of them where in running condition after the EMP. I took the time to call Don and Mat and warned them that they might attempt to send out someone to flank us or to move to the vans before long and to be ready for them. Knowing both of them were ready I again went back to scanning the building. As more than thirty seconds had gone by I took the time to squeeze off a round into the gas tank area of the closest van, punching a new set of holes though and though the van. Just as I had squeezed off the shot, a series of shots rang out to our south, followed by the unmistakable sound of an RPG rocket motor followed closely by an explosion. Don's voice came over the radio, "Scratch three more rag heads from this side," he said, "looks like they have some heavy weapons with them. Haven't seen one of those damn thing since Nam, anyway he wasted that one into the ground about half way between us after I shot his ass, looks like they were making a break for it towards the river." "Good job, keep a close eye out. I don't know what they will try next but we need to get this wrapped up before dark," I replied.

Thinking hard, I really did think these guys were some of the terrorists that had hit the water plant. We had killed at least five of them, but I was figuring that each van had at least four shooters. But what did they have in the vans they were so worried about that would kill all of us. I didn't like what my inner brain was telling me. Could it be some type of chemical weapon? Turning back to my rifle I could see two of the three exploding target canisters Ben had thrown. I glanced over at Ben who was grinning ear to ear, he shrugged, "The third one is there among the vans somewhere, it landed just past the first van I shot." I grinned back, "Why don't you introduce our little friends by shooting that one closest to the window on this side." I keyed my mic and give Don and Mat a heads up just before there was a rifle shot followed by a tremendous explosion beside the ferry building. Peering though my scope I could see that all the windows on this side of the building were gone. "Well," I said to Ben, "I bet we have their attention now." Switching my radio back to our original frequency I said, "Last chance, send the girl out now or your vans go up in flames next." The reply came back in the next instant, "Hold on, let's talk about this." Holding the mic button down I turned to Ben, "Ben shoot the next van." The terrorist screamed back into the radio, "We are letting the girl go. Do not shoot the vans anymore!" I keyed the radio again, "I'm tried of talking, just so you know I grew up playing with the lion's tail, so get the girl with all of her equipment out here within the next 30 seconds or your vans and everything in them are history." The reply came back, "Look, let's talk about this." Calling out to Ben, he didn't wait for me to finish telling him to shoot again, before another shot rang out and hit another of the vans. This time the guy screamed into the radio, "Ok, Ok, Ok, she is coming out, just stop shooting the vans!" I replied, "With all of her gear to include the radio." "Yes, yes she is coming out with all of her gear, just take her and go," the man replied. Ben ask, "What was that about playing with a lion's tail about?" "It is a old Persian children story, I threw it out there to confuse them, I'll tell you the story later."

Beth appeared in the door of the building. She grabbed her bike laying beside the door and began pushing it towards us. Ben and I were both glued to our scopes as she walked, I could tell she had been though hell and that she was limping. Ben started to get up and I stopped him, "Let her get behind cover before you help her. Get a poncho liner out of my bike trailer and cover up Jeff before she sees him. The last thing we need right now is for her to be freaking out. After you do that, bring me my zombie ax and that DP-12 with a bandolier of shells over here." Ben cast me a questioning look and I replied, "We are going to make sure these guys are not on our back trail. Go get that shotgun for me and then help Beth."

Turning back to my rifle, I cranked up the zoom again, I had never played with this model of scope before but I knew the basics. This model had the setup that automatically compensates for bullet drop and also had an illuminated green ranging reticle. It was really overkill for this short of range and I would have to zoom it out again to hit anything as the higher zooms were meant for much longer ranges. I could see a couple guys peeking out the windows attempting to see what was going on. The radio crackled in my ear, "Is Beth ok?" I replied, "Yes Mat, Beth is ok, shook up but ok. Focus on what you're doing and keep your head down." Ben squatted down next to me and laid the DP-12 and bandolier of shells down and handed me my zombie ax. I waved him away towards Beth, who had reached us and had sat down beside Jeff's body. I could see she was crying and Ben sat down beside her talking to her.

Keying the radio, I said, "Ok here is how this is going to go. Don, you and Mat get ready, I'm going to flush these guys out if I can, take them down as they come out." With that said I dialed down the zoom on my scope and focused on the target canister by the vans. Squeezing the trigger I mentally cussed as I watch my round strike about three inches high. Hey this was only about my fourth or fifth shot with this rifle give me a break. The rifle was sighted in for 200 yards, not the 100 or so yards I was shooting right now. My second shot was on target and a very satisfying explosion took place in front of the ferry building. Using the rest of the magazine I proceeded to place a round into each of the vans engine blocks. Reloading I used another magazine to finish the job on the vans. The big rounds from the .308 were making sure that these vans would never again hit the road. By this time I could tell the guys inside the building were extremely unhappy with me. Two men rushed out the front door and attempted to get inside the second van only to be dropped by Don before they got ten feet from the door. By my math that left six to eight more in the building.

Getting back on the radio I ask Mat and Don if they could see any propane tanks around the main building. Don came back with a negative, but Mat said he could see one of the big long tanks out back of the main building. I told Mat to shoot up that tank but not to waste more than a magazine on it. About that time Ben came back over to me and tapped me on the shoulder. As I looked at him, he pointed over towards Beth and shrugged his shoulders. I told him to take over here and to shoot anyone that showed in the windows. With that taken care of I slid back and moved over to Beth. She was sitting beside Jeff's body with her knees pulled up to her chest, arms wrapped around her knees, sobbing and rocking back and forth. As I approached I spoke her name. Her head jerked up and I could see she wasn't tracking well with the wild look in her eyes. She flinched hard when the last exploding target went off when one of Ben's shots found it. I began speaking softly to her, "Beth, you're safe now." She looked up at me and said, "It's all my fault, I didn't think and now Jeff is dead because of me, its all my fault." I remained quiet for several seconds thinking over my options. I could try and comfort her or I could be honest and make her deal with the results of her actions. I really didn't have time to deal with her self-pity party at this moment in time. "Yes, you are correct. This is mostly your fault that Jeff got killed, but we all need for you to get your shit together and help us right now. We have to finish this and get the hell out of here before all this draws everyone within miles to this location," I said. Beth's eyes flashed with anger, she had been seeking comfort and assurance that it wasn't her fault. But I didn't have the time or inclination to baby her, which just was not going to happen. She needed to deal with it, accept it, and learn from it. New world, new rules, time to grow up.

About that time a loud whooshing sound came from the direction of the ferry building. I heard Mat's excited voice on the ear bud explaining that it was the large propane tank in back of the building on fire. I knew it wouldn't explode from just shooting it, but had hoped that it would vent enough to do exactly what it was doing. Hopefully it would be hot enough and close enough to the main building to catch it on fire. I told Mat to watch for leakers attempting to get away from the building. More than likely they would try and make it to the river hoping we didn't have that side covered. I called over to Ben, "Watch for the remaining guys to make a break for it any minute now, the building will be on fire before long. Ben, make it really uncomfortable for them with a couple dozen slugs from the DP-12. Start at one corner and put a round every foot or so at the height of the bottom of the windows. Just walk your fire across the room, start on the second floor than move down to the first floor." Turning back to Beth, I saw she was still glaring at me, I said, "Beth as I said, Jeff's death is mostly your fault, but we can't undo it and we as a group need you to snap out of it and help out. There will be time to mourn his death later. Right now we need to know how many guys were in that group?" Her eyes were still flashing anger but she had stopped crying, "Ten," she flatly stated. "Are you physically ok?" I ask. "Yes, I'm fine, just some bruises is all," she spat out, "not that you care." Turning from her I keyed my mic, "All, we could still have five or six hostiles inside that building." Turning back to her I said, "Beth, what type of weapons do they have?" "They each have an AK and a pistol mostly, I also saw a couple of bolt action rifles, oh and one shotgun. They said they got those from the guy that lived here, after they had killed him and his wife. It was horrible, they made me sit behind the counter where both of them were lying. The woman was naked and had been beaten really bad. They were bragging that they had all raped her but that she was old and no fun so they beat her to death and that they were going to keep me for entertainment and were going to kill all of you guys and take all of our equipment."

"Ok Beth, good, now are you ready for some pay back?" I ask. Beth picked up her rifle and inserted a new magazine, she nodded to me. "Get up there beside Ben and shoot anyone that comes out of that building," I said. Moving up to Ben, I

210

reached out and took the DP-12 from Ben. Checking to make sure it was fully loaded I walked back to the trailer and pulled out a second bandoleer filled with OO buckshot. Jacking out the rounds from the DP-12, I reloaded with every other round being a slug followed with a round of OO buckshot. Crisscrossing the bandoleers I looked like an actor in an Italian spaghetti western. "Ben, when I radio to you guys I want you to lay down a base of fire into the lower floor of the building. When I tell you to switch I what you to switch your fire to the second floor. You two take turns, one of you fires until you're empty than the next one starts, just keep a steady stream of fire going into the windows. Don't burn though all your ammo, just a round every couple seconds. Got it?" Both Ben and Beth nodded their understanding. Couching down I moved to the southeast towards Don's position. Keeping to the trees, out of sight of the building it only took me a few minutes to get to Don's position.

Arriving at Don's position I laid down on the ground about three feet to his left. "Hows it going?" I ask. "All quiet here, don't think they can stay in there much longer, it looks like the fire is really beginning to take hold," said Don. Before I could say anything back, what appeared to be a white t-shirt on a mop handle began waving at the front door. I called everyone on the radio and told them to hold their fire. One of the men holding the flag stepped out of the door and yelled, "The building is on fire and we want to surrender and be turned over to law enforcement." I yelled back, "Really you have only two choices, stay and burn or drop all of your weapons and come out and lay down on the drive way. Those are your choices. No more talking just decide." The guy must have just quit his job at NASA, he yelled back, "We want to surrender to the local law enforcement." Breaking my own word, I yelled back, "Make your choice, step back inside or we will shoot you. The next person we see that doesn't come out with his hands up we will shoot. Move back inside now!" I followed this up with one slug from the DP-12 into the wall about three feet from the man's head. The man ducked and ran back inside the building.

A few minutes went by when a man called out that they were surrendering and coming out. Six men came out in a single file line. Just as I said they came towards us with their hands up in the air. After about fifty feet I yelled for them to stop, "That is far enough, keep your hands on top of your heads. Do it now, no talking, the first to not comply I will shoot. Do it now!" The group jerked to a halt with their hands on their heads. Keying my radio I ask Ben if he could see anything going on. Ben replied, "The second guy from the right is arguing with the guy next to him about something, he appears to be really upset about something." Standing up behind a tree I brought the DP-12 into a low ready position, "Ok," I yelled, "I want you guys to spread out in a straight line, about ten feet apart. Do it now." I watched as they all exchanged looks and began to spread out. One of the men stepped forward and yelled, "Fuck you, just call the cops and turn us over to them. We know our rights!" The others all jumped when a loud boom came from Ben and Beth's position by the footbridge. The man who had challenged my order dropped lifeless to the ground with a shot dead center in his chest. "Sorry boys, but I would say that you really pissed our Lady friend off. Now spread out and get down on your knees and cross your ankles, you know the drill. DO IT NOW!" I yelled. All of them spread out a little further and dropped to their knees and crossed their ankles, but the two on the right were taking their time and were keeping their eyes on me.

Pushing my mic button, "All right everyone, keep a sharp eye on the windows in the building, I think they left someone in there with a rifle to take us out when we come out in the open. I'm going to try and keep dragging this out and see if

212

we can't spot the guy. If you see someone in that building, do not hesitate, take him under fire. If I enter the building stop shooting into the building. Do not shoot me when I come out." Moving from the tree I was standing behind I moved to the next tree closer to the group, briefly exposing myself as I moved. Don whispered into his radio, "Dave there was movement in the second floor window, corner window on the right." Keying my radio twice in rapid secession to acknowledge Don's transmission I moved to another tree, again briefly exposing myself. I stepped out from around the tree and saw the guy on the right eyes slightly widen as he took in all the hardware I was carrying. My M4 was still hanging from its two point sling and he could see my Glocks in the drop down leg holsters. I walked over and stopped about 15 feet from the guy on the right and brought the DP-12 into the ready position pointed directly at him. "If anyone so much as coughs I and my people will cut you in half, you do understand that don't you," I said in a conversational tone.

From the panic I saw in his eyes I knew they had planned something but he hadn't known I would be standing this close to him with a double barreled pump shotgun. Continuing to speak to the nervous man I said, "Go ahead and take your hands off your head and slowly remove your coverall." The man eyes were locked onto the barrels of my shotgun, "I can't lower my hands" the man said desperately. As he said this, the second man in line screamed, "Coward!" and dropped his hands from his head and went for the pistol that had been taped to the small of his back. The next few moments in time stood still for me, I heard Ben's .308 begin firing rapidly with the little sharper cracks for Don's 5.56 even as I began pulling the trigger of the DP-12. As I started to fire I began back stepping and felt the hot breath of a rifle round pass very close to my right cheek. With each back step as my foot hit the ground I fired the shotgun. Aim, squeeze, aim, squeeze, pump, step, aim, squeeze, aim, squeeze, pump. It was over in seconds. I don't know if any of them even got off a round other than the guy left in the building. The OO buckshot and slugs had accounted for at least four of them with Ben or Beth taking the two that had tried to run for it. Walking over to the first guy, I rolled him over and sure enough he had had a pistol taped to him also. Fucking idiots to the end, what a mess I thought. Keying my mic, "Everyone hold tight, I'm going to check the building real fast than we are getting the hell out of here. Keep me covered but be careful." Not saying what I was thinking, which was "And don't shoot me," even though I wanted to.

Quickly shoving in rounds to the DP-12 to replace the ones I fired, I checked each of the bodies outside for any signs of life. They were all dead, some more than just dead, the OO buckshot had really done a number on a couple of them. At that range the 12 gauge had blown holes big enough for fist to fit in. Moving on to the building I could feel the heat as I jerked open the front door and did a quick peek around. There were still racks of snacks in the grocery area and several loafs of bread along with some cans of spam. Looking behind the counter I saw the bodies of the owner and his wife just like Beth had described. Laying the DP-12 on the counter I quickly grabbed a stack of plastic shopping bags and began emptying shelves into the bags. As quick as I filled four of the bags I ran over to the door and set them outside. I called Don on the radio, "Get over here and help me. Move these bags back onto the grass," I said. The store seemed to explore with heat as I saw flames shoot out of the staircase. Sweeping as many cans off the shelf into bags as I could I managed to get three more trips before I grabbed my shotgun and headed out the door for the final time. I hated to leave anything but the second floor could give out at anytime and we had managed to get a lot of it.

Calling Beth and Ben I told them to get the bikes with the trailers down here ASAP. Pulling Don to the side I ask him to get Mat and find a shovel. We needed to get Jeff buried and get out of here before any of the locals showed up. Don took off around the building to meet up with Mat as Beth and Ben came up to me on the bikes. "Guys we need to get as much of this stuff loaded as we can and do it fast. I would suggest emptying one of the trailers and stacking the bottom full of canned goods. I need to check a few things and I'll be right back and give you a hand." Walking down the loading ramp towards the ferry, I examined the bodies of the three men Don had taken down as they attempted to flank us. Two of them were armed with Glock 19's and each had four magazines. The third man had a shotgun and also had a Glock 17. The shotgun was a Remington 870 set up as a tactical shotgun. I frisked all the bodies and kept all the money and ammo they each had. This bunch must have hit several targets around the District before the EMP hit. A quick look inside one of the vans confirmed there were several dozen computers hard drives and sledge hammers. This had to have been planned for a long time, leaving me to wonder again if the whole nation had been hit or just the east coast. Carrying the weapons back to where Beth and Ben were still packing I dropped them off and headed up to the six that had tried to ambush us. Much as the others, these had the same, Glock 19's and 17's. I really hated to leave any weapons but if it came down to extra pistols or food, the food wins. Piling all the pistols together I consolidated all of the fake identification cards and pocket litter from the Iranians in one bag and walked over and stuffed them into my ruck. Digging around in my ruck I found a large freezer Ziploc bag and stuffed it into a cargo pocket. Glancing over at Mat and Don, they were over by a large oak tree working on Jeff's grave.

I turned to Jeff's body and went though all of his pockets for personal items. Taking everything he had I placed all of the items into the Ziploc for safekeeping. Going over to Jeff's bike I opened his pack and got out his poncho liner and his tent foot print tarp. Spreading out the footprint, I smoothed out his liner on top and then gently rolled Jeff onto the edge of the liner and tarp. Folding his arms across his chest, I wrapped the liner and tarp around him and secured it with 5/50 cord at his ankles, knees, waist, and shoulders, leaving his face uncovered but with enough material left over to cover his face after everyone had a chance to say good-bye. Walking over to Don and Mat I offered to take a turn at the shovel but Mat refused saying he would do it. They were already down about four feet and were just finishing squaring off the corners and edges. From the corner of my eye I could see Ben and Beth were finishing up re-loading the trailer with the supplies and were pushing their bikes up to the second stack of weapons. Turning in their direction I told them to just take one a piece and six magazines as backup weapons. I walked over to them and saw Ben was going over the weapon with Beth. I went ahead and cleared the rest but one and carried them over to Jeff's grave. Taking the cleared weapons I dropped them in the grave. Carrying the last Glock 19 with one full magazine over to where Jeff laid I gently slid it under his hands. "Just in case," I said and rewrapped the poncho liner to cover the pistol. I turned to see everyone standing there and all of them had tears in their eyes. Standing I said, "Lets get him moved over next to his grave. Help me lift him." With Ben, Mat, and Don's help we lifted Jeff as gently as we could and carried him over next to his grave. Beth followed a short distance behind us, we could all clearly hear her sobbing as she walked.

I have always hated funerals, a few years back I had had to go to six funerals over the course of two months and I swore than that if I could avoid it the next one I went to would be my own. To me a funeral is a personal event, whether it is family or just a friend it was not something to be shared with anyone. Call it denial or avoidance or whatever you want, I really don't care what you label it. We each deal with our grief our own way. We gently laid him down and briefly just stood there staring down at him. All of us in slight disbelief that he was gone and each hoping that he would just get up and say something totally inappropriate. Don cleared his throat, "He was a fine young man. I didn't know him well but the few times he had been a guest at my house he was always willing to lend a hand without being ask. He will be missed." "Ah come on Grandpa," Mat said, "wasn't it you that always told him he was an ass and that his smart aleck mouth would get him shot, stabbed, or hung one of these days." It came out as a half laugh half sob, but it did lift the mood. Ben added, "It was always funny how he would always hit on every good looking girl but he was scared to death of them if they showed the least amount of interest in him. He had a girl back home that he had been dating since middle school. He always said that the day he graduated he was going to ask her to marry him."

I stepped up to the group, "I, like Don, did not know him well but I'm a pretty good judge of character and he was a good solid man that I trusted enough to cover my back when there was trouble." Everyone turned to Beth, who was still quietly crying. Mat moved over to her and gently took her in his arms and whispered something to her. She buried her face into his chest and said, "I am so sorry, I wish this day never happened," as the sobs took over. I caught Mat's eyes and motioned him to take her away. He turned her and helped her over to the base of the large oak tree. Mat came back over and jumped down into the grave, I followed Mat and we took Jeff from Ben and Don and gently laid him in the bottom of the grave. Once we had him laid down I motioned Mat to get out, as Mat climbed out I took two of the gold coins we took off the bikers from my pocket and gently laid the coins on Jeff's eyes. I wrapped the poncho liner and tarp around his face and stood and climbed out of the grave. I looked around and ask if anyone could say a prayer over him. Don stepped forward and in a voice that would have done any small town preacher proud, he recited the Lord's Prayer. After he was finished, I reached down and grasp a handful of dirt and let it trickle though my fingers into the grave. Each of the others did the same and Ben grabbed the shovel and began to fill in the grave.

Going over to Don and Mat I told them to make sure everything was packed up and that we would be moving out as soon as we could. I then walked back over to the remaining three pistols and the pile of magazines. Giving one each to Don and Mat and split the remaining mags between all of us. Taking mine I slid it into the top pouch of my chest rig, dropped in a couple of mags in my right hand pouch and the rest into my pack. Next I gathered up Jeff's DPMS and the DP-12 and secured the DPMS in Mat's bike trailer and strapped the DP-12 and the bandoleers to my ruck sack in my trailer. Noticing the empty loops in the bandoleers I pulled out a partial box of OO buckshot and refilled the loops.

Ben came over and ask about a marker for Jeff's grave. "Ben none of us will ever forget where he is buried and it won't matter to anyone else. Most men could not ask for more than to be buried where they fell on the battlefield surrounded by their dead enemies. Jeff will be fine without a marker." Ben nodded and headed over to his bike to get ready to go.

Epilogue

With everyone on their bikes and ready to move out I told them to stay up by the footbridge and to keep a good watch to our east as I headed down to try and figure out why the Iranians were so concerned about us shooting up their vans. Approaching the vans carefully, I went to the second van because that was the van the men had attempted to get to earlier. Leaning into the passenger side window, which Ben had so thoughtfully removed for me, I could see the vague out line of three barrels stood on end down the center fine of the van. Pulling my flashlight out of my vest I shined the light on the barrels. Each of the barrels where clearly marked as chlorine. Calling everyone on my radio I instructed Don and Beth to stay with the bikes and for Ben and Mat to come down and help me. With their help we were able to push the van over to the boat ramp and let it roll down into the river. It hit with a hard splash and began floating down the river as it filled with water. Within five minutes the van disappeared under the water and was done from sight. Moving back to our bikes we all headed down to the ferry and pushed our bikes onto the ferry. Turning back to the fully engulfed ferry building I sighed and felt exhausted. It had been a hell of a day. Now we just needed to get to the other side of the river and head for the mountains. The first steps are always the hardest, or so they say.

Made in the USA
Columbia, SC
02 November 2019